CHARLES WILLEFORD

THE SHARK-INFESTED CUSTARD

Charles Willeford was a highly decorated (Silver Star, Bronze Star, Purple Heart, Luxembourg Croix de Guerre) tank commander with the Third Army in World War II. He was also a professional horse trainer, boxer, radio announcer, and painter. Willeford, the author of twenty novels, created the Miami detective series featuring Hoke Moseley, which includes *Miami Blues*, *Sideswipe*, *The Way We Die Now*, and *New Hope for the Dead*. He died in 1988.

NOVELS BY CHARLES WILLEFORD

High Priest of California

Pick-up

Wild Wives

The Black Mass of Brother Springer

Lust Is a Woman

The Woman Chaser

Understudy for Death

Deliver Me from Dallas

Cockfighter

The Burnt Orange Heresy

The Hombre from Sonora

Miami Blues

New Hope for the Dead

Sideswipe

The Way We Die Now

The Shark-Infested Custard

THE SHARK-
INFESTED
CUSTARD

THE SHARK-INFESTED CUSTARD

A Novel

by

CHARLES WILLEFORD

VINTAGE CRIME/BLACK LIZARD
Vintage Books
A Division of Random House, Inc.
New York

FIRST VINTAGE CRIME/BLACK LIZARD EDITION, DECEMBER 2005

 Published in the United States by Vintage Books, a division of Random House, Inc., New York, and in Canada by Random House of Canada Limited, Toronto. Originally published in the United States by Underwood-Miller, Lancaster, Pennsylvania, in 1993.

Part I of *The Shark-Infested Custard* was first published as "Strange" in the story collection *Everybody's Metamorphosis* in 1988 in an edition of 446 hardcover copies from the private press of Dennis McMillan; part II was first published as "Kiss Your Ass Goodbye" in 1987 in an edition of 442 hardcover copies, also from Dennis McMillan.

Cataloging-in-Publication Data for *The Shark-Infested Custard* is on file at the Library of Congress.

Vintage ISBN-10: 1-4000-3251-2
Vintage ISBN-13: 978-1-4000-3251-8

www.vintagebooks.com

146119709

What is very sweet, bright yellow, and extremely dangerous?
–old Miami riddle

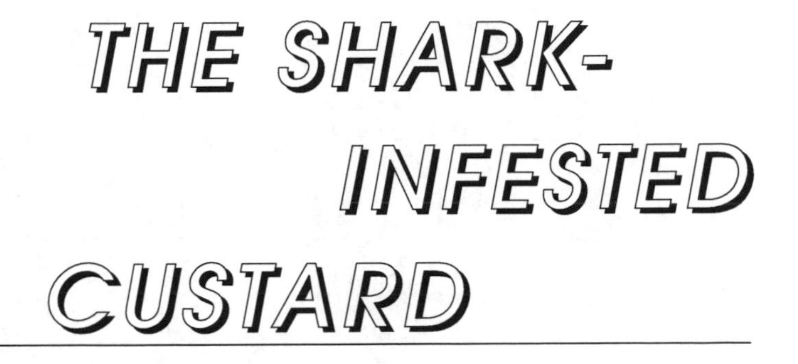
THE SHARK-
INFESTED
CUSTARD

Part 1

Larry "Fuzz-O" Dolman

In Florida, the guilty party who spills everything to the State Attorney first *gets immunity...*

1

It started out as kind of a joke, and then it wasn't funny any more because money became involved. Deep down, nothing about money is funny.

There were four of us at the pool: Eddie Miller, Don Luchessi, Hank Norton, and me—Larry Dolman. It was just beginning to get dark, but the air was still hot and muggy and there was hardly any breeze. We were sitting around the circular, aluminum table in our wet trunks. Hank had brought down a plastic pitcher of vodka martinis, a cup of olives, and a half-dozen Dixie cups. That is one of the few rules at Dade Towers; it's all right to eat and drink around the pool so long as only plastic or paper cups and plates are used.

Dade Towers is a singles only apartment house, and it's only one year old. What I mean by "singles only" is that only single men and women are allowed to rent here. This is a fairly recent idea in Miami, but it has caught on fast, and a lot of new singles only apartments are springing up all over Dade County. Dade Towers doesn't have any two-or three-bedroom apartments at all. If a resident gets married, or even if a man wants to bring a woman in to live with him, out he goes. They won't let two men share an apartment, either. That's a fruitless effort to keep gays out. But there are only two or three circumspect gays in the 120-apartment complex, and they don't bother anyone in the building. The rents are on the high side, and all apartments are rented unfurnished. The rules are relaxed for women, and two women are allowed to share one apartment. That rule is reasonable, because women in Miami don't earn as much money as men. And by letting two women share a pad, the male/female ratio is evened out. So some of the one-bedrooms have two stewardesses, or two secretaries, living together. Other women, who have more money, like school teachers, young divorceés, and nurses, usually make do with efficiencies. If a man wanted to, he could get all of the women he wanted simply by hanging around the pool.

Under different circumstances, I don't think Don, Hank, Eddie and I would have become such good friends. But the four of us were all charter members, so to speak, the first four tenants to move into Dade Towers when it opened. And now, after a solid year together, we were tight. We swam in the pool, went to movies together, asked each other for advice on the broads we took out, played poker one or two nights a month, and had a good time, in general, without any major fights or arguments. In other words, we truly lived the good life in Miami.

Eddie Miller is an ex-Air Force pilot. After he got out of the service, he managed to get taken on as a 727 co-pilot. Flying is just about all Eddie cares about, and eventually he'll be a captain. In the meantime (he only flies 20 hours a week), Eddie studies at the University of Miami for his state real estate exam. That's what many of the airline pilots do in their spare time; they sell real estate. And some of them make more money selling real estate than they do as pilots, even though real estate is a cutthroat racket in Dade County.

Hank Norton has an A.B. in Psychology from the University of Michigan. He has a beautiful job in Miami as a detail man, or salesman, for a national pharmaceutical firm. He only works about ten or fifteen hours a week, when he works at all, and he still has the best sales record in the U.S. for his company. As the top detail man in the field the year before, his company gave him a two-week, all-expenses paid, vacation to Acapulco. He is a good-looking guy, with carefully barbered blond hair and dark, Prussian-blue eyes. He is the best cocksman of the four, too. Hank probably gets more strange in a single month than the rest of us get in a year. He has an aura of noisy self-confidence, and white flashing teeth. His disingenuous smile works as well on the doctors he talks with as it does on women. He makes about twenty-five thousand a year, and he has the free use of a Galaxie, which is exchanged for a new model every two years. His Christmas bonus has never been less than two thousand, he claims.

Don Luchessi makes the most money. He is the Florida rep for a British silverware firm, and he could make much more money than he does if the firm in Great Britain could keep up with his orders. They are always two or three months behind in production and shipping, and Don spends a lot of time apologizing about the delays to the various department and jewelry stores he sells to. What with the fantastic increase of the Miami Cuban population, and the prosperity of the Cubans in general, Don's business has practically doubled in the last four years. Every Cuban who marries off a daughter (as well as her friends and relatives, of course) wants the girl to start off her married life with an expensive silver service. Nevertheless, even though Don makes a lot more money than the rest of us, he is paying child support for his seven-year-old daughter and giving his wife a damned generous monthly allowance besides. As a Catholic he is merely legally separated, not divorced, and although he hates his wife, we all figure that Don will take her back one of these days because he misses his daughter so much. At any rate, because of the money he gives to his wife, by the end of the year he doesn't average out with much more dough than the rest of us.

Insofar as I am concerned, what I considered to be a bad break at the time turned out to be fortuitous. I had majored in police science at the University of Florida, and I had taken a job as a policeman, all gung-ho to go, in Florence City, Florida, two weeks after I graduated. Florence City isn't too far from Orlando, and the small city has tripled in population during the last few years because of Disney World. After two years on the force I was eligible to take the sergeant's exam, which I passed, the first time out, with a 98. They were just starting to build Disney World at the time, and I knew that I was in a growth situation. The force would grow along with Florence City, and because I had a college degree I knew that I would soon be a lieutenant, and then a captain, within a damned short period of patrolman apprenticeship.

So here I was, all set for a sergeancy after only two years on the force. None of the other three men who took the exam with me was even close to my score. But what happened, I got caught with the new ethnic policy. Joe Persons, a nice enough guy, but a semiliterate near-moron, who had failed the exam for five years in a row, finally made a minimum passing score of 75. So the Board made him a sergeant instead of me because he was black. I was bitter, of course, but I was still willing to live with the decision and wait another year. Joe had been on the Florence City force for ten years, and if you took seniority into account, why not let him have it? I could afford to wait another year. But what happened was incredible. The chief, a sharp cracker from Bainbridge, Georgia, called me in and told me that I would be assigned to Sergeant Persons fulltime to do his paperwork for him. I got hot about it, and quit then and there, without taking the time to think the matter out. What the chief was doing, in a tacit way, was making it up to me. In other words, the chief hadn't liked the Board's decision to make Joe Persons a sergeant instead of me any more than I had. By giving me the opportunity to do the sergeant's actual work, which Persons was incapable of handling, he was telling me that the next vacancy was as good as mine, and laying the groundwork to get rid of Sergeant Persons for inefficiency at the same time.

I figured all this out later, but by that time it was too late. I had resigned, and I was too proud to go back and apologize to the chief after some of the angry things I had said to him.

To shorten the story, although it still makes me sore to think about the raw deal I was handed in Florence City, I came down to Miami and landed a job with National Security as a senior security officer. In fact, they could hardly hire me quickly enough. National has offices in every major city in the United

States, and some day—in a much shorter period than it would have taken me to become the chief of police in Florence City—I'll be the director of one of these offices. Most of the security officers that National employs are ex-cops, retired detectives usually, but none of them can write very well. They have to dictate their reports, which are typed later by the girls in the pool. If any of these reports ever got out cold, without being edited and rewritten, we would lose the business of the department store industry receiving that report in five minutes flat. That is what I do: I put these field reports into some semblance of readability. My boss, The Colonel, likes the way I write, and often picks up phrases from my reports. Once, when I wrote to an operator in Jacksonville about a missing housewife, I told him to "exhaust all resources." For about a month after that, The Colonel was ending all of his phone conversations with, "Exhaust all resources, exhaust all resources."

So down at National Security, I am a fair-haired boy. Four years ago I started at $10,000, and now I'm making $15,000. I can also tell, now, from the meetings that they have been asking me to sit in on lately, "just to listen," The Colonel said, that they are grooming me for a much better job than I have already.

If this were a report for National Security I would consider this background information as much too sketchy, and I would bounce it back to the operator. But this isn't a report, it's a record, and a record is handy to keep in my lock-box at the bank.

Who knows? I might need it some day. In Florida, the guilty party who spills everything to State's Attorney *first* gets immunity....

2

We were on the second round of martinis when we started to talk about picking up women. Hank, being the acknowledged authority on this subject, threw out a good question. "Where, in Miami," Hank said, "is the easiest place to pick up some strange? I'm not saying the best, I'm talking about the easiest place."

"Big Daddy's," Eddie said.

I didn't say so, but I agreed with Eddie in my mind. There are Big Daddy's lounges all over Miami. Billboards all around Dade County show a picture of a guy and a girl sitting close together at a bar, right next to the bearded photo of Big Daddy himself, with a caption beneath the picture in lower case Art type: *"Big Daddy's– where you're never alone...."* The message is clear enough. Any man who can't score in a Big Daddy's lounge has got a major hang-up of some kind.

"No," Hank said, pursing his lips. "I admit you can pick up a woman in Big Daddy's, but you don't always score. Right? In fact, you might pick up a loser, lay out five bucks or so in drinks, and then find her missing when you come back from taking a piss."

This was true enough; it had happened to me once, although I had never mentioned it to anyone.

"Think, now," Hank said. "Give me one surefire place to pick up a woman, where you'll score, I'll say, at least nine times out of ten."

"Bullshit," Don said. "Nobody scores nine times out of ten, including you, Hank."

"I never said I did," Hank said. "But I know of one place where you *can* score nine times out of ten. Any one of us at this table."

"Let's go," I said, leaping to my feet.

They all laughed.

"Sit down, Fuzz," Hank said. "Just because there is such a place, it doesn't mean you'll want to go. Come on, you guys—think."

"Is this a trick question?" Eddie said.

"No," Hank said, without smiling, "it's legitimate. And I'm not talking about call girls either, that is, if there're any left in Miami."

"Coconut Grove is pretty good," Eddie said.

"The Grove's always good," Hank agreed, "but it's not a single place, it's a group of different places. Well, I'm going to tell you anyway, so I'll spare you the suspense. The easiest place to pick up a fast lay in Miami is at the V.D. clinic."

We all laughed.

"You're full of it, Hank," Don said. "A girl who's just picked up the clap is going to be turned off men and sex for a long time."

"That's what I would have thought," Hank said. "But apparently it doesn't work that way. It was in the *Herald* the other day. The health official at the clinic was bitching about it. I don't remember his name, but I cut out the piece and I've got it up in my apartment. He said that most of the girls at the clinic are from sixteen to twenty-two, and the guys and girls get together in the waiting room to exchange addresses and phone numbers because they know they're safe. They've all been treated recently, so they know there's no danger of catching anything. Anyway, according to the *Herald*, they've brought in a psychologist to study the problem. The health official wants to put in separate waiting rooms to keep the men and women apart."

"Would you pick up a girl in a V.D. clinic?" Don asked Hank.

Hank laughed. "Not unless I was pretty damned hard up, I wouldn't. Okay. I'll show you guys the clipping later. Here's a tougher question. Where's the *hardest* place in Miami to pick up a woman?"

"The University of Miami Student Union," Eddie said solemnly.

We all laughed.

"Come on, Eddie," Hank said. "Play the game. This is a serious question."

"When a man really needs a piece of ass," I said, "any place he tries is hard."

"That's right," Eddie said. "When you've got a woman waiting for you in the sack, and you stop off for a beer, there'll be five or six broads all over you. But when you're really out there digging, desperate, there's nothing out there, man. Nothing."

"That's why I keep my small black book," Hank said.

"We aren't talking about friends, Hank," I said. "We're supposed to be talking about strange pussy."

"That's right. So where's the hardest place to pick up strange?"

"At church—on a Sunday," Eddie said.

"How long's it been since you've been to church?" Hank asked. "Hell, at church, the minister'll even introduce you to a nice girl if you point one out to him."

"But who wants a nice girl?" Eddie said.

"I do," Hank said. "In my book, a nice girl is one who guides it in."

"If that's true," I said, "every girl I've ever slept with has been a nice girl. Thanks, Hank, for making my day. Why don't we give up this stupid game, get something to eat, and go down to the White Shark and play some pool?"

"Wait a minute," Eddie said, "I'm still interested in the question. I want to know the answer so I can avoid going there and wasting my time."

"A determined man," Don said, "can pick up a woman anywhere, even at the International Airport. And you can rent rooms by the hour at the Airport Hotel."

"It isn't the airport," Hank said. "As you say, Don, the airport's not a bad place for pick-ups. A lot of women, usually in pairs, hang around the Roof Lounge watching the planes take off."

"We give up, Hank," I said. "I've had my two martinis, and if I don't eat something pretty soon, I'm liable to drink another. And on my third martini I've been known to hit my best friend—just to see him fall."

"Eighty-six the Fuzz," Eddie said. "Tell us, Hank." Eddie poured the last drink into his Dixie cup.

"Drive-in movies," Hank said.

"I don't get it," Don said. "What's so hard about picking up a woman at a drive-in, for Christ's sake? Guys take women to drive-ins all the time—"

"That's right," Hank said. "They *take* them there, and they pay their way in. So what're you going to do? Start talking to some woman while she's in her boyfriend's car, while he's got one arm around her neck and his left hand on her snatch?"

Eddie laughed. "Yeah! Don't do it, Don. The guy might have a gun in his glove compartment."

"I guess I wasn't thinking," Don said.

I thought about the idea for a moment. "I've only been to a drive-in by myself two or three times in my whole life," I said. "It's a place you don't go alone, usually, unless you want to catch a flick you've missed. The last time I went alone was to see *Two Lane Blacktop*. I read the script when it came out in *Esquire*, and I really wanted to see the movie."

"I saw that," Eddie said. "Except for Warren Oates in the GTO, none of the other people in the movie could act."

"That isn't the point, Eddie," I said. "I didn't think the movie was so hot either, although the script was good. The point I'm trying to make is that the only reason I went to the drive-in was to see *Two Lane Blacktop*, and it didn't come on until one-oh-five a.m. Where're you going to find anyone to go to the drive-in with you at one in the morning? And when I didn't like the movie either, I wanted to kick myself in the ass."

"I don't think I've ever been to a drive-in alone," Don said. "Not that I remember, anyway."

"Well, I have," Hank said, "just like Larry. Some movies only play drive-ins, and if you don't catch them there you'll miss them altogether."

"I've been a few times, I guess," Eddie said, "and you'll always see a few guys sitting alone in their cars. But I've never seen a woman alone in a car at a drive-in, unless her boyfriend was getting something at the snack bar."

"Let me tick it off," Hank said. "First, if a woman's there, she's either with her parents, her husband, or her boyfriend. Second, no woman ever goes to a drive-in alone. They're afraid to, for some reason, even though a drive-in movie's safer than any place I know for a woman alone. Because, third, a man would be stupid to look for a broad at a drive-in when there're a thousand better places to pick one up."

"That's the toughest place, all right," I said. "It's impossible to pick up a woman at a drive-in."

Hank laughed. "No, it isn't impossible, Larry. It's hard, but it's not impossible."

"I say it's impossible," I repeated.

"Better than that," Eddie said, "I'm willing to bet ten bucks it's impossible."

Hank, shaking his head, laughed. "Ten isn't enough."

"Add another ten from me," I said.

"I'll make it thirty," Don said.

"You guys aren't serious," Hank said.

"If you don't think thirty bucks is serious enough," Eddie said, "I'll raise my ten to twenty."

"Add another ten," I said.

"And mine," Don said.

"Sixty dollars is fairly serious money," Hank said. "That's twice as much dough as I'd win from you guys shooting pool at the White Shark."

"Bullshit," Eddie said. "We've offered to bet you sixty hard ones that you can't pick up a broad at the drive-in. And we pick the drive-in."

"You guys really love me, don't you?" Hank said, getting to his feet and rotating his meaty shoulders.

"Sure we love you, Hank," I said. "We're trying to add to your income. But you don't have to take the bet. All you have to do is agree with us that it's impossible, that's all."

"What's my time limit, Eddie?" Hank said.

"An hour, let's say," Eddie said.

"An hour? Movies last at least an hour-and-a-half," Hank said. "And I'll need some intermission time as well to talk to women at the snack bar. How about making it three hours?"

"How about two?" I said.

"Two hours is plenty," Don said. "You wouldn't hang around any other place in Miami for more'n two hours if you couldn't pick up a broad."

"Let's compromise," Hank said. "An hour-and-a-half, so long as I get at least ten minutes intermission time. If the movie happens to run long, then I get more time to take advantage of the intermission, but two hours'll be the outside limit. Okay?"

"It's okay with me," I said.

"Then let's make the bet a little more interesting," Hank said. "For every five minutes under an hour, you add five bucks to the bet, and I'll match it."

Hank's self-confidence was irritating, but I considered it as unwarranted overconfidence. We took him up on his addition to the bet, and we agreed to meet in Hank's apartment in a half-hour.

We all had identical one-bedroom apartments, but we furnished them so differently none of them looked the same. I don't have much furniture, but the stuff I've got is unique. On Saturday nights I often get the early Sunday edition of the *Miami Herald* and look for furniture bargains in the Personals. That's how I got my harpsichord. It was worth at least $850, but I paid only $150 for it. I can pluck out "Birmingham Jail," but I plan to take lessons if a harpsichord teacher ever moves to Miami. I'm not in any hurry to complete the furnishings; I'm willing to wait until I get the things I want to keep.

Eddie has a crummy place, a real mess, but his mother drives down from Ft. Lauderdale every month to spend a couple of days with him, and that's the only time it's clean.

When Don left his wife, he took all of his den furniture, and his living room is furnished as a den. He's got two large comfortable leather chairs, tall, old-fashioned, glass-doored bookcases, and a half-dozen framed prints of "The Rake's Progress" on the walls. When we're watching football and drinking beer in Don's place, it's like being in some exclusive men's club.

Hank, because he doesn't have an office, has almost a third of his living room taken up with cardboard boxes full of drugs and samples of the other medical products his company manufactures. Hank serves as our "doctor." We get our pain killers, cold remedies, medicated soap, and even free toothbrushes from Hank. Before the strict accountability on drugs started, he could sometimes spare sleeping pills and a few uppers. But not any longer. His company counts them out to him now, in small quantities, and he has to account for the amphetamines he passes out free to the doctors he calls on.

Hank's apartment is overcrowded with possessions, too, in addition to the medical supplies. Once he has something, he can't bear to part with it, so his apartment is cluttered. On top of everything else, Hank has a mounted eight-foot sailfish over the couch. He caught it in Acapulco last year, had it mounted for $450 and shipped to Miami. Across the belly, in yellow chalk, he's written, "Hank's Folly." He still can't understand how the boat captain talked him into having the sailfish mounted, except that he was so excited, at the time, about catching it. He's so genuinely unhappy now, about his stupidity in mounting a sailfish, we no longer kid him about it.

When I got to my apartment, I was feeling the effects of the two martinis, so before I took my shower, I put on some coffee to perc. After I showered, I put on a T-shirt, khaki shorts, and a pair of tennis shoes. I fixed a very weak Scotch and water in a plastic glass, and carried it with me down to Hank's apartment.

The other guys were already there. Don, wearing yellow linen slacks and a green knit shirt, was checking the movie pages in the *Herald*. Eddie wore his denim jacket and jeans with his black flight boots, and winked at me when I came in. He jerked his head toward the short hallway to the bedroom. Hank, of course, was still dressing, and a nose-tingling mixture of talcum powder, Right Guard, and Brut drifted in from the bedroom.

Eddie grinned, and jerked his head toward the bedroom. "An actor prepares," he said. "Stanislavski."

"Jesus," Don said, rattling the paper. "At the Tropical Drive-In they're showing *five* John Wayne movies! Who in hell could sit through five John Waynes for Christ sake?"

"I could," I said.

"Me, too," Eddie said, "but only one at a time."

"If you go to the first one at seven-thirty," Don said, "you don't get out 'til three a.m.!"

"I wouldn't mind," Eddie said, "if we all went and took along a couple of cases of beer. It's better than watching TV from seven-thirty till three, and I've done that often enough."

"Yeah," I said, "but you can watch TV in airconditioned comfort. You aren't fighting mosquitoes all night."

"They fog those places for mosquitoes," Eddie said.

"Sure they do," Don said, "and it makes them so mad they bite the shit out of you. Here's one. Listen to this. At the Southside Dixie. *Bucket of Blood, The Blood-Letters, The Bloody Vampires,* and *Barracuda*! There's a theater manager with a sense of humor. He put the barracuda last so they could get all that blood!"

We laughed.

Eddie got up and crossed to the kitchenette table, where Hank kept his liquor and a bucketful of ice. "What're you drinking, Fuzz-O?"

"I'm nursing this one," I said.

"Pour me a glass of wine, Eddie," Don said.

"Blood-red, or urine-yellow?"

"I don't care," Don said, "just so you put a couple of ice cubes in it."

Eddie fixed a scotch over ice for himself, and brought Don a glass of Chianti, with ice cubes.

"The Southside's probably our best bet," I said. "There'll be fewer women at the horror program than at the John Wayne festival. And besides, there's a Burger Queen across the highway there on Dixie. We can eat something and watch for Hank when he comes out of the theater."

"Shouldn't one of us go with him?" Eddie said.

"It wouldn't be fair," Don said. "I don't think he'll be able to pick up any women there anyway, but it would be twice as hard to talk some woman into getting into a car with two guys. So we let him go in alone. As Larry says, we can watch the exit from across the Dixie Highway."

Hank came into the living room, looking and smelling like a jai-alai player on his night off. He wore white shoes with leather tassels, and a magenta slack suit with a silk blue-and-red paisley scarf tucked in around the collar. Hank had three other tailored suits like the magenta—wheat, blue and chocolate—but I hadn't seen the magenta before. The high-waisted pants, with an uncuffed flare, were double-knits, and so tight in front his equipment looked like a money bag. The short-sleeved jacket was a beltless, modified version of a bush jacket, with huge bellows side pockets.

Don was the only one of us with long hair, that is, long *enough*, the way we all wanted to wear it. Because of our jobs, we couldn't get away with hair as long as Don's. Hank had fluffed his hair with an air-comb, and it looked much fuller than it did when he slicked it down with spray to call on doctors.

"Isn't that a new outfit?" Eddie said.

"I've had it awhile," Hank said, going to the table to build a drink. "It's the first time I've worn it, is all. I ordered the suit from a small swatch of material. Then when it was made into a suit, I saw that it was a little too much." He shrugged. "But it'll do for a drive-in, I think."

"There's nothing wrong with that color, Hank," Don said. "I like it."

Hank added two more ice cubes to his Scotch and soda. "It makes my face look red, is all."

"Your face *is* red," I said.

"But not as red as this magenta makes it look."

"When you pay us off tonight," Eddie said, "it'll match perfectly."

Hank looked at his wristwatch. "Suppose we synchronize our watches. It is now, precisely...seven-twenty-one. We'll see who ends up with the reddest faces."

We checked our watches. For the first time, I wondered if I had made a bad bet. If Hank lost, I consoled myself at least his over-confidence would preclude my giving him any sympathy.

We decided then to meet Hank at the Burger Queen across from the Southside Drive-In. He would take his Galaxie, and the rest of us would ride down in Don's Mark IV.

Because we stopped at the 7/Eleven to buy two six packs of beer, Hank beat us to the Burger Queen by about five minutes. Don gave Hank a can of beer, which he hid under the front seat, and then Hank drove across the highway. It was exactly seven-forty-one.

We ordered Double Queens apiece, with fries, and then grabbed a tile table on the side patio to the left of the building. The Burger Queen didn't serve beer, and the manager couldn't see us fish our beers out of the paper sack around to the side. We could look directly across the highway and see the drive-in exit.

Unless you're going out to dinner somewhere, eating at eight p.m. in Miami is on the late side. We were all used to eating around six, and so we were ravenous as we wolfed down the double burgers. We didn't talk until we finished, and then I gathered up the trash and dumped it into the nearest garbage can. Don ripped the tops off three more beers.

Below Kendall, at this point on the Dixie Highway, there were six lanes, and the traffic was swift and noisy both ways. Eddie began to laugh and shake his head.

"What's so funny?" I said.

"The whole thing—what else? I know there isn't a hellova lot to do on a Thursday night, but if I ever told anyone I sat around at the Burger Queen for two hours waiting for my buddy to pick up a woman at a drive-in movie— "

"You'd better hope it's at least an hour-and-a-half," Don said.

"I know, I know," Eddie said, "but you've got to admit the whole business is pretty stupid."

"Yes, and no, Eddie," I said. "It isn't really money, either. You and Don both know that we'd all like to take Hank down a notch."

Don smiled. "I think you may be right, Larry."

"I'm not jealous of Hank," Eddie said.

"Neither am I," I said. "All I'm saying is that for once I'd like to see old Hank lose one. I like Hank, for Christ's sake, but I hate to see any man so damned over-confident all the time, that's all."

"Yeah," Eddie said. "I know what you mean."

Don snorted, and looked at his watch. "You'll have to wait until another time, I think. It's now eight-twelve, and here comes our wandering over-confident boy."

Don had spotted Hank's Galaxie as it cleared the drive-in exit, and Hank, waiting to make a left turn, was hovering at the edge of the highway when I turned to look. He had to wait for some time, and we couldn't see whether there was a woman in the car with him or not. He finally made it across and parked in the Burger Queen lot. We met him about half-way as he came towards us—by himself.

"How about a beer?" Hank said.

"We drank it," Eddie said.

"Thanks for saving me one. Come on. I'll introduce you to Hildy."

We followed Hank to the Galaxie. When he opened the passenger door and the overhead light went on, we saw the girl clearly. She was about thirteen or fourteen, barefooted, wearing a tie-dyed T-shirt, and tight raggedy-cuffed blue jeans with a dozen or more different patches sewn onto them. On her crotch, right over the pudenda, there was a patch with a comic rooster flexing muscled wings. The embroidered letters, in white, below the chicken read: I'M A MEAN FIGHTING COCK. Her brownish hair fell down her back, well past her shoulders, straight but slightly tangled, and her pale face was smudged with dirt. She gave us a tentative smile, and tried to take us all in at once, but she had trouble focusing her eyes. She closed her eyes, and her head bobbled on her skinny neck.

"She's only a kid," Eddie said, glaring at Hank.

Hank shrugged. "I know. She looked older over in the drive-in, without any lights, but you guys didn't set any age limit. A girl's a girl, and I had enough trouble snagging this one."

"It's a cop-out, Hank," I said, "and you know it."

"Suit yourself, Fuzz-O," Hank said. "If you guys don't want to pay off, I'll cancel the debt."

"Nobody said he wouldn't pay," Don said. "But the idea was to pick up somebody old enough to screw. You wouldn't fuck a fourteen-year-old girl—"

"That wasn't one of the conditions," Hank said, "but if that's what you guys want, I'll take Hildy home, give her a shower, and slip it to her. I sure as hell wouldn't be getting any cherry—"

The girl—Hildy—whimpered like a puppy, coughed, choked slightly, and fell over sideways in the seat.

"Nobody's going to hurt you kid," Don said.

"She's stoned on something, Hank," I said. "You'd better get her out of there before she heaves all over the upholstery."

Hank bent down, leaned inside the car, and pushed up the girl's eyelids. He put a forefinger into her throat and then grabbed her thin right wrist to check her pulse. He slammed the passenger door, and leaned against it. His red, sunburned face was watermelon pink—about as pale as Hank was capable of getting.

"She's dead," Hank said. He took out his cigarettes, put one in his mouth, but couldn't get his lighter to work. I lighted a cigarette myself, and then held the match for Hank. His fingers trembled.

"Don't play around, Hank," Don said. "Shit like that isn't funny."

"She's dead, Don," Hank said.

"Are you sure?" Eddie said.

"Look, man—" Hank ran his fingers through his fluffy hair, and then took a long drag on his cigarette. "Dead is *dead*, man! I've seen too many...too fucking many—"

"Take it easy, Hank," I said.

"What do we do now, Larry?" Don said. Hank and Eddie looked at me, too, waiting. At 28, I was the youngest of the four. Hank was 31, and Don and Eddie were both 30, but because of my police background they were dumping the problem in my lap.

"We'll take her to Hank's apartment," I said. "I'll drive Hank's car, and Hank'll go with me. You guys go on ahead in the

Continental and unlock the fire door to the north-west stairway. Meet us at the door, because it's closest to Hank's apartment. Then, while you three take her upstairs to the apartment, I'll park Hank's car."

"Okay," Don said. "Let's go, Eddie."

"Don't run, for Christ's sake," I said.

They slowed to a walk. Hank gave me his car keys, and I circled the car and got in behind the wheel.

On the way back to Dade Towers I drove cautiously. Hank sat in the passenger bucket seat beside me, and held the girl's shoulders. He had folded her legs, and she was in a kneeling position on the floor with her face level with the dash glove compartment. He held her steady, with both hands gripping her shoulders.

"How'd you happen to pick her up, Hank?" I said.

"Thursday's a slow night, apparently," Hank said. "There're only about twenty-five cars in there. No one, hardly, was at the snack bar. I got a paper cup from the counter, and went outside to pour my beer into it. Sometimes, you know, there's a cop around, and you're not supposed to drink beer at the drive-in, you know."

"I know."

The girl had voided, and the smell of ammonia and feces was strong. Moving her about hadn't helped any either. I pushed the button to lower the windows, and turned off the airconditioning.

"That was a good idea," Hank said. "Anyway, I got rid of the beer can in a trash basket, and circled around the snack bar to the women's can. I thought some women might come out, and I could start talking to one, but none did. Then I walked on around the back of the building to the other side. Hildy, here, was standing out in the open, not too far from the men's room. She was standing there, that's all, looking at the screen. The nearest car was about fifty feet away—I told you there were only about twenty-five cars, didn't I?"

"Yeah. A lot of people don't come until the second feature, which is usually the best flick."

"Maybe so. The point is, nobody was around us. 'Hi,' I said, 'are you waiting for me?' She just giggled and then she mumbled something.

" 'Who? I said, and then she said, 'The man in the yellow jump suit.'

" 'Oh, sure,' I said, 'he sent me to get you. My name's Hank—what's yours?'

" 'Hildy,' she said.

" 'Right,' I said. 'You're the one, all right. I hope you don't mind magenta instead of yellow.'

"Then she asked me for some of my Coke. She thought I had a Coke because of the red paper cup, you see. So I gave her a drink from the cup and she made a face. Then she took my hand, just like I was her father or something, and I led her over to my car. It was dark as hell in there, Larry, and I swear she looked older—around seventeen, anyway."

"That doesn't make any difference now," I said.

"I guess not. I wish to hell I had a drink."

"We can get one in your apartment."

The operation at Dade Towers worked as smoothly as if we had rehearsed it. I parked at the corner, ten feet from the door. Hank wrapped a beach towel around Hildy, an old towel he kept in the back seat, and Eddie opened the car door. The fire door to the stairway, which was rarely used, only opened from the inside. Don held the door partly open for Hank and Eddie, and they had carried her inside and up the stairs before I drove across the street and into the parking lot. After parking in Hank's slot and locking the car, I shoved Hildy's handbag under my T-shirt.

I knocked softly at Hank's door when I got upstairs. Don opened it a crack to check me out before he let me in. Hildy was on her back on the couch, with the beach towel beneath her. She was only about four-eight, and the mounted sailfish on the wall above her looked almost twice as long as she did. The sail's name in yellow chalk, "Hank's Folly," somehow seemed appropriate. When I joined the group, Hank handed me a straight Scotch over ice cubes.

The four of us, in a semi-circle, stared down at the girl for a few moments. Her brown eyes were opened partially, and there were yellow "sleepies" in the corners. There was a scattering of pimples on her forehead, and a few freckles on her nose and cheeks. There was a yellow hickey on the left corner of her mouth, and she didn't have any lipstick on her pale lips. Her skin, beneath the smudges of dirt, was so white it was almost transparent, and a dark blue vein beneath her right temple was clearly visible. She wasn't wearing a bra beneath her T-shirt; with her adolescent chest bumps, she didn't need one.

"She looks," Eddie said, "like a first-year Brownie."

Don began to cry.

"For God's sake, Don—" Hank said.

"Leave him alone, Hank," I said. "I feel like crying myself."

Don sat in the Danish chair across from the TV, took out his handkerchief, wiped his eyes, and then blew his nose.

I emptied the purse—a blue-and-red patchwork leather bag, with a long braided leather shoulder strap—onto the coffee table. There were two plastic vials containing pills. One of them was filled with the orange heart-shaped pills I recognized as Dexies. The other pills were round and white, but larger than aspirins, and stamped "M.T." There was a Mary Jane, a penny piece of candy wrapped in yellow paper, the kind kids buy at the 7/Eleven; a roll of bills held together by a rubber band; a used and wadded Kleenex; and a blunt, slightly bent aluminum comb.

As I started to count the money, I said to Eddie, "Search her body, Ed."

"No," he said, shaking his head.

"Let me fix you another drink, Ed." Hank took Eddie's glass, and they moved to the kitchenette table. Don, immobilized in the Danish chair, stared at the floor without blinking.

There were thirty-eight dollars in the roll; one was a five, the rest were ones. I emptied the girl's front pockets. This was hard to do because her jeans were so tight. There were two quarters and three pennies in the right pocket, and a slip of folded notebook paper in the left. It was a list of some kind, written with a blue felt pen. "*30 ludes, 50 Bs, no gold.*" There was only one hip pocket, and it was a patch that had been sewn on in an amateurish manner. The patch, in red denim, with white letters, read, KISS MY PATCH. The pocket was empty.

"There's no I.D., Hank," I said.

"So what do we do now," Eddie said, "call the cops?"

"What's your flying schedule?" I said.

"I go to New York Saturday. Why?"

"How'd you like to be grounded, on suspension without pay for about three months? Pending an investigation into the dope fiend death of a teenaged girl?"

"We didn't do anything," Eddie said.

"That's right," I said. "But that wouldn't keep your name out of the papers, or some pretty nasty interrogations at the station. And Hank's in a more sensitive position than you are with the airline, what with his access to drug samples and all. If—or when—he's investigated, and his company's name gets into the papers, as soon as he's cleared, the best he can hope for is a transfer to Yuma, Arizona."

Hank shuddered and sat down at the coffee table beside me in the straight-backed cane chair. He opened the vial holding the pills that were stamped "M.T."

"Methaqualone," Hank said. "But they're not from my company. We make them all right, but our brand's called 'Meltin.' There're twenty M-T's left in the vial, so she could've taken anywhere from one to a dozen—or more maybe. Four or five could suffocate and kill her." Hank shrugged, and looked at the girl's body on the couch. "The trouble is, these heads take mixtures sometimes of any and everything. She's about seventy-five pounds, I'd say, and if she was taking a combination of Dexies and M.T.'s, it's a miracle she was still on her feet when I picked her up." He tugged on his lower lip. "If any one of us guys took even three 'ludes, we'd sleep for at least ten hours straight. But if Hildy, here, was on the stuff for some time, she could've built up a tolerance, and— "

"Save it, Hank," I said. "The girl's dead, and we don't know who she is—that's what we need to know. The best thing for us to do, I think, is find the guy in the yellow jump suit and turn her over to him."

"What guy in what yellow jump suit?" Eddie said.

Hank told them what the girl had said, that she was waiting for a man in a yellow jump suit.

"Do you think it was her father, maybe?" Don said.

"Hell, no," I said, "whoever he is, she's his baby, not ours."

"How're we going to find him?" Eddie said.

"Back at the drive-in," I said. "I'm going to get my pistol from my apartment, and then we'll go back and look for him."

"D'you want me to take my pistol too, Larry?" Eddie asked.

"You'd better not," I said, "I've got a license, and you haven't. You and I and Hank'll go back. You'd better stay here with the girl, Don."

"I'd just as soon go along," Don said.

"No," I said. "Somebody'd better stay here with the girl. We'll go in your car, Hank." I handed him his keys. "I'll meet you guys down in the lot."

I went to my apartment, and changed into slacks. I put my pistol, a Colt Cobra .38, with a two-inch barrel, into its clip holster, and shoved the holstered gun inside the waistband of my trousers. To conceal the handle of the weapon, I put on a sand-colored lightweight golf jacket, and zipped up the front. Hank and Eddie were both in the Galaxie, Eddie in the back seat, and Hank in the driver's, when I got to the parking lot. I slid in beside Hank.

On our way to the drive-in I told them how we would work the search party. Hank could start with the first row of cars, going from one to the next, and Eddie could start from the back row. I'd start at the snack bar, checking the men's room first, and then look into any of the cars that were parked close to the snack bar. I would also be on the lookout for any new cars coming in, and I would mark the position of new arrivals, if any, so we could check them out when we finished with those already there.

"One other thing," I said. "If you spot the guy, don't do anything. We'll all meet in the men's room, and then we'll take him together. There aren't that many cars, and we should finish the search in about five minutes."

"What if he isn't there?" Eddie said.

"Then we wait. I think he'll show up, all right. My worry is, he might not be alone, which'll make it harder to pick him up. But there aren't that many guys wearing jump suits, especially yellow ones, so we should be able to spot him easily enough."

"Not necessarily," Hank said. "He might be a hallucination, a part of the girl's trip. Hell, she came with me without any persuasion to speak of, and she would've gone with anybody. She was really out of it, Larry."

"We don't have to look for the guy, Hank," I said. "If you think it's a waste of time let's go back and get the girl and dump her body in a canal some place."

"Jesus, Larry," Eddie said, "could you do that?"

"What else do you suggest?"

"Nothing," Eddie said. "But before we do anything drastic, I think we'd better look for her boy friend in the jump suit."

"That's why we're going to the drive-in," Hank said.

I took a five and a one out of my wallet, and had the money ready to pass across Hank to the girl in the box-office the moment Hank stopped the car. Hank had cut his lights, but I regretted, for a moment, not taking my Vega instead of returning in his Galaxie. The Galaxie, because it was leased by Hank's company, had an "E" prefix on the license plate. But because there were three of us in the car instead of only one, it was still unlikely that the girl would make an earlier connection with Hank.

We parked in the last row. The nearest car was three rows ahead of us. As we got out of the car, Eddie laughed abruptly. "What do we say," he said, "if someone asks what we're looking in their car for? Not everybody comes to this fingerbowl to watch the movie, you know."

"Don't make a production out of it," I said. "Just glance in and move on. If somebody does say something, ask for an extra book of matches. That's as good an excuse as any. But look into each car from the side or back, and you won't get into any hassles. Remember, though, if you do spot the guy, keep on going down the line of cars as before. Don't quit right then and head for the men's room. He might suspect something."

A few minutes later we met in the men's room. I lit a cigarette, and Eddie and Hank both shook their heads. I wasn't surprised. I hadn't expected to find any man in a yellow jump suit. In fact, I suspected that Hank had made up the story. And yet, it was wise to get all three of them involved. I had realized, from the beginning, that I would have to be the one who would have to get rid of the girl's body, but it would be better, later on, for these guys to think that they had done everything possible before the inevitable dumping of the kid in a canal.

"Okay," I said. "To make sure, let's start over. Only this time, you start with the first row, Eddie, and you, Hank, start with the back. It won't hurt anything to double-check."

"If you really think it's necessary," Hank said.

"We've got to wait around anyway," I said.

They took off again. It wasn't necessary, but I wanted to keep them busy. They didn't have my patience. These guys had never sat up all night for three nights in a row at a stake-out in a liquor store. But I had. I went around to the back of the snack bar, where it was darkest, and kept my eye on the box-office entrance, some hundred yards away. Two more cars, both with their parking lights on, came in. The first car turned at the second row and squeezed into an empty slot. The second car, a convertible, drove all the way to the back, and parked about three spaces to the right of Hank's car. If you came to see the movie, it was a poor location, so far from the screen, and angled away from it. A man got out of the car, and started toward the snack bar.

I caught up with Hank, and pointed the man out as he came slowly in our direction, picking his way because his eyes weren't used to the darkness. "I think we've got him, Hank," I said. "Go straight up to him and ask for a match, and I'll circle around in back of him."

"What if he's got a gun?" Hank said.

"I've got a gun, too. Hurry up."

When Hank stopped the man, I was behind him about ten yards or so. He gave Hank a light from his cigarette lighter; then he heard me and turned around. I clicked the hammer back on my .38 as he turned.

"Let's go back to your car, friend," I said.

"A stick-up in the drive-in? You guys must be out of your fuckin' minds," he said.

"Stand away from him, Hank," I said. "If he doesn't move in about one second, I'll shoot his balls off."

"I'm moving, I'm moving," the man said. He put his arms above his head and waggled his fingers.

"Put your arms down, you bastard," I said. "Cross you arms across your chest."

When he reached his car, a dark blue Starfire, with the top down, I told him to get into the passenger side of the front seat. Eddie, breathing audibly through his mouth, joined us a moment later.

"Okay, Hank," I said, "the same as with the girl. You drive on ahead, get Don, and have the fire door open for us. Eddie'll drive this car, and I'll watch the sonofabitch from the back seat. Okay, friend, put one hand on top of the dash, and pass over your car keys with the other."

"No dice," he said. "If you guys want my dough, go ahead and take it, but I ain't leavin' the drive-in—"

He sat erect in the seat with his arms crossed, looking straight ahead. He was wearing a yellow jump suit, and from the cool way he was taking things I knew that he was the right man. I slapped the barrel of the pistol across his nose.His nose broke, and blood spurted. He squealed, and grabbed for his nose with his right hand.

"Cross your arms," I said.

He quickly recrossed his arms, but he turned his head and eyes to glare at me. "Now," I said, "slowly—with one hand, pass over your car keys to the driver." He kept his right forearm across his chest, and dug the keys out of his left front pocket. Eddie slid into the driver's seat, shut the door, and took the keys.

"Get going," I said to Hank, who was still standing there. "We'll be right behind you."

Hank walked over to his car. I climbed over the side of the Starfire, into the back seat, and Eddie started the engine.

"Wait till Hank clears the exit before you pull out," I said to Eddie.

"Where're you guys takin' me, anyway?" the man said. "I got friends, you know. You're gonna be sorry you broke my fuckin' nose, too. It hurts like a bastard." He touched his swollen nose with his right hand.

"Shut up," I said, "and keep your arms crossed. If you move either one of your arms again, I'm going to put a round through your shoulder."

Eddie moved out, handling the car skillfully. He drove to the extreme right of the row before turning onto the exit road, and without lights. There was a quarter-moon, the sky was cloudless, and we'd been in the drive-in so long by now that we could see easily.

When we reached the fire door at Dade Towers, Don and Hank were waiting for us. I ordered the man in the yellow jump suit to follow Don, and Hank followed me as we went up the stairs. Eddie parked the convertible in a visitor's slot across the street, and came up to Hank's apartment in the elevator.

While we were gone, Don had turned on the television, but not the sound. On the screen, Doris Day and Rock Hudson were standing beside a station wagon in a suburban neighborhood. She was waving her arms around.

The man in the yellow jump suit didn't react at all when he saw the dead girl. Instead of looking at her, he looked at the silent screen. He was afraid, of course, and trembling visibly, but he wasn't terrified. He stood between the couch and the kitchen, with his back to the girl, and stared boldly at each of us, in turn, as though trying to memorize our faces.

He was about twenty-five or -six, with a glossy Prince Valiant helmet of dark auburn hair. His hair was lighter on top, because of the sun, probably, but it had been expensively styled. His thick auburn eyebrows met in the middle, above his swollen nose, as he scowled. His long sideburns came down at a sharp point, narrowing to a quarter-inch width, and they curved across his cheeks to meet his moustache, which had been carved into a narrow, half-inch strip. As a consequence, his moustache, linked in a curve across both cheeks to his sideburns, resembled a fancy, cursive lower case "m." His dark blue eyes watered slightly. There was blood drying on his moustache, on his chin, and there was a thin Jackson Pollock drip down the front of his lemon-yellow poplin jump suit. His nose had stopped bleeding.

Jump suits, as leisure wear, have been around for several years, but it's only been the last couple of years that men have worn them on the street, or away from home or the beach. There's a reason. They are comfortable, and great to lounge around in—until you get a good profile look at yourself in the mirror. If you have any gut at all—even two inches more than you should have—a jump suit, which is basically a pair of fancied up coveralls, makes you look like you've got a pot-gut. I've got a short-sleeved blue terrycloth jump suit I wear around the pool once in awhile, but I would never wear it away from the apartment house. When I was on the force and weighed about 175, I could have worn it around town, but since I've been doing desk work at National, I've picked up more than twenty pounds. My waistline has gone from a 32 to a 36, and the jump suit makes me look like I've got a paunch. It's the way they are made.

But this guy in the yellow jump suit was slim, maybe 165, and he was close to six feet in height. The poplin jump suit was skin tight, bespoken, probably, and then cut down even more, and he wore it without the usual matching belt at the waist. It had short sleeves, and his sinewy forearms were hairy. Thick reddish chest hair curled out of the top of the suit where he had pulled the zipper down for about eight inches. He wore zippered cordovan boots, and they were highly polished.

"What's the girl's name?" I said.

"How should I know?" he said. "I never seen her before. What's the matter with her, anyway?"

"There's nothing the matter with her," Don said. "She's dead, now, and you killed her!" Don started for him, but Hank grabbed Don by the arms, at the biceps, and gently pushed him back.

"Take it easy, Don," Hank said. "Let Larry handle it." When Don nodded, Hank released him.

"Step forward a pace," I said, "and put your hands on top of your head." The man shuffled forward, and put his hands on his head. "Here, Don," I said, handing Don the pistol. "Cover me while I search him. If he tries anything shoot him in the kneecap."

"Sure, Larry," Don said. His hand was steady as he aimed the .38 at the man's kneecap.

"I'll hold the pistol, Don," Hank said, "if you want me to."

Don shook his head, and Eddie grinned and winked at me as I went around behind the man in the jump suit to frisk him.

"Leave him alone, Hank," I said. "Why don't you fix us a drink?"

I tossed the man's ostrich skin wallet, handkerchief, and silver ballpoint pen onto the coffee table from behind. He didn't have any weapons, and he had less than two dollars worth of change in his front pockets. He had a package of Iceberg cigarettes, with three cigarettes missing from the pack, and a gold Dunhill lighter.

At his waist, beneath the jump suit, I felt a leather belt. I came around in front of him, and caught the ring of the zipper. He jerked his hands down and grabbed my wrists. Don moved forward and jammed the muzzle of the gun against the man's left knee. The man quickly let go of my wrists.

"For God's sake, don't shoot!" he said. He put his hands on top of his head again.

"It's all right, Don," I said.

Don moved back. I pulled down the zipper, well below his waist. He wasn't wearing underwear, just the belt. It was a plain brown cowhide suit belt, about an inch-and-a-half in width. I unbuckled it, jerked it loose from his body, and turned it over. It was a zippered money belt, the kind that is advertised in men's magazines every month. If he had been wearing the belt with a pair of trousers, no one would have ever suspected that it was a money belt. I unzipped the compartment. There were eight one-hundred dollar bills and two fifties tightly folded lengthwise inside the narrow space. I unfolded the bills, and counted them onto the coffee table.

"That ain't my money!" the man in the yellow jump suit said.

"That's right," Eddie said, laughing. "Not any more it isn't."

"I'm telling you, right now," the man said, "that dough don't belong to me. You take it, and you're in trouble. Big trouble!"

I sat down at the coffee table, and went through his wallet. Eddie sat beside me in another straight-backed chair. Hank set scotches over ice in front of me. He held an empty glass up for Don, and raised his eyebrows. Don shook his head, but didn't take his eyes off the man in the yellow jump suit. Hank, with a fresh drink in his hand, leaned against the kitchenette archway, and stared at the man.

There were three gas credit cards in the billfold: Gulf, Exxon, and Standard Oil. The Gulf card was made out to A.H. Wesley, the Exxon to A. Franciscus, and the Standard card was in the name of L. Cohen. All three cards listed Miami addresses. There was no other identification in the wallet. There was another eighty dollars in bills, plus a newspaper coupon that would entitle the man to a one-dollar discount on a bucket or a barrel of Colonel Sanders' fried chicken. There was a parking stub for the Dupont Plaza Hotel garage, an ivory toothpick in a tiny leather case, and a key to a two-bit locker. Bus station? Airport? Any public place that has rental lockers. And that was all.

"I've never seen a man's wallet this skimpy," I said to Eddie.

"Me either," Eddie said. "I can hardly fold mine, I got so much junk."

"Which one is you?" I said, reading the gas credit cards again. "Cohen, Franciscus, or Wexley?"

"I don't like to use the same gas all the time, man," he said, then he giggled.

I got up and kicked him in the shin with the side of my foot. Because I was wearing tennis shoes, it didn't hurt him half as much as he let on, but because he was surprised, he lost some of his poise.

"Look, you guys," he said, "why don't you just take the money and let me go. I haven't done anything—"

"What's the girl's name?" I said.

"I don't know her name. Honest."

"What's her name? She told us she was waiting for you, so there's no point lying about it."

"Her name's Hildy." He shrugged, yawned, and looked away from me.

"Hildy what?"

"I don't know, man. She worked for me some, but I never knew her last name."

"Doing what?" I said.

"She sold a little stuff for me now and then—at Bethune."

"Mary Bethune Junior High?"

"Yeah."

"Did you drop her off, earlier tonight, at the drive-in?"

"No. I was supposed to collect some dough from her there, that's all."

"Do you know how old she is?"

"She's in the eighth grade, she said, but I never asked how old she was. That's none of my business."

"So you turned her on to drugs without even caring how old she was?" Hank said. "You're the lowest sonofabitch I've ever met."

"I never turned her on to no drugs, man," the man said. "She was takin' shit long before I met her. What I was doing, I was doing her a favor. She lives with her mother, she said. Her mother works at night, over at the beach, she said. And her father split a couple of years back for Hawaii. So Hildy asked me if she could sell some for me. She was trying to save up enough money to go to her father in Hawaii. That's all. And the other kid, a black kid, who used to sell for me at Bethune, he took off for Jacksonville with fifty bucks he owed me. I needed someone at Bethune, and I told Hildy I'd give her a chance. She needed the bread, she said. She wanted to live with her father in Hawaii. So what I was doing, I was doing her a favor."

He ran down. We all stared at him. Beneath his heavy tan, his face was flushed, and he perspired heavily in the air-conditioned room.

"I ain't no worse'n you guys," the man in the yellow jump suit said. "What the hell, you guys picked her up to screw her, didn't you? Well, didn't you?"

"You mean you were screwing her, too?" Don said.

"No—I never touched her. She might've gone down on me a couple of times, but I never touched her."

"What do you mean, 'might have'?" Don said. "Did she or didn't she?"

"Yeah, I guess she did, a couple of times. But I never made her do it. She wanted to, she said."

Don fired the pistol. It was like a small explosion in the crowded room. Hank, standing in the kitchenette archway, dropped his glass on the floor. It didn't break. Eddie, sitting beside me, sucked in his breath. The man in the yellow jump suit clawed at his chest with both hands. He sank to his knees and his back arched as his head fell back. The back of his head hit the couch and his arms dropped loosely to his sides. He remained in that position, without toppling, his face in the air, looking up at nothing, on his knees, with his back arched and his head and neck supported by the couch. Don made a funny noise in his throat. There was a widening red circle on the man's hairy chest, as blood bubbled from a dark round hole. I stood up, took the pistol away from Don, and returned the gun to my belt holster. The man in the yellow jump suit had voided and the stench filled the room. I crossed to the TV and turned up the volume.

"I didn't— " Don said. "I didn't touch the trigger! It went off by itself!"

"Sit down, Don," Hank said. He crossed to Don, and gently pushed him down into the Danish chair. "We know it was an accident, Don."

"Eddie," I said, "open the windows, and turn the air-conditioning to fan."

Eddie nodded, and started toward the bedroom where the thermostat was on the wall. I opened the door to the outside hallway. Keeping my hand on the knob, I looked up and down the corridor. A gunshot sounds exactly like a gunshot and nothing else. But most people don't know that. I was prepared, in case someone stuck his head out, to ask him if he heard a car backfire. The sound from the TV, inside Hank's apartment, was loud enough to hear in the corridor. I waited outside for a moment longer, and when no heads appeared, I ducked back inside and put the nightlock on the door.

"Larry," Hank said, "d'you think I should give Don a sedative?"

"Hell, no," I said. "Let him lie down for awhile on your bed, but we don't want him dopey on us, for Christ's sake."

Don was the color of old expensive parchment, as if his olive tan had been diluted with a powerful bleach. His eyes were glazed slightly, and he leaned on Hank heavily as Hank led him into the bedroom.

Eddie grinned, and shook his head. "What a night," he said. "When I opened the damned window behind the couch, I accidentally stepped on the guy's hand. One of his damned fingers broke." Eddie looked away from me; his mouth was twitching at the corners.

"Don't worry about it, Ed," I said. "You and I are going to have to get rid of him, you know—both of them."

"That figures. Any ideas?"

Hank came back from the bedroom. "I'm treating Don for shock," he said. "I've covered him with a blanket, and now I'm going to make him some hot tea."

"Never mind the fucking tea," I said. "I'm not worried about Don. We've got to get these bodies out of here."

"I know that," Hank said. "What do you suggest?"

"We'll put them into the back seat of the convertible, and then I'll drive his car over to the Japanese Garden on the MacArthur Causeway. I'll just park the car in the lot and leave it." I turned to Eddie. "You can follow me in my Vega, and pick me up."

"Okay," Eddie said. I gave Eddie my car keys.

"I'll go with you, if you want," Hank said.

"There's no point, Hank. You can stay here after we load the bodies, and make some fucking tea for Don."

"Wait a minutes," Hank said, "you don't have to—"

"I don't have to what?" I said.

"Cut it out, you guys," Eddie said. "Go ahead, Larry. Get the convertible and park it by the fire exit. I'll bring the girl down first, but it'll take all three of us to carry him down."

"All right," I said. "Except for the money, put the girl's bag and wallet and all their other stuff into a paper sack." I pointed to the stuff on the coffee table. "And we'll need something to cover him up."

"I've got a G.I. blanket in the closet," Hank said.

Taking the car keys to the convertible from Eddie, I left the apartment.

While Eddie and I wedged the girl between the back and front seats on the floor of the convertible, Hank held the fire door open for us. We covered her with the beach towel, and I tucked the end under her head.

"Shouldn't one of us stay down here with the car?" Eddie asked.

"No," I said. "He's too heavy. It'll take all three of us to bring him down. It won't take us long. We'll just take a chance, that's all."

On the way back to Hank's apartment, we ran into Marge Brewer in the corridor. She was in her nurse's uniform, and had just come off duty at Jackson Memorial. She was coming toward us from the elevator.

"I'm beat," she said, looking at Hank. "A twelve-hour split shift. I'm going to whomp up a big batch of martinis. D'you all want to come down in ten minutes? I'll share."

"Give us a raincheck, Marge," Hank said. "We're going down to the White Shark and shoot some pool."

"Sure," she said. "'Night."

We paused outside Hank's apartment. Hank fumbled with his keys at the door until she rounded the corner at the end of the corridor.

"Go inside," I said. "I'd better pull the emergency stop on the elevator. You can take it off after we leave, Hank."

They went inside. I hurried down the hall, opened the elevator door, and pulled out the red knob. There was an elevator on the other side of the building, and the residents who didn't want to climb the stairs could use that one.

Hank and I, being so much bigger than Eddie, supported the man in the yellow jump suit between us. We each draped an arm over our shoulders, and carried him, with his feet dragging, down the corridor. If someone saw us, it would look—at least from a distance—as if we were supporting a drunk. Eddie, a few feet in front of us, carried the folded army blanket and the sack of stuff. It was much easier going down the stairs. I went down first, carrying the feet, while Hank and Eddie supported him from behind. After we put him on top of the girl, in the back of the car, and covered him with the G.I. blanket, I got into the driver's seat. The fire door had closed and locked while we loaded him, so Hank started down the sidewalk toward the apartment entrance.

"Look, Eddie," I said. "Drive as close behind me as you can. If I'm stopped—for any reason—I'm going to leave the car and run like a stripéd ass ape. And I'll need you behind me to pick me up. Okay?"

"No sweat, Larry," Eddie said, "if you want me to, I'll drive the convertible. I'm a better driver than you."

I shook my head. "That's why I want you behind me, in case we have to run for it in the Vega. Besides, I'm not going to drive over thirty, and when I cross the bridge, before the Goodyear landing pad, I'm going to throw my pistol over the side. It'll be a lot easier to throw it over the rail from the convertible."

"Move out, then. I'm right behind you."

I got rid of the gun, leaving it in the holster, when I passed over the bridge, and a few moments later I was parked in the Japanese Garden parking lot. There were no other cars. The Garden itself was closed at night, and fenced in to keep the hippies from sleeping in the tiny bamboo tearoom. But the parking lot was outside the fence. Sometimes lovers used the parking lot at night, but because most people knew that the Garden was closed at night, they didn't realize that the parking lot was still available. Eddie pulled in beside me and cut his lights.

I got some Kleenex out of the glove compartment of my Vega, and smudged the steering wheel and doors of the convertible. I did this for Eddie's benefit mostly; it's almost impossible to get decent prints from a car. Then I got the G.I. blanket and the beach towel and the paper sack of personal belongings. As we drove back toward Dade Towers, I folded the blanket and the towel in my lap.

Eddie said: "What do you think, Fuzz-O?"

"About what?"

"The whole thing. D'you think we'll get away with it?"

"I'm worried about Don."

"You don't have to worry about Don," Eddie said. "Don's all right."

"If I don't have to worry about Don," I said, "I don't have to worry about anything."

"You don't have to worry about Don," Eddie said.

"Good. If you don't scratch a sore, it doesn't suppurate."

"Hey! That's poetry, Larry."

"That's a fact," I said. "When you hit Twenty-seventh, turn into the Food Fair lot. I'll throw all this stuff into the Dempsey Dumpster."

When we got back to Hank's apartment, Don and Hank were watching television. The color was back in Don's face, and he was drinking red wine with ice cubes. Hank had found an old electric fan in his closet, and some Christmas tree spray left over from Christmas. The windows were still open, but the pungent spray, diffused by the noisy fan, made the room smell like a pine forest. I turned off the TV, fixed myself a light scotch and water, without ice, and sat in front of the coffee table. I counted the money, and gave two one-hundred-dollar bills each to Eddie, Hank, and Don, and kept two of them for myself. I folded the remaining money, and put it into my jacket pocket.

"I'll need this extra money to buy a new pistol," I said. "I got rid of mine—and the holster."

"What did you do with it, Larry?" Don said.

"If you don't know, Don, you can't tell, can you?" I looked at Don and smiled.

"What makes you think Don would ever say anything?" Hank said.

"I don't," I said. "But it's better for none of you guys to know. Okay? Now. If anybody's got anything to say, now's the time to say it. We'll talk about it now, and then we'll forget about it forever. What I mean, after tonight, none of us should ever mention this thing again. Okay?"

Hank cleared his throat. "While you and Eddie were gone, Don and I were wondering why you had us bring the girl here in the first place."

"I was waiting for that," I said. "What I wanted was a make on the girl. I figured that if I could find out her address, I could call her father, and have him come and get her. Either that, or we could take her to him after I talked to him. That way, he could've put her to bed and called his family doctor. That way, he could've covered up the fact that she died from an O.D., if that's what it was."

"That wouldn't have worked," Hank said.

"Maybe not. But that was the idea in the back of my mind. You asked me why I brought her here, and that's the reason."

"It would've worked with me," Don said. "I wouldn't've wanted it in the papers, if my daughter died from an overdose of drugs.

"Okay, Larry," Hank said. "You never explained it to us before, is all. I just wonder, now, who those people were."

"The papers will tell you." Eddie laughed. "Look in the *Miami News* tomorrow night. Section C—Lifestyle."

"Don?" I said.

"One thing," Don said, looking into his glass. "I didn't mean to pull the trigger. I'm sorry about getting you guys into this mess."

"You didn't get us into anything, Don," Eddie said. "We were all in it together anyway."

"Just the same," Don said, "I made it worse, and I'm sorry."

"We're all sorry," I said. "But what's done is done. Tomorrow, I'm going to report it at the office that my pistol was stolen out of the glove compartment of my car. They may raise a little hell with me, but these things happen in Miami. So I'm telling you guys about it now. Some dirty sonofabitch stole my thirty-eight out of my glove compartment."

No one said anything for a few moments. Don stared at the

diluted wine in his glass. Eddie lit a cigarette. I finished my drink. Hank, frowning, and looking at the floor, rubbed his knees with the palms of his hands.

"Eddie," I said, "do you want to add anything?"

Eddie shrugged, and then he laughed. "Yeah. Who wants to go down to the White Shark for a little pool?"

Hank and Don both smiled.

"If we needed an alibi, it wouldn't be a bad idea," I said. "But we don't need an alibi. If there's nothing else, I think we should all hit our respective sacks."

Eddie and I stood up. "You going to be okay, Don?" Eddie asked.

"Sure," Don stood up, and we started toward the door.

"Just a minute," Hank stopped us. "I picked up the girl in the drive-in, and bets were made! You guys owe me *money*!"

We all laughed then, and the tension dissolved. We paid Hank off, of course, and then we went to bed. But as far as I was concerned, we were still well ahead of the game: four lucky young guys in Miami, sitting on top of a big pile of vanilla ice cream.

Part 2

Hank Norton

He is only trying to frighten me, and he has succeeded.

4

I had been running around with Jannaire for almost six weeks before I found out that she was married. At ten p.m., Sunday night, when I started to leave my apartment house, planning to buy the early edition of the Monday morning *Miami Herald* at the 7-Eleven store a block away, I knew that her husband, Mr. Wright, meant to kill me.

Dade Towers, the apartment house where I live, covers a triangular block, and the building was constructed to fit all of the lot. Coming toward the building from LeJeune, it looks like the prow of a ship. If you approach it from College Drive it resembles a five-story office building. There is a main entrance on College Drive, with a Puerto Rican blue awning out front, and a telephone system and directory outside the locked door. To get the front door open you consult the posted directory, dial the apartment number, and if someone is at home and if he wants to let you in he pushes a button and a buzzer opens the door. When the door is opened, there is a large tiled patio-lobby, filled with glass and wrought-iron furniture. Beyond the patio is a swimming pool surrounded by a wide grassy border. There are four Royal palm trees inside, and all of the ground-floor apartments on this inner courtyard have back entrances to the lawn and pool.

There is an elevator in the corridor to the left of the patio-lobby, and if you cross the open pool area to the other side of the building, there is another elevator. This second elevator serves the back entrance, and there is a tiled, lighted foyer here, as well, with a glass door leading out to Santana Lane. There is a streetlight just outside the doorway on Santana, and two steps down to the sidewalk. These steps are covered with green "no-slip" strippings. Across the street, on Santana, there is a large parking lot, but it is rarely used. Most of the residents nose into the curb around the building, parking on College and Santana. The Dade Towers parking lot across Santana Lane, which is required by Miami law, is used mostly by visiting guests, or by residents who have a boat on a trailer, or a camper to park—or in some instances, an extra car.

My apartment, 235, is directly above the back entrance foyer on Santana. I almost always park on Santana, and if the spaces are all gone, I park across the street in the lot. But I rarely park on College or enter the building by the front entrance. Whoever it was who shot at me knew that I would come out the back way, and they—or he—would know when I was leaving my apartment because the lights in my second floor apartment would be switched off. All of the residents in Dade Towers have an outside door key, and this key fits the front College Drive entrance, the back Santana entrance, and the two fire doors, as well. The locks haven't been changed in two years, and there are a lot of people in Miami with keys who shouldn't have them. Laundry men, paperboys, ex-residents, airconditioning companies, bug spray people, and who knows how many residents have passed out extra keys to their lovers, male and female? Nevertheless, as apartment houses go in Miami, Dade Towers is safer than most, and the single women who live here like the security. The building, as I said, is two years old, and so far there has never been a robbery.

But because so many unauthorized keys are out, I was going to the 7-Eleven for a newspaper. I planned to crumple big balls of newspaper and scatter them around in my bedroom. That way, if Mr. Wright somehow got into the building, and then managed to get into my apartment when I was asleep, he would kick the wadded newspapers in my bedroom. They would whish or rattle into each other, and the sounds they made would wake me. I hadn't planned on what I would do after I awakened, but the thought of being killed in my sleep, which was one of many possibilities, frightened me. I had been thinking about Mr. Wright's threat ever since five p.m. and by ten that night I was worried enough to take him at his word.

The single shot, fired from a moving, dark blue Wildcat, a car that roared out of the parking lot directly across the street as I stood on the steps of the Santana back entrance, missed my head by a good yard. But it was close enough to scatter a few bits of stucco from the wall, and some of these tiny chips stung my left cheek. The driver was making a right turn as he fired. He was driving with his left hand and firing across his body and out the window with his right. The Wildcat was moving about thirty miles per hour, and the car was about twenty-five yards or more away from me when he fired. The pistol sounded like a sonic boom in that quiet back street, and I figured by the sound that it was either a .45 or a .357 Magnum. With a gun that large, the marksman would have to be an expert to shoot accurately under such conditions, and the miss of a full yard, for which I was thankful, was too close to be a warning shot. Whoever it was, and if it wasn't Mr. Wright it must have been a man he hired (or even a woman), had surely meant to kill me.

A split second after the shot was fired, which was already much too late, because by that time the car had reached LeJeune, I dived for the sidewalk, crawled into the gutter, and tried to wedge my two hundred pounds under a 1967 red Mustang. I got my left leg and left arm under the car, but that was as far as I could go. As I lay there, struggling futilely to get all of me under the car, I could feel my heart thumping away, and my dry mouth seemed to be full of unwashed pennies. I am thirty-two, and I've been in a few barroom fights and in several situations where the danger potential was incredibly high, but this was the first time in my life that I have ever been afraid for my life. As this thought registered, I realized that I was in a vulnerable position. If the gunman circled the block and came back for another shot, here I was, all spread out for him. He could stop his car, aim straight down, taking his time, and...I scrambled to my feet and, running in a half-crouch, the way I had been taught in R.O.T.C. summer camp, I scuttled to the door, fumbled with my keys, and ran up the stairs to my apartment.

Once inside, I put the chain-lock on the door, and poured a double shot of St. James Scotch into a glass and added one ice cube. The quick jolt, which I downed in two medicinal gulps, helped so much I wanted to drink another. But I didn't. I needed a cool head, not a befuddled one, to think things out, to figure out what to do next. Mr. Wright was crazy, a psychopath. He had to be. Nobody, nowadays, shoots a man just because he thinks the man has fucked his wife. I hadn't touched Jannaire. I had intended to, of course, but that wasn't the same thing, and besides, I hadn't know that she was married. If I had known that she was married, I would have made my plans accordingly. She was the most desirable woman I had ever met, and because I wanted her so badly, I had apparently overlooked the telltale signs of her marriage. She had fooled me from the beginning, and for no discernible reason.

The entire pattern was senseless and illogical, beginning with the electronic dating service, "Electro-Date."

5

Larry "Fuzz" Dolman, who also has an apartment in Dade Towers (319), is a friend of mine, and he became my friend—if not what you would call a close buddy—simply because we both happened to live in the same apartment house. We became friends through the accidental sharing of the apartment facilities. We used the swimming pool, and we played poker in the recreation room. We had both moved into Dade Towers when it opened, two years ago, and over this long period of time (two years is considered as a very long residency in a city of transients, like Miami), we had shared enough common experiences, together with Don Luchessi and Eddie Miller, to be more than just acquaintances.

Eddie and I were *close* friends, but Eddie had moved out of the building and was shacking up with a well-to-do widow in Miami Springs. We were still good friends, and we called each other on the phone two or three times a week, but Miami Springs is a long way from the South Miami area, and we rarely got together to do things any longer.

Don Luchessi, who had also lived in the building for a year, after leaving his wife, had finally gone back to her. Don still detested his wife, or said that he did, but she and the priest and her father and mother and her brother had worked on him, and he finally made the sacrifice and was reconciled. He had an eight-year-old daughter he doted on, a spoiled, fat little girl named Marie, and he went back to his wife because of his daughter—not because he wanted to live with his wife again. No man in his right mind would want to live with Clara Luchessi. Clara would never stop talking, and all she ever talked about was her house and the things that were in it. She never left the house, either. She would never come with Don when he came over to visit Larry and me, and when we went to his house we had to listen to Clara talk about army worms, her glass drapes, a new rug-cleaning process she had discovered, and other domestic inanities.

And little fat Marie was also there, never more than six inches away from Don. When he was behind the bar mixing drinks, she was back there with him, "helping" him. If he sat down, she sat on his lap. He had a pool table in his Florida room, but she spoiled the games we tried to play. She always wanted to play, too, and Don would let her. If she missed a shot, she cried and he had to comfort her. If she made one, she crowed. She also cheated, and Don let her get away with it.

Going to Don's house, which could have been a pleasant diversion, what with his heated swimming pool, his regulation pool table, and his well-stocked bar, was spoiled by his wife and daughter.

Clara was a great cook, one of the best cooks in the world, but even her wonderful dinners were ruined for you because she had to tell you exactly how each dish was made, and where the ingredients could be obtained. No one else could get in a word, or force her to change the subject. During Clara's vapid monologue, delivered rapidly in a shrill high-pitched voice, Maria made ugly faces, got down from the table from time to time to play terrible children's records on the stereo, and greedily finished her food as soon as possible so she could sit on Don's lap for the rest of the meal.

There is much to be said for the old-fashioned notion of having women serve the men first, and then eat their own meals at the second table in the kitchen.

For a full year, the four of us had had some good times together, but after Eddie and Don moved out, Larry and I spent more time together than we would have ordinarily. We went to movies together, rather than to go alone; we went out to dinner sometimes, rather than to go alone; and we sometimes went to the White Shark on Flagler Street to drink beer and play pool. We both loved to play pool, and as partners we were a deadly combination. We invariably won more games than we lost. But we didn't have much else in common. And the times were becoming more frequent when I preferred going to a movie, or out to eat somewhere alone, rather than taking Larry along.

Larry had a literal mind, and although I knew him well enough by now to know that he would and did take many things literally, it was a characteristic that one never gets used to completely. His interpretation of movies, for example, was maddening. He was unable to grasp an abstract conception. When we discussed *Last Tango in Paris*, he claimed that the reason Brando's wife had purchased identical dressing gowns for her husband and her lover was because she got them on sale. This absurd, practical interpretation of the identical dressing gowns makes Larry seem almost feminine in his reasoning, but there was nothing effeminate about him. He was tough, or as the Cubans in Miami say, *un hombre duro*—a hard man.

As an ex-cop, Larry had an excellent job at National Security, the nation-wide private investigation agency. He was a senior security officer, but not a field investigator, although he had a license, of course. He was an administrator, and worked in the Miami office on a regular forty-hour week. He never went out on investigative assignments. He has a B.A. in Police Science from the University of Florida, and his literal mind, apparently, was not a drawback insofar as his work was concerned. He wasn't allowed to say exactly what it was that he did at National Security, but his work had something to do with personnel assignments, and keeping track of cases and operators in the field. He made about twenty thousand a year, if not more.

Part of Larry's personality problem, although Larry was unaware of any problem, was his inability to taste anything. Something was awry with Larry's taste buds. He was unable to tell the difference between sweet and sour. Everything tasted just about the same to him. One night when were both at Don's house, Larry took two bites out of a wax pear, picking the pear out of a bowl on the sideboard and biting into it without asking Clara if he could have it. The point is, he took the *second* bite before complaining that "this is the worst goddamned pear I ever ate."

The fruit looked realistic, all right, and anyone could have made the same mistake in the dim dining room, but no one with any taste at all would have taken the second bite. Larry would have gone on, in all probability, and eaten the entire pear if Don and I hadn't started to laugh. Clara, of course, didn't laugh. The wax fruit was quite expensive; she had purchased it from Neiman-Marcus' Bal Harbour store. On another night, he ate a colored soap ball in Don's bathroom. There was a full glass of these pastel soap balls in there, and he thought he was eating a piece of candy. He didn't stop to consider that it would be peculiar to keep a jar of candy on a shelf beside the bathtub.

At any rate, Larry's lack of sensuous taste extended into tastelessness in other matters; in the clothes he wore, in his speech, and even in women. But there was nothing wrong with his olfactory organ. He had a keen sense of smell, which is unusual when something is wrong with your taste buds, and in a way, somewhat baffling when you consider that if he could smell the soap, and recognize the smell, why would he eat it under the impression that it was a piece of candy? All he could come up with in this instance was that "It smelled good enough to eat, so I thought it was candy."

When we went out together to eat, either for lunch or dinner, he invariably ordered a club sandwich. A club sandwich is easy to eat, of course, and it has all of the life-sustaining ingredients: turkey, ham, cheese, bacon (sometimes), lettuce, tomato, mayonnaise, three pieces of toast, and usually, pickle and potato chips on the side. At any rate, that was the reason Larry gave for always ordering a club sandwich.

I was sitting by the pool with a beer when Larry joined me, about five-thirty one evening. He told me that he had sent in a coupon and a check for ten dollars to "Electro-Date."

"What for?" I said. "There're about seven single women in Miami for every single man now. It's ridiculous to pay ten bucks for an electronic date. All you have to do is..."

"I know," he said. "I have a book with names and phone numbers, and if I got on the horn, I could have a woman join us here at this table in about ten minutes. But that isn't the idea."

Sitting there, with a secret widening grin, Larry was hard on my eyes. His silk shirt, stained with sweat, was yellow, and his Spanish leather tie was the color of dried blood. His textured hopsack jacket was orange, and his hair, Golden Bear styled, was haloed by the low sun with a 1930s rim-lighting effect. He took off his jacket, and draped it over a metal chair.

"All right, Hank," he said, "let's look at the evidence. If I made a phone call, and arranged a simple date—dinner, a movie, and then back to my apartment for a couple of drinks and a piece of ass—how much would it cost me?"

I shrugged. "About fifty bucks. It depends on where you have dinner, and the number of pre- and post-prandials you drink."

"Not necessarily. When you drive to Palm Beach every month, and you stop for a Coke and a hamburger, how much do you put down on your expense account?"

"Seven or eight bucks, something like that."

"Right. And you've made at least a three-fifty profit."

"About that, but on my expense account I'm entitled to a six-dollar lunch. If I take a hospital administrator to lunch, I can get away with a twenty-dollar tab, or, with drinks, even more."

"Exactly. So if I spend forty bucks on a simple date, and forty bucks is the irreducible minimum nowadays in Miami, and I can charge off the date to my expense account, wouldn't you say that I could get away with an over-all tab of fifty or sixty?"

"Sure. But a personal date, even with an electronic service, will be hard to slip by your office comptroller."

"You're right, Hank. Impossible, in fact. But not by the Internal Revenue Service. I can take the cost of the date off my income tax."

He took out his wallet, flipped it open, and displayed the photostat of his private investigator's license.

He said: "The idea came to me this morning when I saw the ad in the *Herald*. Instead of taking a chance on picking up a broad in a bar or a party who might turn out to be a drag, or a professional virgin, or a husband-seeker, I can get a date through the computer that fulfills most of my requirements in a woman. When I sent in the coupon and the check, I started a new file at the office. What I'm doing, you see, is investigating the possibility of using these woman who sign up with Electro-Date as part-time operatives, to employ when we need them at National Security for special assignments. After each date, I'll fill in a mimeographed form I've devised on the girl, and put it into this new folder. I can then take the expenses of the date, padded, naturally, off my income tax."

"Did your boss authorize this?"

"The Colonel? Hell, no! He'd never okay anything this reasonable. This is my own idea, and I'll spend my own dough. But the point is, if I'm called down by the IRS, I'll have the folder with the info on the girls to show them. I *am* a private investigator, and one of my duties at National is to check background reports on possible employees. My reason for doing this, officially, is personal enterprise. I'm showing initiative, and if the Colonel ever finds out about my plan he'll have to back me up with IRS because he's a great advocate of personal initiative. Besides, it isn't costing National a dime."

"What's the real reason?"

"Compatibility. As I said, the girl who signs up for Electro-Date has to pay fifty bucks for five dates. The male client only pays ten bucks for his five dates. So much for Women's Lib, you see. But she will be favorably disposed to me from the beginning because she has put down on her form what kind of man she wants to date, or *thinks* she wants to date, which is the same thing. And on a first meeting, we won't need any elaborate setting, nor will I have to spend a lot of dough. We'll want to talk, to explore each other, discover our likes and dislikes. No movie, no Miami Beach first-date crap, with the big stage show and champagne cocktails. No. Just me. Honest Larry 'Fuzz' Dolman, and the sincere here's-what-I-think-what-do-you-think heavy rap.

One hamburger, two cups of coffee, at Howard Johnson's, let's say, and I can take fifty bucks off my income tax for a so-called investigation. If I like the woman, and if she likes me, on the second date I'll have her in the sack in my apartment.

"What do you think?"

"I don't know, Fuzz. In a way, it sounds almost brilliant. But it seems to me that women who would sign up for a computer date are either going to be dogs or desperate for a husband."

"That used to be true. The older dating services were mostly match-making matrimonial set-ups, but that isn't true any more. Women have changed..."

"When it comes to wanting marriage, women never change."

"The form will avoid such problems. All I have to do is put down that I want to date a woman who doesn't want to get married. A career woman, or something. Anyway, when I get the questionnaire, I want you to help me with it. You're the man with a degree in psychology, and these data forms have probably got a few catch questions."

"Why not?" I said. "We'll have some fun with it, and you can hardly go wrong on a ten-dollar investment. But if IRS ever calls you down, don't count on me to go down there with you."

However, you can go wrong on a ten-dollar investment, as Larry found out on his first date.

The questionnaire, when it arrived, was not what we expected it to be. What Larry thought, and was led to suspect, was that the form would be a series of multiple choice questions, all of them concerned with the personality traits and characteristics he wanted his ideal girl to have—like the tests they run occasionally in the women's magazines, with the things you like least versus the things you like best in a "mate." *Cosmopolitan* magazine has tests like these all the time, and any person with a fair grounding in psychology, and mine is a good one, can score a hundred every time on such tests.

I was particularly good on testing, anyway, because of my two years as station psychologist at the U.S. Army Pittsburgh Recruiting Station. It was my job then to weed out military misfits, to interview admitted homosexuals, actual and phony, and to make decisions on whether to accept borderline enuresis cases or to send them home. The testing department was also under my supervision, although I had a Master Sergeant who ran this section for me. I was smart enough to let him alone and allow him to do things his own way, and as a consequence I learned a lot from him.

The only disagreement we ever had was about my attitude toward draftees who asked to see me because they were homosexuals, or claimed that they were. Sometimes, oftentimes, they were not, and it was easy enough to tell when they were lying.

When you ask some innocent eighteen-year-old, "What do you do together, you and another man?" and he is unable to tell you because he has no idea of what two men do together, it is obvious that the prospective draftee is lying to avoid the draft. But I would reject him anyway, much to the annoyance of my NCOIC of Testing. The way I figured, if a man was so terrified of the Army that he would say that he was a homosexual, even though he wasn't, he wouldn't make much of a soldier. And the first sergeants, down on the line somewhere, who would have to make a soldier out of him, had enough problems already.

But the questionnaire Larry received from Electro-Date had no questions whatsoever about his preferences in women. It was all about him—his age, his religion, his hobbies, and so on. This information would be transferred to a card, the card would be run through the computer, and then the cards that women had filled out—those that were similar in information to his—would drop out. He would be matched with one of them, and a date would be arranged between the two of them on the telephone by someone at the Electro-Date office.

"What you're going to have to do, Larry," I said, "is lie."

"Why?"

"Because the women who fill out their questionnaires are going to lie, that's why. For example, what's the upper age limit you'll agree to date?"

"Thirty, I suppose. I don't mind dating a woman my own age."

"There you are," I said. "If a woman's thirty-five, and she thinks she can get away with it, she'll put her age down as thirty. So you'd better put down that you're twenty-eight instead of thirty. You still might get an older woman, but at least you'll have some leeway.

"What's your religion, Larry?"

"None, really, but I used to go to the Unitarian Church once in awhile in Gainesville."

"You can't put that down. That's the last thing you want, a date with a Unitarian. They're weird, man."

"I know. They were weird in Gainesville, but they weren't inhibited, either."

"Put down Church of England."

"Episcopalian?"

"No. Church of England. That way they can match you with Episcopalians and lapsed Roman Catholics. If you happen, by chance, to get a real Church of Englander, they aren't concerned with morality, anyway. Episcopalians are all time-servers, and lapsed Catholics have a sense of guilt they're always trying to deny. A girl who thinks that sex is dirty, and feels guilty about it, can be a damned good piece of ass. If you were sincere about this questionnaire, I'd say to put down Roman Catholic, because you'd probably get a lot of nubile Cuban girls. But they'll all be looking for a husband."

"How young?"

"Look at the newspapers. Usually, Cuban girls are married by the time they're sixteen. If they're nineteen and still single, they're desperate, Larry."

"Let's change Church of England then, and put down Roman Catholic."

"Why?"

"A desperate girl is ready for anything."

"You'll be flooded, Larry. Except for priests you're probably the only single thirty-year-old 'Catholic' in Miami who's eligible and unmarried."

"I like that. What about occupation?"

We had some fun with that one, but finally decided upon "Dietician." We figured that he would probably get a few nurses that way, or at least some healthy girl who was an organic food freak. We added an extra degree, making him an M.A., and provided him with some interesting hobbies: making models of World War I airplanes, collecting old bottles in the Keys, and spelunking for buried treasures.

Three days later Larry dropped by my apartment to have a drink, on his way to his first arranged date. We are about the same height, but he weighs twenty pounds more than I do. In his new white sharkskin suit, red silk shirt, with a white-on-white necktie, red socks, and white alligator-grained Ballys, he looked like a friendly giant.

"How do you like the suit?" he said. "Coat and trousers, four hundred bucks. If it wasn't for the expense account, I couldn't have afforded a suit like this."

"You're really pushing the IRS to the wall," I said.

"Not at all. The new suit comes under the allowance for uniforms, and a man has to dress for his job. If I have to date these women, in the pursuit of my investigations, I have to make myself attractive. Right?"

"What's the girl's name?"

He looked at a slip of paper, and grinned. "Shirley Weinstein."

I laughed. "That sounds like a nice Catholic girl."

"I don't give a damn," he said. "She might even be a Catholic, for all we know. A lot of people think my name is Jewish, you know. Dolman sounds Jewish, if you don't know any better. But no one would make that mistake with my old man, especially on St. Patrick's Day when he used to go around town wearing an orange tie and looking for trouble."

"Where does she live?"

"Miami Beach. Where else? In the Cresciente condominium on Belle Isle."

I whistled. "Those apartments start at a hundred thousand, and that's for a one-bedroom, with one-and-a-half baths. I've seen the ads."

"What's the easiest way to get there?"

"The Venetian Causeway is the quickest, I think. Another short one?"

"I'd better not. What are you doing tonight?"

"I thought I'd call Eddie. Maybe we can get together for some pool at the White Shark. If he can't get away, I'll probably take in a flick. But report in when you get back. I'd like to know how it goes."

I called Eddie, but he was flying to Chicago at eleven p.m. and couldn't drink. He said he'd call me when he got back. This was his last flight for the month, and then he would have at least three days off.

After hanging up, I found myself envying Larry. It was such a strange and formal way to meet a woman it was bound to be interesting. I didn't envy him the girl—Shirley Weinstein—I could pretty well imagine what she would be like, but the formality of the idea was attractive.

Women were not a problem for me. I could telephone two girls I knew in Hialeah, and if they were home, I could drive over and have a three-way orgy. There were a dozen names or more in my book, and half of these girls, if they had a date, would break it to go out with me if I called and asked them. Or, if I wanted some stranger, I could cruise around and pick up a new broad within an hour or so.

But lately, it seemed, the women I screwed were all alike, as if they were cut out of the same batch of cookie dough. The stewardae *were* alike, and practically interchangeable. Their apartments looked as if they were all furnished by the same decorator. The clear plastic air-filled chair, the Budweiser bottle pillow, the *Rolling Stone* Mark Spitz poster (the one with Spitz lifting his trunks to reveal his pubic hair), the bottle of Taaka vodka, the tall stack of plastic glasses on the Kentone coffee table, the Port-au-Prince voodoo doll on the pillow, and the bed made up with garish Peter Max sheets—never with a bedspread—and the fresh uniform; always a clean, fresh uniform in a plasticene bag just back from the cleaners, hanging on a black wire hanger on the closet door; never inside the closet. Only the color of their eyes, hair and uniform was different. After a while, a few months back, while I was on my stewardess kick—with one leading me into another as I met the roommate, and she moved, and then I met *her* new roommate, who introduced me to her best friend, and then onto the next—they all blurred together.

They were even the same in bed, as if they had attended the same sex classes and had to pass an examination on *The Sensuous Woman, The Joy of Sex,* and the collected novels of John O'Hara.

Stewardesses never wanted to screw; with them it was all A.C.F.—anilingus, cunnilingus, and fellatio. You were lucky if one in ten would let you put it in. And there were more than 25,000 stewardesses living in Miami, all hot-eyed and eager to get a husband. They even smelled the same. Like milk. They usually wore musk oil, the scent that is supposed to bring out a true and personal odor, and that odor was milk; raw unpasteurized milk.

Nurses were a little better, but they had their peculiarities, too. At least one hand, but usually both hands, had to be touching you at all times; on the arm, the shoulder, the leg, and an arm was always around your waist when you walked. And a nurse's taste in civilian clothes was abominable. They looked great in their white uniforms, brisk, clean, and iodoformy, but then they would put on a red dress or a purple pants suit, or a peasant blouse and a plaid skirt, and they looked as if they had closed their eyes and grabbed something out of a Goodwill clothing bin. But nurses were all right, much better than stewardae. They were earthy, dependable, predictable, and almost always on time.

The problem, of course, was me. Not the stewardesses, not the nurses, but me. I was bored with their conversational subjects, flying schedules and ports of call, hospital schedules and patients. I had been through the same conversations again and again, and I didn't want to listen to them any longer. But people always talk about their work, and it was only natural for them to talk about their flying and floor schedules. I just didn't want to listen to them, that was all.

With Rita and Tina, the two Cuban girls in Hialeah, there was no talk at all. I didn't even know where they worked, or what they did for a living, although I had a hunch that they were divorcees on alimony. I would bring over a bottle of scotch, undress as I fixed a drink, and then we went to it, all three of us, without any discussion. It didn't cost me anything, but a man has to be in the right mood for an orgy...

I left the apartment and went out to a John Wayne re-run, *The Train Robbers*, probably the worst western the Duke ever made.

7

I had just finished watching the eleven o'clock news when Larry knocked on my door. He took off his jacket, refused a drink—he was already a little tight—and put a pot of water on to boil for instant coffee. He spooned two heaping teaspoonfuls of instant into a cup, and I asked him how it went.

"It was different," he said, after a long pause. "I've never had a date quite like it, and I had a much better time than I expected. It was weird, and gross, and yet I had a hellova good time."

He removed his tie and began to roll it around his finger the way I had taught him to do. I always do this, no matter how drunk I am when I get home. By rolling your tie into a tight roll, and putting it away in a drawer all rolled, it will be ready to use the next time without a wrinkle.

"This apartment," Larry said, "the Weinstein apartment, is on the top floor, the twelfth—not the penthouse, but the top floor. The Cresciente is on the bay side of Belle Isle, not on the ocean, but up this high, and on the southeast side of the building, with a screened veranda on both corners, there's a beautiful view of the Miami skyline and the ocean too.

"One hundred and fifty thousand hard ones, it cost."

"How do you know?"

"Irv told me. Mr. Weinstein. He was happy to tell me. He could hardly wait to tell me. Three bedrooms, three-and-a-half baths, a living room, a dining room, and a recreation room with a snooker table."

"A pool table..."

"No, a *snooker* table, regulation size, and two high pool room chairs, too. Irv had them made of rattan and fitted with custom cushions."

He stirred his coffee, and sat down across the coffee table from me.

I pointed the gadget at the TV set and switched it off. Larry said:

"The date didn't cost me a dime. I'd planned on taking Shirley to Wolfie's, or some place like that. I was a little nervous about this idea when I saw the Cresciente, but I was going to go through with it, anyway. But they had other plans. Mrs. Weinstein had fixed dinner, and on this first date they thought it would be best if we all just sat around and got acquainted with each other. Oh, yeah, they kept calling me 'Doctor.'"

"Did you go along?"

"Sure. Except I told them I was a Doctor of Philosophy. They didn't know the difference. I think the people down at Electro-Date must've told them I was a doctor. If it had been you, instead of me, you could've passed yourself off as an M.D. easy because you got all that medical jargon down. But they were just as happy with a Ph.D. They figured I was a college professor, at first, but I told them I was working as a private investigator for National Security, and that I was planning to write a book later on the philosophy of security."

"What's that?"

"How do I know? You're always saying I can't think in abstract terms, but it went down okay with the Weinsteins."

"What about the girl?"

"I don't know about the girl. Shirley didn't say much. Her mother dominated the dinner conversation, and then I played snooker with Irv. So Shirley didn't get to say much of anything."

"Was she pretty?"

"It's hard to tell, really. These Jewish girls all look alike to me, you know, at least the ones on Miami Beach. She'd had a nose job but they took off too much, as they usually do. Somehow, that Irish *rétroussé* nose never quite fits a Jewish face. If you'd studied as many mug shots as I have the last few years you'd know what I mean. She had nice hair, though, black, long, and straight down her back—almost down to her ass. She wore round, lightly tinted blue glasses, and a full-length granny dress. She had a weight problem, I think—at least her face was chubby—but she was fighting it. She hardly ate anything at all at dinner."

"What did they feed you?"

"Whitefish, with the heads on and all, some kind of meat and tomatoes and cheese casserole, and a Caesar salad. I didn't eat any whitefish. I don't like to see a fish with the eye staring up at you, and I was afraid of bones. Besides, by the time dinner was served, I was a little looped.

"Irv, you see, likes to drink, but I could tell he isn't allowed to have very many unless there's somebody else around. As soon as I'd drink half my drink, and it was Chivas and soda, too, he'd say, 'Let me freshen that for you, Doctor,' and he'd whip over to the bar. He'd add a couple of jiggers to his glass, too, except that he was drinking a full drink every time, not half-a-drink like me. The old lady noticed it, too, but she couldn't say anything to him with me there. Old Irv was really putting the stuff away."

Larry sipped his coffee, and said: "He's a retired furrier, about fifty-five or -six, somewhere in there."

"What about the girl? Shirley?"

"Under thirty. I don't know how much under thirty, but she was definitely under thirty, and she was unhappy about the situation, the date. I knew she wanted to go out, to get away from her parents, but there wasn't any way to work it. And after dinner, once I started to play snooker, I didn't want to go out anyway. Irv is a good player, and he beat me the first game. But I beat him the second two games. His problem, he doesn't play enough with other people. He probably practices a lot, and you know how it is when you practice, you try a lot of shots you wouldn't consider seriously in competition because they're too risky. So he would try some of these risky shots, and he missed a lot. I haven't played any snooker for four or five years, and I didn't really get my eye back until the middle of the second game. I wish I'd known about the snooker table, I'd have taken my own cue stick along..."

I laughed. "Shirley would've appreciated that," I said. "Bringing your cue stick along on a first date."

Larry laughed. "Yeah. But what I mean is the way it worked out."

"Did Shirley play, too?"

"No. She just sat in one of the high chairs and watched. She didn't say anything then, and before dinner and during dinner she didn't really get a chance to say anything. Her mother talked all the time, a real brittle woman, with a head of bleached blonde hair that looked like it was carved out of sandstone. You knew how hard it was by just looking at it."

"What did she talk about?"

"In a couple of weeks or so, all three of them are going on an around-the-world cruise. She talked about that. For the last year-and-a-half Shirley's been in Israel, living on a *kibbutz*. When they went to visit her there, Irv and Helen, they were so appalled by the living conditions they brought Shirley home. The water was alkaline, they had outside johns, the food was bad, the place was unsanitary, and they worked the shit out of poor Shirley. They had her running a buzz saw, making furniture. Shirley, I gathered, didn't want to come home, although she didn't say anything at the table. But this 'round-the-world trip is supposed to be a present to make up for it. That was the implication, anyway. Shirley hardly opened her mouth, but she looked at me a lot.

"Then, on purpose, but trying to pass it off, Helen, Mrs. Weinstein, said that the cruise would be a honeymoon gift for Shirley, if she wanted to take advantage of it."

"That was pretty blunt, Larry. Did they think, all this time, that you were Jewish?"

"I think so, yes. Irv didn't care, but Helen stiffened up when I finally said I was a Catholic. And it upset Helen, too, when I said that I thought *they* were all Catholics and that that's what they'd told me at Electro-Date."

"They didn't tell you that at Electro-Date."

"I know, but that's what I said. Can you imagine some poor bastard getting married and having mother- and father-in-law along in the same cabin for three months?"

"They'll find someone. He's got money, this guy."

"Irv's got money all right. He's rich, man. And a damned good snooker player. Why don't you and I got out for snooker some night? Did you ever play it?"

"I used to, but I don't even know where there's a table in Miami."

"We could play over at Irv's. He said to call him any time I wanted to play. But that's out, I suppose. I'm not interested in the girl, and if I went back, it might give her a false idea."

"Did you get a chance to talk to her alone? You said she didn't talk much, but you haven't told me anything she said."

"Well, we didn't talk alone until I actually left. When I got ready to leave, her mother called her into the kitchen for a minute, and Irv went to get my coat. I'd taken it off when we played snooker, and left it in the rec room. When I opened the front door, Shirley said, 'I'll ride down to the lobby with you.'

"We got into the elevator, and about the sixth floor she pulled out the red emergency knob and stopped the elevator. I was still a little high, and when the elevator stopped suddenly that way I lurched against the wall. She looked into my eyes, through those blue-tinted glasses of hers, and said: 'Are you circumcised, Larry?'

" 'No.' I said.

" 'Let me see it,' she said.

"I took out my cock and showed it to her. She looked at it for a long time, as though she'd never seen a dong before, at least an uncircumcised dong, and then said, 'I don't care.'

"'What do you mean,' I said, 'you don't care?'

"'I mean,' she said, 'that it doesn't matter to me whether you're circumcised or not.'"

"She was propositioning you, Larry. That is, she was telling you that she was available."

"I know that, Hank. I put it away, zipped up, and took the elevator off emergency. It really turned me off, man, not that I was turned on by her in the first place, but it was all so weird, standing there with half-a-buzz on, you know, with my dong out, and the way she stared at it. Maybe a soft, uncircumcised prick isn't a beautiful thing to see, but it's mine, you know, and that curious, scientific look she had, the blue-tinted glasses, the way she leaned over, with her hands on her hips—I don't know, Hank, I just don't know. For a moment there, it scared me. I had a funny feeling, or a premonition, that it would never get hard again.

"Anyway, when we got down to the lobby, I gave her a good-night kiss, a long slobbery one. And she responded, too. But there was nothing there, man, nothing. My balls were ice cubes. So much for the first date. I think I'll put down about thirty-five bucks for this one on my expense account, and call it a night."

Larry rose, and picked up his white jacket. He put his rolled white tie into the left jacket pocket.

"Something's wrong with the computer at that electronic dating service," I said. "You couldn't have been matched any worse if you'd picked up a lez at a gay bar."

"I know. Tomorrow I'm going to call Electro-Date and raise holy hell. Even though I'm not a Catholic I said I was a Catholic and I'm entitled to either a Catholic or to someone who has lied about it the way I did."

I laughed. "Say that again."

Larry grinned. "I can't."

After Larry left, I thought about this strange evening for a few minutes, and then went to bed myself. The dating service didn't enter my thoughts again until I ran into Larry with his second date at Don's birthday party, a week later.

That's when I met Jannaire.

8

There were more than twenty cars parked on Don's lawn and along the curb and on neighboring lawns by the time I got to his house for his birthday party. The quiet of the suburban neighborhood was bothered by gibbering drums which pulsed above the shattering rise and fall of voices from the poolside patio. I learned later that some maniac had given Don a birthday present of three LPs of the authentic tribal drums of Africa.

Clara Luchessi, in a losing effort to keep as many people out of her house as possible, had centered the festivities around the pool and patio. The bar, the tables loaded with catered food, and even two green-and-white striped tents, with extra swimming trunks and bikinis, one tent marked HE and the other SHE, as dressing rooms, were outside. There were no emergency latrine facilities at poolside, however. One still had to go inside the house to use the john, or else pee in the pool.

There was a lopsided pile of birthday presents on a card table at the far end of the pool. I added mine to the pile and checked the birthday card again to make certain the tape would keep it secure on the package. My present to Don was in poor taste, but it wasn't really for Don's benefit—it was for Clara's. I had found a used copy, almost in mint condition, of George Kelly's *Craig's Wife*, in Maggie's Old Book Shop, and I had talked Maggie into giftwrapping it for me. Don would read the play and laugh, knowing it was a joke. But if Clara read it, she might, quite possibly, take some of the pressure off Don around the house.

The soft night air was muggy, with the humidity at ninety percent, according to my car radio, but a warm heavy breeze huffed across the patio from the flat green fairway beyond the back of the house. Don's backyard pool was merely an easy lay away from the No. 8 green of the Miccosukee Country Club. Around the edges of the yard, and along the fairway border, Clara had placed lighted candles. They were upright in sandfilled paper sacks, and the surprisingly good light made the faces of the guests slightly distorted because they were lit from below. There was a strong electric light above the bar, however. The bartender, Joe T., or Jotey, as he was called, was a black man who bagged groceries regularly at the Kendall Kwik-Chek. All four of us guys had hired Jotey as a bartender at one time or another for parties because he had surprisingly good judgment. If someone was about to get overloaded, Jotey would gently taper him off by reducing the alcoholic content of his drinks. Moreover, because Jotey didn't have to go to work at the Kwik-Chek until ten a.m., he would come back willingly, early the next morning following a party, and clean everything up for an extra ten bucks.

"Mr. Norton," Jotey said, as I reached the bar; "a J.B. and soda." He grinned, and handed me my drink.

"It's a lot better than Glen Plaid," I said.

Jotey winked, and waited on another customer, Nita Peralta, Don's chubby Cuban secretary. I admired her costume, a silk white-and-red awning striped mini-skirted dress, tied around her bulging middle with a red silk sash. She also wore strawberry mesh stockings and green patent leather boots. Not wanting to get into a conversation with Nita, I moved away from the bar.

I knew a few of the people slightly—Don's married friends—but most of the guests were middle-aged strangers. The older men, many of them accompanied by their wives, were Don's customers, I supposed, invited to his birthday party so he could write it off legitimately as a business expense. Despite the heat, many of these older men wore dinner jackets and business suits. In Miami, the word "informal" on an invitation does not mean dinner jackets, it means sports shirts, Bermuda shorts, and tennis shoes or sandals. But older men, as a kind of compromise, almost always wear a suit and tie to "informal" parties. A suit for a businessman, like a soldier's uniform, is always correct, even though it's equally uncomfortable.

The weather in Miami is precisely the same as the weather in South Vietnam, and it's a damned shame that we cannot dress accordingly. When I call on doctors and visit hospitals, my company insists that I wear a suit and tie. I must keep my hair cut short, although the young doctors I see sometimes have bushy curls down to their shoulders. The rapport I gain with the older, far-right doctors, I lose with the younger far-left doctors.

I spotted Don right away. He was seated, with his daughter Marie on his lap, on the far side of the pool. He was talking to a middle-aged Cuban in a blue chalk-striped wool suit, and from the earnestness of their conversation, they were undoubtedly talking business. Don sold a lot of his English silverware to Cubans, he told me. His Cuban customers made up almost thirty percent of his business.

I decided to talk to Don later. Clara was at the other end of the patio, pushing the baked beans and potato salad. I wondered, maliciously, if she counted the red plastic spoons and forks after the guests left.

Eddie Miller had told me on the phone that he would be staying overnight in Chicago and would miss the party, so I searched for Larry. I ambled about, nodding pleasantly, but not stopping, to avoid talking to anyone. I knew that Larry would be there soon, because there could be no date cheaper than to take a woman to a free birthday party, and he said he would be coming with a new Electro-Date. After listening to his story about the Weinstein date, I was curious to see what the dating service would come up with next.

Movement helped a little, but the dull pain in my stomach was undiminished. I had gained five pounds, and when I gain five pounds I eat only one meal a day, at noon, until I have dropped back to 195. Eating once a day enables me to lose the necessary amount, and I can still have a few drinks besides.

Ordinarily, I return to one meal a day as soon as I hit 200, but somehow I had crept up to 205 before I noticed it. As an additional psychological crutch to maintain my weight at a sturdy 195, I have all my clothes tailored. If I zoomed, suddenly, to 210, for example, I would need an entirely new wardrobe. And at the moment, at 205, my trousers were uncomfortably tight at the waist. I wore the tails of my sport shirt outside my paints to gain an extra eighth of an inch. It was all I could do to stay away from Clara's groaning buffet, but I was afraid to go near it.

I stood for a minute or so, nibbling on an ice cube and watched a wide-assed girl climb out of the pool across the water, and then returned to the bar for another drink.

I was on my third drink, and still hungry, when Larry arrived. He was wearing his white suit, his "dating uniform," and he moved like a snow-covered mountain through the crowd as he headed for the bar. The woman trailed him, and I didn't get a good look at her, even when he got to the bar, because she was on the other side of him. Larry put his birthday gift on the bar, a greasy, clumsily wrapped package in green tissue paper, and ordered two bourbons with Coke chasers. He was that way. He always ordered for himself and the woman he was with without asking what she wanted. With drinks, it didn't matter so much, but they corrected the order in a hurry when he ordered club sandwiches and they wanted a steak and a salad.

"What's that?" I said, tapping the package.

Larry grinned. "Don's birthday present. I got him a Colonel Sanders thrift-pack. Nine pieces of cold chicken. And I wrapped it myself."

"Your gift is worse than mine," I said. "I got him a book."

"Not really," Larry said. "I thought the thrift-pack might remind him of his batching days with us at the building."

"It will. But I don't think Clara will appreciate it."

"I hope not."

I picked up the greasy package, put it on the card table with the others, and returned. This time I got a good look at Larry's date. She was beautiful enough to know that the world would always be on her side.

Then I got a whiff of her, the full heady aroma, and it was like a hard right to the heart, a straight punch, with the entire weight of the body behind it. An odor, a smell, is almost indescribable, except, perhaps, in terms of other smells, but in one word Jannaire smelled Woman. I mentioned musk oil earlier, and the futile hope that it will bring out a person's individual odor. Most of the time it doesn't; it simply smells like musk oil on the user. It seems as if most of the women in Miami and half of the gay men use it, but this impression is false. If there are five women sitting together in a room, and if only one of them is wearing musk oil, it is so powerful that it blends with the perfumes the other four women are wearing, giving the surreptitious sniffer the impression that all five women are muskily anointed.

The musk smell on Jannaire was faint, because her own smell, or reek, to be more exact, of primeval swamp, dark guanoed caves, sea water in movement, armpit sweat, mangroves at low tide, Mayan sacrificial blood, Bartolin glands, Dial soap, mulberry leaves, jungle vegetation, saffron, kittens in a cardboard box, Y.W.C.A. volleyball courts, conch shells, Underground Atlanta, the Isle of Lesbos, and sheer joy—Patou's Joy—overpowered the musk oil. I was overwhelmed by the nasal assault, overcome by her female aroma, and although I could not, at the time, define the mixture—nor can I now, exactly—there wasn't the faintest trace of *milk*. Here was a woman.

"Jannaire," Larry said, "this is Hank Norton, my best friend. Hank. Jannaire."

She looked up at me with gold-flecked fecal-beige eyes. She was about five-two, but she looked shorter in gold flats. Her straight, dark brown hair, parted in the center and loose to her shoulders, was a dark bronze helmet, and it clung flat to her head as if she had just broken water after a shallow dive. There was at least a sixteenth of an inch of white showing beneath her pupils, and her bold dark eyes revealed the full optic circle. She wore a gold knee-length dress, shapeless at the waist and unbelted, with tiny golden chains for shoulder straps.

She raised her arm as Larry handed her the bourbon and

Coke, and a thick tuft of black steelwool under her arm bugged out my eyes. Except in Swedish and British films, I had never seen a woman with unshaved armpits, and I mentally visualized the same thick inky hair of her bush. Tiny stop-and-go rivulets of sweat inched down my sides as I began to perspire.

"Jannaire..?" I said.

"She doesn't have a last name," Larry said. "She said," he added, in disapproval.

"How do you do, Jannaire?" I took the glass out of her hand, and placed it on the bar. "You don't have to drink that. You can have anything you want."

"I'd like a beer, I think." There was a catch in her voice, and she ended the sentence with a rising inflection. She ended all her sentences with rising inflections, I soon discovered.

"I'll get you one," I said. There was no beer at the bar, but I knew there would be beer in Don's refrigerator.

"Stay here, Jannaire," Larry said. "I've got to make a phone call."

"We'll be right back," I said.

Larry and I entered the kitchen, and he jerked his head toward the hallway. "Let's go into Don's study for a minute."

We entered the study and Larry turned on the desk lamp. "Did you smell her, Hank?" he said. "Driving here from Hojo's in the car I had to turn off the airconditioner and roll the goddamned windows down."

"I'll take her off your hands, Larry," I volunteered casually.

"How? I can't just ditch her. She's liable to report me to Electro-Date, and I've got three more dates coming. Unfortunately," he said bitterly.

"No problem. You said you had to make a phone call. I'll just tell Jannaire for you that your boss sent you out on an emergency mission of some kind. You wait in here a couple of minutes, and I'll take her out to the golf course. That'll give you a chance to say 'Happy Birthday' to Don and bug out."

"You don't have to do this for me, Hank. I got into it, and I..."

"What the hell. You'd do the same for me."

"I'm not so sure that I would. What *is* that smell, Hank?"

"Woman, that's all, woman."

"Did you see her fucking armpits? I've never seen a woman with unshaved armpits before, have you?"

"No, but it kinda turns me on."

"It turns me off! After I finish the three other dates, I'm going back to stewardae. The hell with this income tax dodge. I keep running into one goddamned fantasy after another."

"Is Jannaire a Catholic?"

"She must be. There isn't a Protestant in American who'd let hair grow under her arms."

"Okay, Larry. Give me a couple of minutes," I said, "and I'll get you out of it."

"Right. I'll just talk to Don a second, and split. It's a lousy party anyway, isn't it?"

"They always are."

I got two cans of beer out of the refrigerator, and rejoined Jannaire at the bar. Jotey, behind the bar, was pointing out Don and Clara to her with his long black forefinger.

"Let's go out by the golf course to drink these," I said. "If people see us with beers, they'll all want one."

I popped the tops and handed her a can as we walked toward the No. 8 green, and skirted the sand trap. The green was on a gentle berm of filled earth, and we sat on the grassy slope facing the lighted back yard. The row of candles along the border made the milling people around the pool resemble actors on a stage set, with the candles serving as footlights.

"Where's Larry?" she said.

"I don't know how to tell you this, Jannaire, but he said he simply couldn't stand you. So he left, and I promised to take you home."

"I could tell he didn't like me," she said, "but you don't have to take me home. I can get a cab back to the Hojo's on Dixie."

"Why Hojo's?"

"That's where I left my car."

"Larry's crazy," I said. "You're the most attractive woman here tonight. Perhaps you said something to irritate him. Larry's very sensitive, you know."

"I don't know what it could be. I know he didn't believe me when I told him I didn't have any last name, but it's true. I had my name changed legally to Jannaire five years ago."

"From what?"

"That's what he asked. But that's the way things always go with me. Men either like me or they don't from the first moment we meet. And more men dislike me than like me. It's always been that way, ever since high school."

"What do you do, Jannaire?"

"About men, do you mean?"

"No. I *like* you. We've already got that established. Work, I mean."

"Many of the women here tonight would know—a lot of them, I think. I design clothes, pant suits, mostly, under the trade name of Jannaire. I also own the Cutique, on Miracle Mile in the Gables."

"Cutique?"

"Awful, isn't it? But they remember the name, women do, and they come back. I also own two apartment houses, and I'm a silent partner in a few other business ventures. I keep busy."

"I don't understand this dating business, then. Why would a woman as attractive as you, and with some money besides—and a business—sign up with Electro-Date?"

She laughed. "Does Larry tell you everything?"

"No, but we're friends, and we live in the same building. And he did tell me about Electro-Date."

"To tell you the truth, Mr. Norton..."

"Hank, for Christ's sake. I'm not going to call you Miss Jannaire."

"All right, Hank. That's an odd name, too, isn't it?"

"Come on, back to the truth about the electronic dating."

"I happen to own twenty percent of Electro-Date, and it isn't doing very well now, although it started out well enough. Miami is much too small for accurate matching, which is always half-assed at best, but there're too many dating services competing. Anyway, when someone really bitches, as Larry did after his first date, they call me. I study the application questionnaire and sometimes take the next date myself. I'm sure if Larry and I had had a chance to talk together, as you and I are doing now, I could've overcome his objections to me, whatever they are."

"No," I laughed. "Not unless you shaved under your arms."

"Fuck him, then! Do you want to blow a roach?" She opened her little gold mesh bag, and took out a stick.

"Go ahead," I reached for my lighter, "but I never smoke pot. It doesn't do anything for me, and I've been brainwashed. I'm a detail man, and by the time we've finished our indoctrination course, we never touch anything in the drug line."

"Mary Jane isn't a drug," she protested.

"I know the arguments. And I can counter every one you bring up, too. But in my job, with drugs of every kind available to me, I leave them strictly alone. They scared us badly during training. I'm even nervous about taking an aspirin. And aspirin can be dangerous too. In some people, it burns holes through the stomach lining."

I lit her cigarette. She inhaled deeply, held it in, and said through closed teeth, "What's a detail man?"

"Drug pusher. I'm a pharmaceutical salesman for Lee Laboratories, and my territory includes Key West, Palm Beach, and all of Dade County. I'm supposed to see forty doctors a week and tell them about our products. I brief them, or *detail* one or more of our products, so they'll know how to use them."

"There're a lot of drug companies, aren't there?"

"Sure. And a lot of detail men, and a lot of doctors. But my job, especially for Lee Labs, is one of the best jobs in the world, if not the best. I work about five hours a week, when I work at all, and I make a decent living."

"How can you call on forty doctors in five hours?"

"You can't. I fake it, turning in my weekly report from the info in my files. Also I telephone from time to time—the doctors' secretaries—to make sure the doctor hasn't died on me since the last time I actually called on him. But I can usually make ten or fifteen personal calls in an afternoon when I want to. And if I set up a drugs display for one day in a hospital or medical building, that counts as forty calls for the week. I like my work, though, and I'm really a good salesman. I feel sorry for doctors, the poor overworked bastards, and I like to help them out."

"Do they always let you in? Just like that?"

"Most of them do. There are three kinds of doctors, you see. It's impossible for a doctor to read everything put out by the drug companies on every drug, but a few try. They all need a detail man to explain what a drug does, its contraindications, and so forth. So one doctor refuses to see detail men, and reads all of the literature, or tries to, himself. Another doctor never reads anything, but depends entirely on a detail man to brief him. The third kind doesn't read anything or see any detail men either. And if you happen to get this guy for a doctor, your chances for survival are pretty damned slim."

"So they see you, then?"

"Most of them, but you can't always overcome their prejudices or their ignorance. For example, I might ask a doctor, 'What do you know about migraine?' Half the time, he'll tell me that migraine headaches are psychosomatic, and that you can't do anything for them. He doesn't want to listen, you see. His mind is made up. In a case like that, you say, 'Okay,' and get onto something else. But when you're lucky, you'll run into an intelligent doctor, and he'll say, 'I don't know a damned thing about migraine. I get four or five cases a week, and I can't do anything for them.'

"So then you tell him. It so happens that we've got a product that reduces or even stops migraine headaches. What happens, you see, is that tension, or something, nobody knows what it is exactly, causes the blood veins in your temples to constrict. Now this isn't migraine, not yet. But these veins can't stay constricted too long because you've got to get blood to your head. What happens, pressure builds, and the man can feel his migraine coming on. Then, all of a sudden, the tight veins open up and a big surge of blood gushes through these open vessels, and there's your migraine headache. What our product does is keep the veins closed. They open eventually, but gradually, slowly. Without the sudden surge of released blood, the headache is either minimized or it doesn't come."

"How did you learn all that?"

"Well, in this case, we had a two-day conference in Atlanta, with all of the detail men from Lee Labs in the Southeast present. We had a doctor who has spent his life studying migraine. He briefed us, and our own company research men who finally developed the drug briefed us. We had two films, and then some Q. and A. periods. Then we all got drunk, got laid, and flew back to our own territories. But the thing is, a doctor who came out of medical school ten years ago, let's say, was told that you couldn't do anything about migraine. 'It's psychological,' they told him. So he still believes it, and he won't listen to you. And if he doesn't read anything, and he won't listen to you, if a patient has a migraine and goes to him, he'll tell him that the headache's all in the mind. It's a shame really, because such people can be helped by our drug."

"I've never had a migraine."

"They're pretty bad. They can last for hours, or even for days, sometimes. You're nauseated, and you lie flat on your back in a dark room with a wet towel over your eyes. It'll go away, eventually, but when a person gets a warning it's coming—you know, the tightening of the temples and so on—he has time to take our product and prevent the damned thing—or at least to reduce the force of it."

"Here," she said, passing me the stick, "take a drag. Sharing is part of the high, you know."

To please her, I took a short toke and returned the butt.

There was a happy shout, and I watched the guests gathering near the bar. It was time for Don to open his presents.

I rarely talked about my work, and not always truthfully when I did talk about it. But I had opened up to Jannaire, and probably bored the hell out of her. She had seemed interested, however, and the subject was interesting—at least to me. I wanted her to like me. She was a mature woman, at least thirty, I figured, and I couldn't talk to her about inconsequential matters the way I did with younger women. I also realized, sitting there, that I hadn't dated or slept with a woman older than twenty-five since I came to Miami. I wanted to kiss Jannaire. In fact, I wanted to rape her, right there on the No. 8 green, and yet I was reluctant to put my arm around her, afraid that I would be premature. Talking with Jannaire gave me an entirely different way of looking at a female.

"Do you want to watch Don open his presents?" I said.

"Not particularly. I should go, I think. I haven't even met the host or hostess..."

"This isn't a good time to meet them, either. Suppose we go somewhere and talk? To my apartment, perhaps?"

She laughed. "Apparently you like me better than Larry did."

"I'll just say 'so long' to Don, and wish him a happy birthday. Do you really want to meet him?"

"No, not in the middle of the big production number."

It was a production number. A circle of chattering bodies surrounded Don and the card table loaded with presents. Don sat in a chair beside the table, while his daughter, glorying in being the center of attention, opened the presents, one at a time, and handed them to him for inspection. Don would read the card aloud, and the guests laughed or applauded his loot. Clara, with a pencil between her teeth like a horse's bit, held a yellow legal pad. She would write the donor's name down, make a cryptic note of the present, and later on she would write nice letters of thanks, which Don would sign as his own. It was a grim business.

I stepped up to Don, put a hand on his shoulder. "Happy birthday, Don," I said in an undertone. "I'm splitting."

"What the hell is this?" He said unhappily. "Eddie is in Chicago, Larry just left, and now you—my best friends, for Christ's sake!"

I grinned. "Look what I'm leaving with—no, don't look now, and you'll understand."

I nodded politely to Clara, and ran after Jannaire, who was already at the end of the patio and opening the gate in the Cyclone fence that led to the street.

As I drove down Dixie Highway toward Hojo's I hugged the right lane and drove as slowly as I could get away with, wondering why I had exaggerated the healing properties of mygrote. Mygrote was effective in at least three cases in ten of migraine, but it sure as hell wasn't the cure-all I had claimed for it in my discourse to Jannaire. I never lied to doctors about the product, so why had I snowed Jannaire? I was trying to impress her, I decided, but I was going about it in the wrong way. Jannaire was more than just another cunt, and I would have to use other tactics to impress her, if that was what I wanted to do.

"Look," I said, clearing my throat as we stopped at a red light at Sunset Drive, "I've got two tickets to the Player's Theater tomorrow night. It's *The Homecoming*, a Pinter play. Perhaps you'd like to see it."

"Yes, I'd like very much to see it. But not if you're going to tell Larry Dolman."

"Tell him what?"

"That you're dating me, and that I have a partial interest in Electro-Date."

"Why not?"

"For one thing, he works for National Security, and I don't want those snoops to know anything about my business. For another, I've been lining up Larry's next date in my mind, and I don't want him to suspect that I had anything to do with it, you see. I have a hunch that he could be very nasty if he had a grudge."

"He could. I advise you not to play any tricks on him."

"Oh, I won't." She laughed. "The trick'll be his problem, not mine!"

"I don't tell Larry everything. But going to the play will just be the first date, Jannaire. My overall plan, after I convince you how sweet and charming I am, is to get you into the sack. Eventually, anyway; I'm not going to rush it."

"A woman admires frankness, Hank, but you're awfully crude."

"Not crude," I laughed. "Basic."

I parked in the Hojo lot. She leaned toward me, kissed me on the lips, banging her wet hot hard tongue against my teeth. I felt the flames of her furnace breath for a second, and then she was out of the car before I realized what happened.

"I'll meet you at the theater," she said, waving, and climbed into her silver-gray Porsche. As she backed out of the slot, I noticed that the little car had battered front fenders.

There was no way, as I thought back on this first encounter, to tell that Jannaire was married. A married woman cannot easily get out of the house for two nights in a row. She had gone to Don's birthday party with Larry, and the next night she went to the play with me. Two nights later, I met her downtown at the Top of the Columbus for cocktails and dinner. The following week I had lunch with her twice, once at Marylou's Soul House, and once at LaVista. The lunches were both short, lasting less than an hour and a half each time, but she arrived on time, and left hurriedly because of business appointments.

My hours, the few hours I put in each week, were flexible, but Jannaire was always busy with her boutique (the Ugh! "Cutique"), her real estate interests, her designing, her clients, and with her home and husband. But I never, not once, suspected that she was married, or even that she had *ever* been married.

The evidence, however, or the clue, was always there, but I had failed, in my infatuation, my frustration—and there were times when her peculiar admixture of odors made me almost insane with desire—to recognize the obvious evidence.

She always met me somewhere, and she always drove home alone. I had never picked her up at her apartment, and I never had an opportunity to drive her home. With the number of separate dates we worked in during a period of almost six weeks—perhaps sixteen dates altogether—I should have suspected something.

The problem was, I was always trying to get her to come to my apartment. I had never concentrated on getting her alone at her place because she said that her aunt from Cleveland was visiting her for the season. She had established this house guest early, and I had accepted the aunt as a fact of coexistence. Also, from time to time, Jannaire would make an excuse to turn down a date because she was doing something or other with her aunt. That was another peculiar thing; why did she give me her home telephone number? I had no ready story prepared to explain to a jealous husband why I was calling his wife. I had no objections to running around with a married woman, of course, but to run around in Miami, visiting public places (I had even taken her to The Mutiny, the private club at Sailboat Bay) could have—in fact, it *did*—place a man's life in jeopardy. *My* life.

Except for the single, swift erotic kiss I got on parting—never on greeting—a kiss that always promised everything and delivered nothing, I was no closer to seducing Jannaire after six weeks than I had been on the first night at Don's house. I had cupped her breasts in the car a couple of times, as we were driving somewhere, and they were as firm as clenched fists. But that was all. When I propositioned her, which I did two or three times during each date, she merely smiled and changed the subject or smiled and continued to ask me questions about myself. As a consequence, Jannaire knew a great deal about me, but I knew very little about her.

I have never been in love. I'm not even sure that I know what love is, in fact, or whether I would recognize it if it ever happened to me. But I was not, in the sense that the term is used generally, in love with Jannaire. All I really wanted with Jannaire was to screw her and screw her and screw her, and that was all. But that "all" was getting to be an obsession.

It was Sunday morning.

Saturday night, Eddie Miller and I had gone to the White Shark to play pool and drink a few beers. The place was crowded, and it was hard to get the pool table. Once we got it, when our turn came to challenge the winners, we were able to hold it all right, but on our last game we played an old man and Sadie. Sadie, who owns the White Shark, also works the bar (The White Shark is a beer-and-wine bar only), and she had to keep leaving the game to serve customers, usually when it was her turn to shoot. The old man took a maddeningly long time to make his shots, and the single game of eight-ball we played with Sadie and the old man lasted for almost an hour. Eddie decided to quit.

Two or three times during the evening, Eddie, preoccupied with something, had started to tell me what was troubling him, but each time he changed his mind.

I knew, or thought I knew, what was bothering him. He was still living with the wealthy widow in Miami Springs, a move he had made stubbornly against the advice of Larry, Don, and myself, and he had now discovered, I suspected, what a mistake he had made. The woman, who was still attractive, with a good, if rather lush, figure, was almost twice as old as Eddie, and she was undoubtedly smothering him. He wanted to talk about it, but was too embarrassed. I would not under any circumstances have pulled an "I told you so," and Eddie knew me well enough to know this, but he was still reluctant to talk about his problems. I didn't push him. He would eventually come around with his problem, whatever it was, and I would advise him as well as I could.

We left the White Shark at eleven p.m., Eddie to drive home (to the widow's house in Miami Springs), me to drive home alone to Dade Towers. He handed me a folded sheet of paper as we stood for a moment in the parking lot to suck in a little fresh, humid air.

"What's this?" I said.

"For now," Eddie said, "just put it in your pocket. D'you

remember that game we played one night? The night you had us all make a list of everything we had in our wallets? Then you had a psychological analysis of each one of us from our lists..."

"Sure, I remember. But it wasn't fair as far as you and Larry were concerned. I knew you guys too well already. But I hit the girls pretty well, I thought."

"I thought so, too. I don't know how you did it, but that little chick I had, the Playboy bunny, turned as white as rice when you got onto her about her father..."

"I can explain how I reached that conclusion. What she..."

"I don't want an explanation, Hank. We all laughed at the time, and you said yourself that it was inaccurate, at best, but I was impressed as hell. I never said so, Hank, but I was. I really was."

"It isn't a trick, Eddie. There is *some* validity to the analysis, but it's too general to be conclusive, for Christ's sake. On Larry's girl, the chubby brunette, I could say positively that she was a poor driver and she knew she was a lousy driver, because she had all of her earlier driver's licenses in her wallet. She had kept old ones, even when she got her new and current license. And she admitted, as I recall, that I was right. She felt, she said, that she really didn't deserve a driver's license, and it made her feel more secure to have as many as possible."

"That was sharp to spot that, though. I was impressed by that analysis."

"Hell, Eddie, you could've made the same comment. I was lucky on that one. She could've just had her current license, and I never would've figured out that she was, or thought she was, a lousy driver. Actually, she was a pretty good driver. She never had an accident, she said. If more people thought they were lousy drivers and drove more carefully, there'd be fewer accidents."

"I know. I know. That isn't the point. But what I've given you is a list of the shit Gladys carries in her handbag. In her wallet, and in her handbag, too. And as a favor—I hate to ask this, Hank—I'd like you to kind of look it over and give me an analysis of Gladys some time."

"Is there anything else you want to tell me about the problem, Ed? I mean, if there's something specific, I might be able to do a better job, even though it won't actually prove anything about what kind of woman she is."

"No, there's nothing specific I want to get into. I think I know what kind of woman she is anyway. Besides, I don't want to prejudice you any. I want you to be objective, as objective as you can, as if Gladys was a stranger, you know. I already know you don't like her..."

"I never said I didn't like her."

"I know you didn't. But I still want you to be objective." Eddie looked away from me, and took a rumpled Lucky Strike out of his beatup package. This was a sure sign that he was nervous. Eddie, to my envy, only smoked one package of Luckys a week. This single pack, by the end of the week, was usually wrinkled and battered because he carried it with him all the time. Sometimes he would go for two full days without even thinking about smoking a cigarette. I smoked two packs a day, and if I was drinking at night, I often went through a third. So when he did light a Lucky, it was easy to see he was agitated about his problem.

"That old trick of yours came back to me the other night, and I decided to try it," Eddie said. "On Gladys, but without her knowing anything about it. So this morning, when she took some clothes out to the washer in the utility room, I grabbed her purse and made this inventory—the one I gave you." He blushed, and took a deep drag on his Lucky. "I found out something about her already I didn't know. She's forty-seven, not forty-five. She lied to me, Hank. She told me she was only forty-five. But it was on her driver's license, her age, I mean, forty-seven."

I nodded. "She might be even older than that," I said. "She might've lied to the Highway Patrol, too. A woman who'll tell a black lie to her lover wouldn't hesitate to tell a white lie to the Highway Patrol."

"Jesus, Hank! Cut it out, will you? It's bad enough she's forty-seven without making her fifty, for Christ's sake!"

"I didn't say she was fifty. All I said was that she might've taken off a couple of more years on her license. The possibility is there, isn't it?"

"I asked you to be objective, Hank."

"I am being objective. That's what psychological analysis is, looking at every possible angle. There's nothing tricky about a wallet survey, Eddie. It just happens that we had this professor at Michigan, a Harry Stack Sullivanite, he was, who taught us how to look for shortcuts. We played this game in class with each other, and it was fun because it was so half-assed. The reason I got good at it was because I tried it again when I was staff psychologist at the Pittsburgh Recruiting Station. For example, if a draftee told me he was gay, and then I looked into his wallet and found a couple of condoms, a picture of his girl friend, and about five scraps of paper with girls' names and phone numbers on them, the evidence was contrary to what he said. It also worked the other way, with gays who claimed that they weren't gay, guys who wanted to get into the Army. I remember one sonofabitch..."

"Look, Hank, just go over the list for me, the one I gave you, and do what you can. It might be helpful to me. Okay?"

"I'll do it tomorrow."

"There's no hurry, man. Next week, the week after—I don't give a shit. Okay?"

"Sure, Eddie. I'll call you."

"I'm sorry, Hank. I got a lot on my mind these days. And that old man in there tonight drove me up the fucking wall."

"We should've gone to a flick. The White Shark's too crowded on a Saturday night."

"I couldn't have sat through a film. Goodnight, Hank."

So on Sunday morning, after I finished typing my sales reports and had them ready to mail out to Atlanta the next morning, I pulled out the inventory Eddie had given me of Gladys Wilson's handbag. As I started to unfold it, a long yellow legal-sized sheet of paper, the phone rang.

It was Jannaire. The call was unexpected, because she had told me that she and her aunt were going to spend the weekend in Palm Beach.

"My aunt went to Palm Beach, Hank, but at the last minute yesterday afternoon I begged off. I tried to call you last night, but you didn't answer your phone."

"I went out to play some pool, but I was home by eleven-thirty, baby."

"I called around nine, I think it was."

"You said you were going to Palm Beach, so..."

"I know. But I was lonely as hell last night. I wonder if you could come over for awhile this afternoon—around twelve-thirty or so, and I'll fix us brunch. Did you have breakfast, or are you still just eating one meal a day?"

"All I've had this morning was coffee. I'll be there at twelve-twenty-nine. What shall I bring?"

"Just yourself. Park in the street, not in the driveway. That's the arrangement I've got with my neighbors downstairs. They use the driveway one month, and I use it the next. And this month they're parking in the driveway. You've got my address?"

"Your address and your number."

"Push the bell twice so I'll know it's you."

My heart was beating a little faster when I racked the phone. At last, I thought, my patience has paid off. I refolded Eddie's list without looking at it, and threw it into the waste basket. Eddie's problems were probably unsolvable anyway.

I had about an hour and fifteen minutes to shave, shower, select the right clothes, and get ready for what I could envision as the greatest afternoon in the sack I had ever had.

10

Jannaire lived on LeJeune, in Coral Gables, in a two-story two-apartment duplex. Her apartment was the one on the top floor. There was hardly any yard in front of the duplex, and there were no garages. The neighbors below, whoever they were, had parked both of their cars in the short circular driveway.

I had forgotten, when she told me on the phone to park in the street, that there was no parking allowed on LeJeune in the Gables. LeJeune is the main four-lane artery that leads from Coral Gables to the airport, so parking is wisely prohibited. I drove around the corner and parked on Santa Monica. As I walked back I noticed that Jannaire's Porsche was also parked on Santa Monica, half-hidden by a huge pile of rotting vegetation that should have been collected weeks before.

I buzzed twice, and Jannaire pushed the buzzer from upstairs to open the door. The stairs, in the exact center of the duplex, were steep, and I wondered, as I climbed them, what this architectural horror did to the unhappy people living below, with the big wedge slanting through the middle of their downstairs living room. Of course, architects do terrible things like that in Miami to build houses with additional space on small lots; but Jannaire, with the top apartment, certainly had the better deal of the two.

Jannaire was wearing a shorty nightgown and a floor-length

flimsy peignoir, both sea-green. Her long brown hair was held in place with a silk sea-green headband. She didn't wear any make-up, not even the faint pinkish-white lipstick she usually wore during working hours, and her remarkable odor, which reminded me—perhaps because of the colors she wore—of the Seaquarium at midday, assailed and stung my nostrils like smelling salts. But instead of my eyes watering, my mouth watered, and I felt the firm stirring of an erection. The dark tangle of inky pubic hair was an irregular shadow clearly visible beneath the two thin thicknesses of gown and peignoir.

She kissed the air, not me, trailed two fingers lightly across my cheek, and told me to sit down. I sat on the long white couch, and gulped in a few quick mouthfuls of airconditioned air as she went into the kitchen to get the coffee.

The room was furnished ugly with oversized hotel-lobby-type furniture. There were two Magritte lithos on one lime wall, and an amateur watercolor of the Miami Beach skyline on another. A third wall, papered with silver wallpaper streaked with thin white stripes, held a blow-up photograph of Jannaire, taken when she was about nine or ten years old. The blow-up, about three by four feet, was framed with shiny chrome strips. In black and white, it held my interest, whereas the rest of the furnishings only indicated Jannaire's taste for impersonality. Everything else in the room, except for the blow-up photo and perhaps the two Magrittes, would have served as lobby furniture for any of the beach motels north of Bal Harbour. There were even two lucite standing ashtray stands, holding small black metal bowls filled with sand. There were no books or magazines, and two droopy ferns, in brown pots, looked as though no one had talked to them in months.

I studied the blow-up photo, astonished that such a pudgy, unattractive child, squinting against the bright sun in her eyes (the shadow of the male photographer—probably her father—slanted across the foreground of the lawn) could turn into such a lovely woman. For a moment, the photo reminded me of Don's daughter, Maria, and I shuddered. I was immediately cheered, however, when I thought that there could be a similar future for

Maria. Perhaps Maria, too, would be a beautiful woman some day; and for Don's sake, I hoped so.

Jannaire returned with the coffee, and set the silver service on the glass coffee table. I drank my coffee black, which I hated to do, and pointed to the blow-up.

"Whatever possessed you, Jannaire," I said, "to blow up that snapshot of yourself?"

"How do you know it's me? Do I look like that?"

"Not any more you don't, but it's you, isn't it?"

"No, it isn't me. It's my younger sister. She's dead now, and that was the only photograph of her that I had. She had others..." She shrugged, and twisted her lips into a rueful grimace "...but she burned most of her personal things before she killed herself."

"I'm sorry," I said. "It's always sad when a child commits suicide..."

"She wasn't a child when she died. She was twenty-two."

"That makes it even worse," I said.

Jannaire stared at me for a long moment with her glinting, sienna eyes, shook herself slightly, and said, "Yes, it does. Now, what would you like for brunch?"

"Do you have a menu?"

"No, but if you tell me what you want, I'll tell you what you can have."

"I'll have you, then."

"Scrambled eggs? Bacon? Ham?"

"No. Cottage cheese, with grapefruit segments, two four-minute eggs, fried eggplant, and an eight-ounce glass of V-8 juice."

"You don't much care what you eat, do you?"

"Not if I can't have you, I don't. And that's the truth when I'm only eating once a day. I'd rather eat things I don't like when I'm dieting this way, because I'm not tempted to eat any more of the same later on in the day. And I'll have a St. James and soda, too."

"I'll give you Chivas instead, and fried plantain instead of eggplant, but otherwise, you'll get the breakfast you ordered."

"Good! I hate plantain worse than eggplant, but it's just as filling."

That was the beginning of a strange afternoon.

I could not bring myself to believe that Jannaire did not want me to seduce her. I tried everything I could think of, but I got nowhere. After eating the bland, unappetizing breakfast, and I ate alone because she had either eaten already or said that she had, I had two more scotches, switched over to beer when I began to feel them, and talked and talked. I grabbed her, I kissed her, and she got away from me. Once I chased her and got one hand between her thighs from behind, but she cleverly eluded me, fled to the back bedroom and locked the door. She stayed in there for almost an hour, while I drank two more beers, saying she wouldn't come out again unless I promised to let her alone. I promised, reluctantly, and she came out—this time fully dressed, wearing one of her slack suits.

I was sulky, pissed off and puzzled. There are ways to play the game, and there are certain unwritten rules to be followed. There are variations to the rules, which make the game interesting, but reliable patterns eventually emerge, one way or another, sets of clues, so to speak, and the game is either won or lost. I have won more games than I have lost because I have practiced the nuances and studied the angles a little closer than most men are willing to do. The discernible pattern, insofar as Jannaire was concerned, was the waiting game. By playing hard-to-get and yet by always holding out the musky carrot, I had recognized the classic pattern of her play early in our acquaintanceship.

She had called me for a date, or a meeting, almost as often as I had called her. She also, when we had met at a bar or a restaurant, paid her half of the tab, thereby establishing her independence. I didn't mind that. Tab-sharing, five years ago, was a rare phenomenon, but during the last couple of years it has happened as often as not—or at least an *offer* to pay half is made frequently. The insight required is to gauge whether the woman's offer is sincere, or merely a half-hearted gesture to indicate a show of independence. If it were the latter, and you guessed wrong, accepting the proferred cash, you could quickly lose the girl and the game. But there was no doubt with Jannaire. She would pick up the check, put on her reading glasses, total it silently, and hand me the correct amount of cash for what she had ordered. She didn't share tipping, of course, and in this respect I admired her perceptiveness. Women, when they tip at all, and most women truly hate to leave a tip, undertip—especially in Miami, if they are year-'round residents—whereas men like myself, who have a tendency, on other dates, to return to certain places, usually overtip. Overtipping is one of my faults, but I like to do it because I can afford to do so. By getting out of the tip altogether, but by still paying her share of the tab, Jannaire was able to establish her independence and essential femininity at the same time.

She was a mature woman and well aware of her body. Jannaire had admitted to twenty-nine, so I doubt that she was much more than thirty-one. She was beautiful enough to pick and choose. For every man she turned off by her earthy body odor and underarm hair, and she flouted the latter by wearing sleeveless tops, and taking off her suit jacket in public places—as she had turned off Larry Dolman—she would turn on another man like me who was fascinated by the eccentric, the exotic, the unusual, the untried. Sergeant Weber, my NCOIC at the Pittsburgh Recruiting Station, had told me how sexy luxuriant growths of underarm hair had been to him in Italy during World War II, and to many other GI's, once they got over the initial shock. And it *was* sexy. Jannaire was a woman who wanted to know a man well as a person before going to the mat with him. She didn't have to fall in love with him, or even pretend to be in love with him, but she did have to like him; and the only way that she could tell whether she liked him or not was to get to know him fairly well. Once I had that figured out, I had set out deliberately to make her like me.

I thought I had succeeded. I had made my pitches at every opportunity, but I had made them lightly, and without using any hard sell techniques. Her rejections had never been outright turndowns; she merely changed the subject, or smiled without saying anything. It was the old waiting game, one I was familiar with, and a game I was willing to play.

After all, I had some other things going for me, and I could wait as long as she could—perhaps longer, unless she changed the pattern and decided she didn't like me after all—and she would be a more appreciated lay for the delay. And if I lost, in the long run, there was a good deal of solace in the knowledge that the ratio of women to men in Miami, as I had reminded Larry, was still seven to one.

But here it was, Sunday, pay-off day, and the afternoon had been wasted. What was going on? The brunch invitation, the shorty nightgown, the exposed cleavage of hard, unhampered breasts across the table as I ate the tasteless food, the time and place available—and then, a runaround.

I sulked, sitting in a deep leather arm chair across from the white couch, and glared at her silently when she sat and faced me. She had combed her bronze hair, or brushed it, I supposed, and it was fuller as it touched her shoulders. Her alluring musky odor was fainter now, because of her jacket and slacks, and her freshly painted lips, playing card pink, almost matched the string of imitation pearls, as large as marbles, she wore around her neck.

I quite sulking, making an effort to salvage some dignity, buttoned my flowered bodyshirt, and yawned, stretching out my arms.

Jannaire, I concluded, was a lost cause. I didn't mind losing so much as I minded not knowing why. Although I wanted to leave, I was still curious about the why of the rejection. I was also feeling a trifle logy from the two scotches and six cans of beer, and I had the beginnings of a headache.

She looked at her watch.

"Humphrey Bogart Theater will be on in a few minutes. D'you want to watch TV?"

I laughed. "What's the film?"

"*Knock on any Door.*"

"He doesn't play Bogey in that one."

"We could play checkers."

"We've been playing that all afternoon."

"You can start sulking again if you want to. I think it's kinda cute the way you can pout with your upper lip without moving your bottom lip. How did you learn that, anyway?"

"By hanging around cock-teasers in the ninth grade. I thought I'd forgotten how but I remembered how to do it after chasing you around all afternoon. How did you learn such a good game of checkers?"

"What's the name of the film where Bogey has a plastic surgeon change his face, and then he turns out to be Bogey when the bandages come off?"

"Did you ever read *The Chessmen of Mars*, by Edgar Rice Burroughs?" I asked.

"No, but I read *Tarzan at the Earth Score.*"

"You agglutinated that. When you were a kid you probably asked your mother for a napple."

"I did not."

"Why do you end every sentence with a rising inflection? 'I did not?' "

"Do I sound that way to you?"

"Not really. I can't get the little catch in the middle right."

"You're really angry with me, aren't you, Hank?"

"Not at this moment. I was for a while, but now I'm merely disappointed. Resigned, I suppose."

"I couldn't do it. I meant to, I intended to, and then I couldn't."

"Why?"

"I don't want to talk about it."

"Now I'm getting angry again."

"If you want to learn how to play checkers, why don't you study the game?"

"In other words, somewhere along the line in the last six weeks I made a wrong move, and that cost me the game?"

"Maybe I made the wrong move, Hank."

"I don't think so. Besides, nothing could make me mad enough to hit a woman."

"When you think, you frown, and when you frown your eyebrows meet in the middle."

"You've never met me in the middle. He escaped from San Quentin."

"And this girl in San Francisco took him in. He was trying to prove that he'd been railroaded into prison."

"Framed. You haven't eaten all day."

"I don't eat on Sundays. Sometimes, before I go to bed I..."

"And you don't screw on Sundays either. You watch Humphrey Bogart Theater."

"I have a toasted English muffin, and drink a glass of skim milk."

Downstairs, the door opened, and I listened as footfalls clumped up the stairs.

"Your aunt's back," I said.

"No," Jannaire said, "it isn't my aunt."

I got to my feet as she did. A man entered. He jangled some keys in his right hand a couple of times. Jannaire crossed to his side, put her right arm around his waist, and kissed him on the cheek.

"Mr. Norton," she said, smiling as she turned toward me, "this is my husband, Mr. Wright. And this is Mr. Norton, darling. Mr. Norton's in real estate, and he's been driving me around all afternoon showing me some properties. It was so hot in the car, I invited him up for a beer."

Mr. Wright, her husband, looked disinterestedly at the six empty beer cans clustered on the coffee table. He was in his early forties, and bald in front, but four inches of black side hair had been combed over the bald spot. He was about five-eight, slight, but wiry looking, and about 150 pounds. There was a deep dent in his slightly crooked blade of a nose, and the two deep lines in his thin cheeks were so well-defined they were black, as if they had been drawn with ink. He had a short upper lip, and to make it seem longer he wore a very long—practically a hairline—moustache. He would have been a plain, even an ugly, man, if he hadn't had such clear, penetrating, intelligent eyes. His eyes, bluish purple, with the black arching brows above them, almost made him handsome. There was a ragged pink patch of vitiligo on his forehead. His hands were huge, hands that belonged to a much larger man, and his thick wrists dangled below the two-short sleeves of his blue seersucker suit jacket.

"How do you do, sir?" I said. "I think the acreage west of Kendale Lakes is a good buy for your wife, and I'll be glad to show it to you sometime, Mr. Wright. At your convenience, of course." I looked at the beer cans, and shook my head. "Ha, ha, Mrs. Wright, I'll bet you'll think twice before asking me in for a beer again, won't you? But that sun out there really made me thirsty. Well..." I started toward the door "...you've got my phone number. It was nice to meet you, sir, and now I'd better get on home. My wife'll begin to wonder what happened to me."

"I'll walk you to your car," Mr. Wright said.

He followed me downstairs, right at my heels. I wanted to run, but I walked as casually as possible, matching his shorter pace as we shared the sidewalk.

"Were you showing my wife real estate all afternoon, Mr. Norton?" he said, twisting his head slightly to look up into my face.

"Yes, sir. All afternoon—since one o'clock."

"Whose car did you use?"

It was a trick question. But then, he knew her Porsche. Did he know mine?

"Mine," I said. "Why?"

He took a rotor out of his jacket pocket. "Because I have the rotor to my wife's Porsche."

We reached my car, and I took out my keys.

"Is this your car, Mr. Norton?"

I nodded.

"This car's been parked here all afternoon. I checked it four times, each time on the quarter hour."

I couldn't think of anything to say.

"You've been fucking my wife all afternoon."

"No...I..."

"We've already established that you're a liar, Norton. And you pants are unzipped."

I looked down to see, one of the most foolish things I've ever done in my life, and yet, it would have been impossible not to look down and check. My zipper was *not* down, but what could I say? My mind was benumbed. I fumbled with the keys, and finally got the door open. Mr. Wright stood in the open doorway, and held the door open as I slid under the wheel.

"You cuckolded me in my own house, and in my own bed, Norton. And I'm going to kill you for it." His dark blue, almost purple eyes, stared at me coldly. He slammed the door, and stepped back.

I started the engine, and pulled away from the curb. Through the rearview mirror I could see Mr. Wright jotting something in a black notebook as he looked after my car. He was probably taking down my license number.

He is only trying to frighten me, I thought, and he has succeeded.

11

By midnight, two hours after Jannaire's husband had taken a shot at me, I had reviewed the steps leading up to it, and all I had to show for it was a hodgepodge of contradictions. They didn't hang together, none of them. I could discount Jannaire's lack of a wedding ring. Many married women nowadays don't wear one, feeling rightly or wrongly, that a wedding band is a stigma, a symbol that they are possessed by a man. So that didn't mean much, except, if she had worn one, I would have handled my seduction campaign differently from the beginning.

The aunt, I concluded, was certainly fictitious. On the other hand, when I had used the john in Jannaire's apartment, after the second, no, the third beer, I hadn't seen any evidence of male occupancy in the bathroom. So Mr. Wright—or Wright—I kept thinking of him as *Mister* Wright—was probably sleeping in the guest bedroom, or living elsewhere. She had said, "my husband," so they were still married, not divorced—or perhaps estranged. Estrangement, as the newspapers indicate every day, made him more dangerous than a husband who was safely and happily married and coming home every week with a paycheck. It was the estranged and jealous husbands who were always coming around to shoot their wives, their wives' lovers, and, if they had any, their children sitting in front of the TV set. If a lover was getting some, and they were not, it drove estranged husbands crazy. Almost every day when I picked up the paper I read about some jealous husband shooting up his house, his wife, or pouring sugar into the gas tank of his wife's lover's car.

That could account for Wright's mean-spirited attitude all right, and yet I couldn't be certain. The way he came in, juggling the house keys in his hand, the kiss Jannaire gave him on the check, and the calm way she greeted him—no anxiety showing, that I could recall—was almost as if she were expecting him. And if that were the case, although it seemed crazy to consider such a wild idea, she had set me up. She had set me up for the encounter, and she had planned, but had failed to carry through, to let me spend the afternoon in bed with her. Or so she had intimated—except that she couldn't go through with it.

If I could talk to Jannaire, or talk to Mr. Wright calmly and reasonably for a few minutes, I could straighten the entire matter out.

I called Jannaire's number, and she answered on the third ring.

"Jannaire," I said, "this is Hank. I..."

"Just a minute, Hank."

I waited, and a moment later Wright was on the phone. "Norton?"

"Oh," I said, "you're still there? Listen Mr. Wright, I..."

"Where else would I be, Norton? You're a lucky man, and you've got a lot of guts calling here. But the next time I see you, your guts are going to be spread out on the pavement."

"Listen a minute..."

"You were lucky because the damned Wildcat I rented had this emission control that screwed up the engine. Just as I fired, the car surged and threw off my aim."

"They all do that, surge I mean. The emission control..."

"That's what the man at Five-A-Day Car Rental told me when I turned in the car. So I've got another car now, an older car, and next time you won't be so lucky."

"That's what I want to talk to you about. You're making a bad mistake, and..."

He slammed the phone down.

He was crazy, I decided, and so was Jannaire for living with him, or not living with him, whatever, or for ever marrying him in the first place. He was at least fifteen years older than Jannaire, and she was making plenty of money without him, so *why* had she ever married a nut like that?

I fixed a drink, a normal one-and-a-half ounce scotch, with an equal amount of soda over ice, and noticed that my hands no longer trembled. I wasn't panicky, nor was I terrified. I was merely frightened, but it was a good kind of fear, the way you feel before a basketball game, or before making a speech on safety to a large group. In addition to my fear, and it was a fear I could control, I had an odd feeling of exhilaration, an emotion I hadn't had for several years. It was a feeling that came from thinking. Thinking was something I hadn't done for a long time. How rare it is nowadays to use your mind to think something out, to puzzle over something; and thinking about this idea, my sudden alertness and feeling of well-being startled me.

The sure knowledge, now, that Mr. Wright was going to shoot me, was a challenge and an insult. Did the crazy bastard think that I was going to let him kill me? Did he think I wouldn't fight back? I could feel the anger surge inside me—the way his car had surged when the emission control system grabbed it—and I choked it off. He wasn't angry. His voice had been cool, controlled, and without a trace of passion or anger. He was carrying out some stupid ritualistic code—the old unwritten law of the pre-Korean War years. A man fucks your wife, so you kill him to protect your honor. That was my lousy luck. Not only was I innocent—I hadn't even got so much as a finger in it—I had had the bad luck to run into a middle-aged husband with outmoded and outdated social values.

Wright would never talk with me. The rigid bastard was a damned reactionary, and, if he could, he would shoot me down in cold blood, dispassionately, feeling that he was doing the right thing and that he would be vindicated whether caught and found guilty, or found not guilty under the so-called unwritten law. The worse that could happen to him, the very worst, was a sentence of life imprisonment—if he were found guilty—and a life sentence meant that he would be released, at the maximum, within eight years. If he behaved himself in prison, and that is what reactionaries did—they always followed the rules—he would be released in about three years. For a crime of passion, a one-time killing purportedly done because of an emotional involvement, he could be out in the streets again—with a good lawyer and plea bargaining—within a year-and-a-half, or two years at the most.

If I knew this much, he certainly knew it, too, and there was no doubt in my mind that he would try to kill me. And that is exactly what he would do, unless I killed him first.

So starting right this moment, Mr. Wright, I thought, I am going to be looking for you, and we shall see who will be the first one shot—you, or me.

I unlocked the front door, went to the trash chute down the hallway, and picked up a stack of discarded newspapers. After relocking my door and testing the chain, I crumpled up big balls of newspaper, scattered them on the floor, and went to bed. For a while, I lay on my back, watching the electric numbers flash on the ceiling from my electric clock projector, and I thought I wouldn't be able to sleep all night. But soon I got so sleepy I couldn't keep my eyes open...

12

I have always been a strong swimmer, but my forte has been endurance, not speed. And yet, here I was, flailing my arms in a loose Australian crawl, with minimum kicking, and I was ploughing through the water at three times my normal swimming speed. My head was high and out of the water, and most of my back was high out of the water as well.

The light was gray, misty, and swirling with patches of fog. I could only see about three or four feet ahead. A huge amorphous shape loomed in front of me, but I neither gained on it nor lost water. Whatever it was, we were apparently making the same speed. If I didn't know where I was going, or where I was, what was the hurry? I stopped swimming altogether. Strange. I didn't sink, and my steady pace continued. I sailed through the murky, pleasantly warm water, as if I were being towed. It was at this point that I felt the wide band around my middle. The band wasn't uncomfortably tight, but it was snug. I was tied somehow, and the band around my wrist, attached to something or other (a submarine periscope?), was propelling me at top speed behind the shapeless gray form ahead.

The gray shape swerved sharply to the right, and a moment later I did, too, into absolute blackness. I wasn't frightened, although I was vaguely uneasy and more than a little puzzled. My pace didn't slacken as my chest parted the water. I clasped my hands, and rested my chin on my knuckles, peering ahead into nothing. Then, beyond the blacker shape ahead of me, the darkness began to lighten slightly, and I saw a half-circle of white in the distance. As the white circle became larger, I realized that I was in a tunnel, a curving tunnel, and a moment later I was bathed in hot pink light as I shot out of the blackness. The gray shape ahead of me metamorphosized immediately into a garishly painted wooden duck, much larger than me, and there were sudden splashes of dirty water between the duck's fanning tail and my head. I heard the sound of the shots then, craned my head and neck to the left, and saw the upper body of a man leaning across a wooden plank, perhaps a hundred yards away, aiming a rifle in my direction. For God's sake, I thought, as my arms flailed the water in an effort to increase my speed, he's shooting at me! I recognized, or thought I did, a patch of vitiligo on the man's forehead. *It's Mr. Wright, and he's shooting at me!*

I awoke then. The top black satin sheet was wrapped twice around my body, and the bed was soaked with perspiration. Thunder shook the skies, and torrents of rain sluiced down my bedroom windows. The electricity was off, which usually happens during these heavy Miami thunderstorms, and with it my airconditioning and clocks. It must have been at least 85 degrees in my apartment, although I didn't know at the moment how long the electricity had been off. My heart was still thumping in my chest from the nightmare as I disentangled myself from the sheet and staggered into the bathroom and took a shower.

Roasting in my bed, I thought, must have brought on the nightmare. Except that it wasn't a bad dream, Mr. Wright was real; he was looking for me with his gun, and I was indeed a captive duck in a shooting gallery—unless I did something about it—and soon.

At three a.m. the airconditioning kicked in. The lights were on again, so I fixed a cup of coffee. While the water was boiling I reset my electric clocks from my wristwatch. The power had been off for almost two hours.

In another three hours it would be light outside. The rain had slackened to a drizzle, and the coffee cheered me up some.

I put an LP of the Stones on the stereo, and listened to them sing about the horrors of England, which were, if anything, much worse over there than they were in Miami. I started to cry, something I hadn't done in at least fifteen years.

Why in the hell was I crying? Perhaps I cried because it was three in the morning, but most of all, I felt that I had lost something, something valuable and irreplaceable, even though I didn't know what it could be.

But I didn't go back to bed.

Somehow, the dream had frightened me more, much more, than Mr. Wright's promise to kill me.

13

The sun and my spirits rose but I was still tired and in need of sleep. I thought about taking a dexie or a bennie, or a half of one or the other now, and the second half at noon. One half of a dexie would wake me fully, give me a feeling of alertness, and provide me with the surge of mental energy I needed.

"I can handle it," I thought.

But these fatal words, flashing into my mind, changed it. This was the familiar rationalization we were all warned against during indoctrination, together with other grave dangers that specious learning and unlimited access to drugs faced detail men in the field. Studying, as we did, the symptoms of diseases, the clinical properties of the drugs we touted to doctors—what they could and couldn't do—contraindications and side effects—the danger of self-prescription was always present. And because doctors as a group are not the sharpest body of men one will ever meet, especially if one ever talks to them about subjects other than their work, it is easy to fall into the trap of believing—of *knowing*—that you know as much, or even more, than doctors do.

Doctors work much too hard. They rarely have an opportunity to read anything, including newspapers. They are, as a whole, naive politically, and unworldly concerning money, economics, or even interpersonal relationships. They make a lot of money, but they never have any because they invariably lose it through poor investments, and they spend it—or their families spend it—as if it came from a magic source. Many doctors, including those with the average $75,000 per annum incomes, who own two or three cars and carry a huge mortgage, have little or nothing in reserve. Bankruptcy is a frequent hazard for doctors, and they are then bewildered men, wondering where all the money went. There are exceptions, of course, but I had talked to hundreds of doctors in the last five years, and the overwhelming majority was poorly informed. They knew very little outside of their trade. It becomes easy, then, to fall into the trap and decide that you, who know so much more about the world than doctors, and have the same access to medical books, medical journals and drugs, can prescribe for yourself when you become sick instead of seeing a doctor.

The company had warned us about that, reminding us, at the same time, that the greatest number of drug addicts in the U.S., as an occupational group, were M.D.s. Doctors, of course, used the same kind of reasoning that a detail man could fall heir to; they had a practically unlimited access to drugs, and because they knew, or thought they knew, as much as any other doctor, they also had a tendency to prescribe drugs for themselves.

"I can handle it," they thought, and they would pop a bennie to get through a six a.m. operation, and then another bennie at ten a.m., to get through their hospital rounds, and then, because they were bone-tired, and beginning to get sleepy by one or two p.m., and they had an office full of waiting patients to get through, they would take a couple of more bennies that afternoon. And so it would go, with emergency calls at night, and the first thing they knew they would be hooked—on bennies, or dexies, or nose candy, and eventually, on horse.

When you get sick, the company told us, see a doctor. Never, never take a self-prescribed drug of any kind. The rule was a good one, because no one can handle it. No one.

With a shrug, I skipped the bennie, and settled for a close shave and a long cold shower. I put on a pair of gray seersucker slacks and a sportshirt, brewed fresh coffee, and sat down to decide my next move.

Luckily, my reports were made out and ready to mail to

Atlanta. It wasn't essential to call on my doctors during the week. I could fake another set of calls on the following Saturday or Sunday when I made my next report, and it made no difference. The sales in my territory were the highest in the Southeastern District. I could devote fulltime to protecting myself, or better, I could reverse the role. I could hunt down Mr. Wright, and put *him* on the defensive. I didn't want to shoot him, or hurt him in any way, but I had to get him alone somewhere and talk to him. I was positive, if I could only talk to him for a while, and explain how Jannaire had passed herself off as a single, unattached woman, and that there had never been anything physical between us, he would see how foolish it was to come after me with a gun.

Jannaire, in all probability, had told him the same thing by now—that there had been no sex between us—and maybe he had cooled off already, during the night. On the other hand, he might not believe Jannaire. She might have had, for all I knew, a long record of clandestine lovers, and if so, Mr. Wright would discount anything she said.

I had to get a gun. What was the best way to go about getting one, and obtaining a license to carry it? Larry Dolman would know, but so would Alton Thead. I couldn't go to Larry. I didn't want Larry to find out about my predicament. He would help me, of course, but if he did, the nature of our relationship would be altered. He believed that I was screwing Jannaire. Without actually saying so, I had implied as much a few days before when I ran into him at the mailboxes in the lobby. If Larry knew that I had been running around with her for six weeks without getting any, and without even learning that she was married, he would be contemptuous. It was bad enough to be contemptuous of myself, but I couldn't stand it from Larry. In his opinion, and in Don's and Eddie's as well, I was purported to be the greatest cocksman in Miami, and I valued the good opinion of my three friends. If Larry helped me, and I know how eagerly he would volunteer if I asked him for help, it would all come out—the entire story—and he, in turn, would tell Don and Eddie...

The phone rang, a single ring, and stopped. I waited, counting. A minute later, it rang again. This was my private signal. During daylight hours, from eight to five, I never answered the phone unless I was called in this special way. I didn't want anyone from the company to call me from New Jersey and find me at home, particularly if that was the day I was supposed to be in Palm Beach or Key West. My immediate supervisor, Julie Westphal, the district manager in Atlanta, knew about my special ring, but we were close friends. I was his best detail man in the field, and we always had a good time together when he came to see me in Miami. A few women, perhaps a dozen, had been told about the two rings, and also Larry, Don, and Eddie, of course—but no one else. I picked up the phone.

"Hi," I said.

"Tom Davies." The solemn voice paused, and then Tom laughed.

"Tom, you bastard," I said, "how did you get onto my secret ring?"

"I called Julie, in Atlanta. You know I don't give a shit anyway, Hank, whatever you do, but this is an emergency and I had to get a hold of you. I was afraid you might get away this morning and go to Lauderdale or Palm Beach, and it's important that I see you."

"You mean you want me to fly up to New Jersey, Tom?"

"No." He laughed. "I'm flying down to Miami this afternoon, and I'm going to have a six-hour stopover on my way to San Juan. I'm going to spend a week, maybe ten days, with Gonzales in Puerto Rico. But I want to talk to you, and catch a little sleep at the Airport Hotel before I grab the midnight flight to San Juan..."

"Do you want some action, Tom? It's short notice but I..."

"No, but thanks, Hank. I'm really tired—I'll tell you about it when I see you. And I imagine Gonzales has got a few things planned for me anyway in San Juan. So what I'd like you to do is book me a room at the Airport Hotel—I'll be in about five-thirty—and we'll get together for awhile at six, in my room." He lowered his deep voice a full octave. "It's important, Hank. Very important."

"Sure, Tom. No sweat. And if you decide you want some action I can probably take care of that, too. I know a couple of girls in Hialeah who like to play sandwich, and if you say the word, I'll..."

"Not this time, Hank. It's business. I haven't slept for twenty-four hours now, and I just want to get a little sack time before midnight, that's all."

"Okay, Tom. I'll see you at the hotel—in the lobby—it's at the end of Concourse Four—at six o'clock."

"Good! We'll have a drink, and talk..."

I called the Airport Hotel and made a reservation for Tom Davies.

My throat was dry, and I was a little irritated at Julie for giving out the information about my special ring. But Julie and I were good friends, and if it hadn't been important, very important, Julie sure as hell wouldn't have given the Vice-President of Sales this privileged information. Tom Davies, of course, was a damned nice guy, and he had been in the field himself, long before he became a district manager and then a vice-president, so he knew what the score was, and how we operated. Perhaps they all knew, the entire executive group in New Jersey, including old Ned Lee, who had founded the company. But we played the game, and we pretended to be working our asses off in the field. And some of us, at least some of the time, actually did work like hell. I certainly had, during my first year, but when your sales are up you are can slack off. If they go down, as they will eventually if you quit pushing your product to doctors for several months and they learn about new ones from other companies they want to try, then you've got to get out there and hustle again. All the same, I wondered what it was that was so important that Tom Davies, the Vice-President of Sales, would take a layover in Miami to talk to me about in person instead of telling me on the phone.

I hadn't seen Tom Davies in about eight months, not since the last Atlanta meeting, when we had had a hellova good time. We had picked up two showgirl types, big Southern broads six feet tall, and we had stayed over in Atlanta an extra day with these giantesses. When he was working Tom was a serious man, but he also knew how to unwind when the time came. We had had a lot of fun with those enormous women. But whatever it was Tom wanted to talk to me about, it would have to wait until six p.m.

Right now, I needed to do something about getting a pistol, and my best bet was Alton Thead, J.S.D.

14

My adjustment year in Miami, after getting out of the army, had been a grim and confusing period. I had hated Pittsburgh, a cold and miserable city, and I had made no friends among its residents. I drank and ran around with some of the other officers from the Recruiting Station, and our conversations were usually centered on what we were going to do and where we were going to go after we got out of the service. It had never entered my mind to go home to Michigan. Dearborn, if anything, was a colder and more miserable city than Pittsburgh, and with fewer opportunities.

When a man is finally discharged he is entitled to travel pay to the home of his choice, and when my time came I selected Miami. I had never been here before, but I knew that it was subtropically warm, and I figured that a city of a more than one million people was large enough for me to find a place for myself.

I had saved very little money, and I took the first halfway decent job I could find, working as an insurance claims adjuster, which gave me $9,000 a year and a free use of a car. Eight years ago, it was still possible to live on nine thousand a year—if not very well.

I had the G.I. Bill coming, and I considered going to graduate school and working on a Ph.D. My undergraduate degree in Psychology was virtually worthless, but I did not like the field well enough to spend three years torturing rats and doing the other boring things I would have to do to get a terminal degree.

The idea of going to Law School occurred to me after I was assigned to a reserve unit. This small unit, which I was forced to join and remain with for three years after my discharge from active service, was a Military Government Team (Res.). We met at seven-thirty a.m. on Sunday mornings, ostensibly for four hours, but rarely stayed for more than two. The size of the team varied from twelve officers to twenty-five during the three years I served with it. We took turns giving fifty-minute lectures, usually on some political or government subject, as assigned by our commander. He was a lieutenant colonel on Sundays, who worked in a gas station during the week. After pumping gas and changing tires all week, he gloried in his Sunday morning elevation to military power, and made the Army Reserve experience much worse for us than it should have been. We—the other junior Reserve officers—became unified in our hate for this gas pump jockey C.O., and I made a few good friends in the unit. Four or five of the other officers were lawyers, and as I talked with them over coffee after the Sunday morning meetings, I thought that the law might be a way to escape from my deadend job as a claims investigator.

The Law School entrance examination, which I had feared, turned out to be fairly easy, and I passed it with a high score. More than half of the exam was concerned with graphs, charts, and math—which surprised me—but because math and statistics had been my best subjects at Michigan State, I scored high enough on these sections to make up for the other sections, where my scores were merely average.

I was accepted and I matriculated in the University of Miami night school program. All I had to do was to go to classes for four nights a week for four years, and I would have a J.D.—Juris Doctorate. My first four courses were Torts, Insurance, Reading and Writing for Law, and Introduction to Law, on Monday, Tuesday, Wednesday, and Thursday nights, in that order. Two weeks into the semester, I dropped the first three courses, and I would have dropped Introduction to Law, as well, if it hadn't been for Alton Thead, who taught the course.

Law is dull, but that isn't the only reason I dropped out. In my job as adjuster, I frequently had to call on people at night, and this conflict made it difficult to attend night classes. My office hours during the day made it impossible for me to find time to study, which meant that I would have had to spend every Saturday, all day, in the Law Library. Sunday mornings were spent at Reserve meetings, and our strict C.O. was a stickler for attendance. If you missed three meetings without obtaining permission to be absent in advance, and he was reluctant about giving permission, too, he would write a letter recommending that you be recalled to active duty for another year. We all lived in fear of this possibility, and he was very anxious to exercise this power.

A seven-day week is not a hardship if a man truly wants to become a lawyer. It is a matter of putting in the fours years, of serving the time, and a great many young men stick with it. But to do so requires more than a negative motivation, and my sole motivation for matriculating was that I did not want to be a graduate student in Psychology.

But it was the example of Alton Thead who persuaded me to give up Law School, although he did not set out deliberately to do so. Thead is a fine man, and he has a brilliant mind. He was entertaining, forceful, witty, and fascinating in the classroom, and he relished talking about his own experiences as a practicing lawyer.

Thead had attracted nationwide notoriety in the late 1950s when he found a Jewish male who was willing to sue his parents for circumcising him as a baby. This was the most difficult part, Thead told us in class, finding a young Jew who was willing to go along with this radical suit. Thead's case, of course, was a good one. Circumcision is a violation of a man's human rights, and the unlawful mutilation came within the province of the newer and stronger state legislation designed to protect the "battered child." Circumcision is not necessary medically, except in about four percent of those male children who are circumcised, and Thead had lined up more than a dozen doctors to testify to this fact to the court. Legally, the parents of the young man were in a poor position. They had "tradition" on their side as a precedent, but little else. They had doctors, too, but the best arguments they could muster were those of "sanitation." The fact that a circumcised penis is easier to keep clean than one that is not is a poor excuse for the mutilation of a baby's body and for violating his rights as a human being. Thead's other major argument, which would have been more cogent today, now that the country, as a whole, is more liberally educated sexually, carried little weight with the jury in the '50s. And this clincher (in my opinion, anyway) was that the glans of a circumcised penis becomes tough, and because of the loss of sensitivity, anywhere from twenty to thirty percent of a man's pleasure in sex is lost when the foreskin is removed.

Thead lost the case, which certainly would have had nationwide ramifications if he had won, and he appealed to the Florida Supreme Court. He lost there, too, on a five-four split decision, and then appealed to the U.S. Supreme Court. The U.S. Supreme Court refused to review the case, and that was the end of it. Eventually, I suppose, another lawyer will take it up again, and the mutilation of boy babies in this country will be stopped; but Thead's mistake, which he acknowledged, was in using a Jewish male instead of a WASP. The religious tradition was too much to overcome, all at once, and he should have sued on behalf of a Protestant male instead, avoiding the religious issue altogether.

After losing this case, Thead became involved in an income tax dodge, and almost became disbarred. He advised a Palm Beach client about a tax dodge, and the man was caught later on by the I.R.S. The disgruntled client spread the word that Thead, after advising him, had informed the I.R.S. about the dodge in order to collect the ten percent informer's fee. Several anonymous letters were sent to the Bar Association, but nothing was proved. But once the false rumor got around, Thead had to close his Palm Beach office for lack of business.

He then obtained a private investigator's license in Miami Beach, and lost it through some mysterious technicality—or loophole—discovered by the City Commission. Thead could not tell us the reasons why because the information was still privileged, between Thead and an unnamed client, but he would be able to reveal it some day in his autobiography, he said.

At any rate, Thead had returned to the Harvard Law School and earned a doctorate in Judicial Science, and then obtained a teaching position at the University of Miami Law School.

If the practical practice of law had given such a hard time to a man as brilliant as Thead, I thought, there was little future in it for me. Besides, there are more lawyers per capita in Miami than in any other city of comparable size in the United States—and I intended to make Miami my permanent home. During that single semester, while I took Thead's introductory law course, we became friends. We were not close friends, but we had a relationship a little deeper than the usual teacher-student friendship because he knew that I was dropping out of Law School at the end of the term.

I hadn't seen Dr. Thead for about three years. Two or three times during the last three years I had driven over to the university to see him, but I hadn't been able to find a place to park. This morning, however, I intended to see him even if I had to park illegally, which I finally had to do. All of the visitor slots were filled, taken in all probability by law students too cheap to buy a five-dollar student decal, so I was forced to park on the grass between a coconut palm and a "No Parking—Anytime" sign.

Eight years ago, there were always a few law students wearing coats and ties, but not any longer. The law students, like the undergraduates, wore the new poverty uniform—jeans, T-shirts, ragged blue work-shirts, beards, shoulder-length hair and beads, and they frowned in disapproval as I crossed the courtyard. My suit, and relatively short hair, alienated me, I supposed, and the dirtiest looks came from the students who were my age or older. But I am used to these intolerant looks, and I had other, more important things on my mind. I had called Thead before driving over to the university, and I knew that he was waiting for me.

Thead grinned at me when I entered his cubby-hole office, and stopped writing on his legal pad. He was thinner and smaller than I remembered. I took off my jacket and sat in the single visitor's chair. Wearing a half-smile, Thead looked at me from behind his glasses, and nodded. He took a pack of crumpled short Camels out of his shirt pocket, untangled a boomerang from the cellophane, straightened it, and managed to light it without taking his eyes off mine. This was a neat trick, and I had forgotten how disconcerting it could be.

"You look prosperous, Hank," he said. "How much are you making nowadays?"

"Twenty-two thousand, expenses, and a free Galaxie." I shrugged. "And I usually get a Christmas bonus."

"That's two thousand more than I make, and I don't have the use of a free car, so why did you finally decide to visit the old loser?"

"I've tried a few other times, Dr. Thead, but there's no place to park around here. I'm in a 'no parking' area now, and when I asked you for your unlisted home phone, you wouldn't give it to me."

"I finally took the phone out, Hank. An unlisted number doesn't work. Somehow, and there are dozens of ways, students got the number and called me at home. If someone really wants to see me badly enough, he'll find a way, even if he can't find a place to park."

"That's true." I grinned. "A very good friend of mine has a problem, and asked me to help him out. I said I would if I could, and that's why I came to you."

He grinned. "Good. I was afraid that you had gotten into some trouble."

"No, sir. It's a friend. A man has threatened his life, and even took a pot shot at him, and he doesn't know what to do about it."

"The shot missed, I take it?"

"Yes, but it was quite close. Should he ask for police protection?"

"He could, but he wouldn't get it. What did he do—screw the man's wife?"

"No, but the man thinks he did."

"What makes him think so?"

"The situation he was in made it look bad, that's all. But there's no doubt that the husband is serious. He really intends to shoot my friend."

"In that case," Thead said, "your friend had better shoot him first. If he pleads self-defense, he won't get more than two or three years."

"How about a license to carry a gun?"

"It takes a little time. How much time does your friend have?"

"Not much."

"To get a license, it's necessary to write the chief of police a letter and request one. The reason the weapon is needed must also be stated, and it has to be a good one, like carrying large sums of money. In your case, it would be simple. As a detail man, you carry drug samples in your car, and you need to protect them from theft, right?"

"All my friend carries is credit cards, Dr. Thead. Very little cash."

"How many credit cards?"

"American Express, Diner's, MasterCard, and three or four gas cards, I guess."

"There you are, then. Stolen credit cards are worth fifty or sixty bucks apiece on the black market. So there's two-fifty or three hundred bucks already. That's a large sum of money, Hank, even in Miami. The next step is going to the police range. To get a license to carry a weapon, a man has to qualify on the range with his own pistol. The initial fee, if he qualifies on the range and his application is approved by the chief, is seventy-five bucks, plus a twenty-five dollar annual fee after that. So the initial outlay is some spare time, and a hundred dollars. The license is good for Dade County only. If he wants to take the pistol into other counties he has to get another separate license from each county."

"What about carrying a pistol without a license?"

"A man's permitted to carry a pistol in his car, as long as it isn't hidden. He can put it on the seat beside him in plain view. If he keeps it in the glove compartment, the compartment must be locked at all times. They have to let a man carry a gun in his car, Hank. Otherwise, he wouldn't be able to drive home with it from the gun shop, you see."

"So there's no problem in buying a gun?"

"None at all, if you've got the price."

"Thanks, Dr. Thead. I'll tell my friend."

"I'll bet you will. And because he's your friend, Hank, there's no fee for all this valuable information."

"He can afford a fee, Dr. Thead. Send me the bill, and I'll see that he sends you the money."

"No fee, Hank. I'd hate to pay the tax on it. When are we going to have lunch?"

"I'll have to call you. My boss is flying in tonight, and I've got a lot of things to do today, but I'll call you soon."

"Please do, Hank. You've put on a few pounds, haven't you?"

"A few, but I still do my fifty push-ups every morning, and I'm on a diet again. I can take off ten pounds in a week. The next time you see me, I'll be back down."

I got up and put on my jacket. It was cool in his office, and there were several things I wanted to talk about with Thead, but I had taken enough of his time already. Besides, I didn't want to confide in him. It was too embarrassing.

"Hank?"

"Sir?"

"Perhaps you'd better tell me your friend's name?"

"Why?"

He shrugged, and then he grinned. "In case the police find his body, I can tell them what his name was."

I shook my head and smiled. "No use you getting involved, Dr. Thead. If something happens to him, I'll tell them his name."

"All right—but call me soon."

Outside in the hot sun again, I felt as if I were walking under water as I crossed the courtyard toward the narrow strip of lawn where I had parked my Galaxie. Except for two Cuban refugees, looking for goodies in a Dempsey Dumpster, there were no suspicious looking people around. I lit a cigarette, and climbed into my car.

15

The explosion, when I turned on the ignition, was instantaneous, but the engine caught. My foot jammed down involuntarily on the gas pedal, and the engine roared. The engine fan, turning at high speed, forced thin wings of black smoke from under the hood on both sides of the car. For a moment, there had been a high shrill whistle before the explosion. I was startled, and my mind was benumbed by the sudden, unexpected noise. Conscious now of the racing engine, I turned off the ignition, unfastened my seat belt and climbed stiffly out of the car.

I wasn't hurt and, looking at the hood, I couldn't see any damage to the car. There was only a faint remnant of smoke wisping out from under the closed hood. I was joined by a half-dozen curious, bearded students. One of them grinned.

"Looks like somebody pulled a trick on you," he said.

"Did any of your guys see anyone around my car?" I said, looking at them. They shuffled back a pace or two. There was some silent head-shaking.

I opened the driver's door, reached under the dash, and pulled the knob to unlock the hood. There was a scattering of gray flecks of paper littering the engine. A student leaned over to look at the engine, picked up a thin red-and-white wire, and traced it to the battery. The wire was split, and scraped to the copper at the ends, and two thin strands were wound around the terminals. There were some short lengths of the red-and-white wire mixed with the shredded bits of gray paper.

"A Whiz-Bang," the student said. "It can't hurt your car any. It just whistles and makes a loud firecracker bang when you turn on the ignition."

I nodded. "But my car was locked. How'd he get inside to open the hood?"

"Maybe you didn't lock the car."

"I always lock it."

"In that case," he said, "he must've unlocked it."

All of the students were grinning now. I grinned, too, trying to make a joke of it. "I'm parked illegally," I said, "so maybe one of your campus cops played the trick on me—as a warning."

One of the students stopped grinning, and frowned. "It isn't really funny, you know," he said. "A man could have a heart attack being shook up like that."

"It scared me all right," I admitted, dropping the hood and checking to see that it was locked, "but I can take a joke. So if one of you guys did the wiring, there's no hard feelings."

"No one here did it," the first student said. "You can buy those Whiz-Bang devices over at Meadows', but that's not the kind of trick anyone would play on a stranger."

"It was probably someone who knew me, who recognized my car." I shrugged and got into the car again and closed the door.

The students, bored now, drifted away. I turned on the ignition, and switched on the airconditioning. I lit a cigarette, and then stubbed it out. My mouth was too dry to smoke. Then I noticed the small three by five inch card half-hidden beneath the seatbelt on the passenger's side. Printed, in neat block letters, with a ballpoint pen, it read: "IT'S YOU I WANT, LUCKY, NOT AN INNOCENT STUDENT. NEXT TIME YOU WON'T BE SO LUCKY, LUCKY. BETTER SAY YOUR FUCKING PRAYERS."

I put the card into my shirt pocket, swiveled my neck and looked out the back window. The courtyard and the first two-story building of the Law School were behind me. Straight ahead, through the front window, was the vast student union parking lot, with cars as thickly clustered as fruitflies on an overripe mango. Students, some going toward the Ring Theater, shuffled along in sandals. Others were leaving the student union to attend classes, but I didn't see a middle-aged man wearing a seersucker jacket. Apparently Mr. Wright had followed me and rigged the gag explosive device on my car, but how had he got into the car without a key? I was positive that I had locked the car. It's the kind of thing a man does automatically, but being positive wasn't enough. From now on I would have to be absolutely sure.

I left the university, and circled about through the quiet back streets of Coral Gables, checking the rearview mirror to see if I were being followed. These were all placid neighborhood blocks, with very little traffic, and there were no cars behind or in front of me when I finally reached Red Road and turned toward Eighth Street—the Tamiami Trail—or, as the Cubans call it, *Calle Ocho.*

My stomach burned, partly with hunger but mostly with fury—an indignant kind of fury caused by the pointlessness of the trick bomb. A real bomb would have killed me, and I could understand Wright's reluctance to place a real bomb in the car when he might have inadvertently killed a passing student as I triggered it, but there was still no point in using a firecracker bomb—just to prove that he could have blown me up with a real bomb as easily. He was making a game, or a joke out of my life—or death—or, more logically, he was giving me a second warning, when the shot was warning enough, to make me more alert, or perhaps, a more worthy opponent for him. Perhaps he was trying to make certain that I would try to protect myself against him? Was he giving me a sporting chance because he didn't want to shoot a "sitting duck?"

Whatever his intentions were, I did not intend to let the joke throw me off. I was trying to outguess Mr. Wright, and there was a possibility that he had had a cooling off period, and that he had placed the trick bomb under the hood to show me that he was no longer angry enough to kill me, to carry out his original threat. But if that were true, why would he leave such a threatening note?

I shrugged away these speculations, knowing how useless

they were. I knew nothing about Wright the man, the husband, or the killer. To stay alive, I would have to assume—without forgetting it for a second—that Wright meant to kill me, and the best way to prevent him from doing so would be to kill him first.

16

After Twenty-Seventh Avenue, driving east, Eighth Street is a one-way, four-laned street. The neighborhoods on both sides, as well as the stores, are almost entirely Spanish-speaking—Cuban, and Puerto Rican, with a scattering of Colombians. There are always two or more people in a car in Little Havana, usually several, and as they—the occupants—drive along, they all talk at once, using both hands, including the driver. Sometimes, a Cuban driver, to make a point to someone in the back seat, will take his hands off the wheel altogether, turn around, and with many gestures, talk animatedly to his passengers in the back while he is still traveling at forty miles per hour. One drives cautiously on Eighth Street, and even more so after it becomes a one-way street. I was looking for the Target Gun Shop, a parking place, and out for other drivers.

I parked on the south side of Eighth, locked my car, and waited for a chance to jaywalk to the other side. The Target Gun Shop had been easy to find. The front of the building was a huge target, with wide, alternating black and white stripes narrowing down to a big circular black bullseye that included the top half of the front door. Running across the street, when my chance came, and heading for that black bullseye door, gave me a queasy feeling.

The store inside, dark and delightfully airconditioned,

was much larger than it had appeared from the street. One half of the building was devoted to guns and ammunition, with a half-dozen long glass display cases filled with pistols. There were tables loaded with hunting equipment, holsters, ammo belts, and other war surplus camping equipment. The other half of the building, with a separate entrance inside the store, was an indoor shooting range.

I looked into the display cases at the wide selection of weapons, bewildered by the variety of choices. A middle-aged Cuban, with fluffy gray sideburns, waited on me. His English was excellent, with hardly any accent.

"Look as long as you like," he said, smiling, "and if you want to examine one of the pistols, just tap on the glass and I'll take it out for you."

"I think I'll need some help," I said. "I need a pistol, but they all look about the same to me."

"No, sir. They are not the same. Do you need a weapon for target practice, or merely for protection?"

"Protection?" I looked at him sharply.

He shrugged. "A man must protect his home."

"Yes," I said, "I need a pistol for protection."

"What do you know about guns?"

"Not much, except what I learned in the Army. One thing—when you look at the riflings inside the barrel, it means you've got a muzzle velocity of one hundred yards per second for each complete twist. Eight complete turns in the barrel means eight hundred yards per second."

He laughed, and shook his head. "Not exactly. It would also depend on the bore size, the load, and the barrel length, but these things are not important with small arms. For short range protection, muzzle velocity doesn't mean so much. A nice short-barrelled thirty-eight, is a good buy for protection. If you're a very good shot you might prefer a forty-five. But if you are not a marksman, I suggest a thirty-eight, and the ammo's a lot cheaper."

He showed me several .38s and I selected a Police Special with a three-inch barrel. It was a delight to hold it in my hand.

The price was $280.00, which was more than I had expected to pay for a used pistol, but I handed him my MasterCard.

He filled out the bill of sale and registration papers and asked me to sign them. I slipped the pistol into my hip pocket, and he laughed.

"Hold on, Mr. Norton. I have to have the gun registered. You'll be able to get it in seventy-two hours—three days from now."

"Three days? I need it for protection now."

"That's the time it takes. We do the paperwork for you, you see, but I can't let you take a weapon out that hasn't been registered downtown with Metro. It's the law."

"Okay. Can you rent me a pistol for three days, until mine is registered?"

"That's—just a minute, Mr. Norton. You'd better talk to Mr. Dugan." He went down the counter, and came back with an older, red-haired man who looked as if he had rinsed his face with tomato soup.

"We aren't in business to rent pistols, Mr. Norton," Mr. Dugan said.

"I understand that, but I carry pharmaceutical supplies in my car, and they need protection until I get the pistol registered."

"Who did you vote for in the last election?"

"That's a personal matter, Mr. Dugan," I said.

"Yes, it is, if you want to keep it personal. Do you mind showing me your voter's registration card?"

"Of course not."

The moment he saw my registration card his stiff attitude changed. He smiled, shook my hand, winked, and returned the card. "For a fellow Republican," he said, "we're willing to bend a little, but we have to be careful, you know. Some of these knee-jerk liberals and independents that come in here—well, I don't have to tell you, Mr. Norton." He turned to the Cuban salesman. "Take care of him, José."

I left the Target Gun Shop with a newly-blued, short-barrelled .38; two boxes of ammunition (100 rounds); a soft, plasticene holster, with a chrome clip to hold the holster and gun inside my trousers; a Hoppe's gun cleaning kit; and a free bumper sticker, reading: "WHEN GUNS ARE OUTLAWED, ONLY OUTLAWS WILL HAVE GUNS."

17

When I got back to my apartment I cleaned and oiled the .38 and got used to handling it. I aimed at various things in the living room and squeezed off some dry-run shots, trying to become familiar with the trigger pull. But I was a little afraid of the pistol. The concept of buying a pistol is one thing; to actually buy and own one and have it in your hand is something else—a step across a dividing line that changes you into a different kind of man. A pistol is often referred to as "the difference," because a man five feet tall with a pistol has made up the difference between himself and an opponent six feet tall. But what I was feeling, as I fooled around with the pistol in my living room, was a psychological difference. I felt a combination of elation and dreadful excitement, together with an eagerness to use the damned pistol—to use it on Mr. Wright.

But I was not a good shot. My Army experience with weapons, as a member of the Adjutant General's Corps, was primarily familiarization firing. During an R.O.T.C. summer camp I had had to qualify with a rifle on the range, but we had only fired five rounds apiece with a .45 on the pistol range, just to give us an idea of what it was like to shoot one.

I boiled four frankfurters and ate them with a bowl of cottage cheese. Every few minutes, I would to the window, and peak out to check my car. Until this business with Wright was resolved, I would be unable to work. I couldn't park in strange parking lots, nor beside doctors' offices—not if Wright had access to my car. Nor was my car safe on Santana, even though I could look out the window once in awhile to check on it. I couldn't watch it all night—not when I slept.

I had to do something now.

It was two p.m., and much too early to go to the airport, but I would be safer there if I could lose or elude Wright beforehand. I was too restless and jittery to stay in the apartment.

I loaded the pistol, slipped it into the holster, and left the building. I had debated putting the bumper sticker on my car, but decided against it. If Wright saw the bumper strip, he might jump to the correct conclusion that I had armed myself, and it seemed to me that I would have a slightly better advantage if he didn't know that I had a weapon.

I had lost Wright, I was certain, when I circled about through the Coral Gables residential sections before going to the gun shop. But the chances were good that he was following me again. To pick up again all he had to do was to return to my apartment house and wait for me. So although I didn't see him, I made some elaborate maneuvers to lose him in case he was somewhere around.

No one knows Miami any better than I do. I've explored most of Dade County by car. I drove downtown on I-95, left the freeway at Biscayne, and then took the MacArthur Causeway to Miami Beach. I drove up Collins, then came back to Miami via the Venetian Causeway, and picked up I-95 South. Then, by a dangerous maneuver and quite unexpectedly, I cut from the far right lane over to the left lane on a tire-screeching four-lane diagonal cross and made the downtown First Street exit ramp. Anyone following me would have had to know I was going to make this suicidal lane switch to stay with me.

I parked at the Miamarina, had a cup of coffee, and then took the Airport Expressway at a leisurely forty miles per hour to the International Airport. I drove up the departure ramp, turned into the terminal parking building across from the Eastern gate, and parked on the top floor. I locked the .38 in the glove compartment (it is not good to be caught with a loaded pistol in an airport). I locked the Galaxie and rode the elevator down to the departing passenger entrance.

It was four-fifteen p.m. I spent the next hour and a half slowly sipping two tall John Collinses at the Airport Lounge, well pleased with myself at the clever way I had lost Mr. Wright, while I waited to see Tom Davies, the Vice-President for Sales.

18

The two drinks, together with the illusion of security I felt at having given Wright the slip, had steadied me, and it was simple to gauge Tom Davies' role when I joined him in his hotel room. Madras is back, and Tom was wearing a new madras suit—predominantly yellow, green, and black—with sixteen-inch cuffed bell-bottoms, a salmon-colored shirt, and a black-and-gold tie. When he met me at the door and didn't take off his jacket when he invited me to fix myself a drink (Jack Daniels Black, water), I perceived that Tom was playing vice-president.

The last time I had been with Tom, about ten minutes before I had passed out, he had been drunk, giggling helplessly, and the two Amazon showgirls we had picked up in Atlanta had been rubbing his naked body with Johnson's Baby Oil. But during this current meeting in the silent soundproof room in the Airport Hotel, mentioning that particular incident would have been undiplomatic. Taking my cue from Tom, I did not remove my jacket. The drink I mixed was very light indeed—a "social" drink, taken genially by the hard-working star salesman in the field.

Tom was wearing his sincere smile, and his manners were muted. Dale Carnegie. I had taken the Dale Carnegie course, and so had Tom; in fact every man in the company had been forced to take it, and the company, of course, had paid the tab. The problem with two men who have both taken and absorbed the Carnegie techniques is to conceal the fact that they are using them on each other. In this respect, Tom was much better at it than I was because, as a Vice-President, with a $70,000 annual salary, plus stock options, he had to be. But I was perceptive enough to realize, or recognize, his superiority in this regard, and all I had to do to maintain my deferential employee role without appearing to be deferential (the company would not tolerate Uriah Heeps) was to talk and act with Tom as if I, too, were making seventy thousand a year. What I had to be very careful about was to never show that I was superior to Tom in knowledge in any area of discussion, and, at the same time, never to reveal abysmal ignorance on any topic discussed. It was quite simple to maintain my role with Tom because he made it easy for me, and I admired his skill.

Besides, you can't shit an old shitter.

Tom had been a detail man in the field, and the district manager for Southern California before he had been promoted to Vice-President for Sales. He was only thirty-five, goal-oriented, and his chances of succeeding old Ned Lee as president of the company some day were better than those of the other vice-presidents I had met in New Jersey.

Tom sat on the edge of the double bed, placed his pale drink on the bedside table, and waved me to the chair by the desk. The chair was more than twelve feet away from the bed, and he was establishing—in case I had failed to notice it already—the distance between us as befitted our roles. He would begin with an apology, and I waited for it silently, wearing my concerned expression.

"I know that six o'clock is an awkward time, Hank, and I'm sorry if you had to break off an engagement of some kind to meet me."

I shook my head. "Not when it's company business, Tom," I said. "Besides, how often do I get a chance to see you?"

I had handled that one neatly, by implying that I had broken an engagement of some kind, and by hinting that I liked him as a person, and not because he was merely a generous boss.

"How well do you know Julie Westphal, Hank?"

"Very well. He's a friend of mine, and I don't say that just because he's the man who hired me. I like him as my district manager and I think he likes me. Julie was damned helpful to me in the beginning, and I learned a great deal from him."

"He likes you, too, Hank," Tom said, nodding his head approvingly. "In fact, he wanted to come down here from Atlanta with me. Do you know why?"

I shook my head.

Tom laughed. "To help me knock some sense into your head, that's why!"

I smiled. "I'm always receptive to more sense. Any man can use more than he has—so what have I done now?"

"What have you done? I'll tell you what you've done! You've become the best goddamned detail man Lee Labs has got in the field, that's what you've done! And I'm going to tell you something else you don't know. You're the highest paid salesman in the company—or did you suspect it already?"

"No," I said. Then I grinned. "But I was a little puzzled when I only got a five hundred dollar raise this year instead of the usual thousand. What's the matter, Tom? D'you guys think you're paying me too much?"

"Frankly, Hank, you weren't supposed to get any raise at all. The only reason you got the five hundred was because I insisted on it. You've had it, Hank. There'll be no more raises. Oh, you'll get your cost of living boosts, of course, and your fair share of the annual bonuses. But your base salary is frozen. As a detail man, you're now in a dead end job."

"I can get by," I said, shrugging. "In fact, I like my job and living in Miami so well, I'd stay with the company even if you paid me a lot less. In this job, helping doctors, which means, in turn, helping sick people, I fulfill myself every single day. It would be pretty hard for me to find a selling job of any other kind as psychologically satisfying."

Tom nodded. "I wish more of our salesmen felt as you do, Hank." He sighed, and shook his head. "However, a dead end job is a dead end job, and you're only thirty-two years old. You were offered the district manager's position in Syracuse, and you turned it down..."

"I explained that..."

"Let me finish, Hank. Sure you turned it down, and I don't blame you. I wouldn't want to live in Syracuse myself. It takes a peculiar and hardy breed of man to brave those Syracuse winters, holding onto ropes as they walk windy streets full of snow, and I was against the idea of asking a man from Florida to take it in the first place. And I told them so emphatically in the executive session. No one held that against you, Hank.

"But then you turned down Cleveland."

"I know, Tom, but Cleveland—Jesus."

"I agree, Hank. 'Cleveland—Jesus!' " He laughed. "The only way we got Fenwick to take Cleveland was to give him a lifetime pass to all the Browns' football games."

"I didn't know that, Tom. In lieu of the salary raise you aren't going to give me, I'll gladly take a lifetime pass to all the Dolphin games."

Tom laughed. "Who wouldn't? For a lifetime pass to the Dolphin games, I'd trade jobs with you myself! But seriously, Hank, those offers—Syracuse and Cleveland—were not made lightly. Any and all promotions are considered in depth. Lee Labs is a quality company, and when we promote a man from the field, we're looking ahead to at least one or two promotions beyond that one. Now, have you ever heard the old saying, 'Three's the charm?' "

I nodded.

"Well, that's it. When the third promotion is turned down, although it rarely happens, we never make another offer. That's it, and I want you to understand this, Hank. So listen carefully, and let me give you the pitch." He paused dramatically, stared into my eyes, nodded three times, and said, "Chicago."

"Chicago? I think I told you once before, Tom—in fact I'm sure I did—that I planned on staying in Miami for the rest of my life. I'm putting down roots here, I love the climate, I..."

"Hold on, Hank. Do you think I'm a fool? Listen to me." He rose, walked toward me, and stopped three feet away. Now I had to look up at him to make eye contact.

"When I said Chicago, I didn't mean that you'd be the

Chicago *salesman*, for Christ's sake! We've already got two detail men in Chicago. I'm offering you the midwestern *district*! If you told me you liked Chicago, or wanted to live there, I'd think you had rocks in your head. But you'll only be in Chicago on weekends as the district manager. Your headquarters'll be there—no office—you'll work out of your apartment and get your mail there, but during the week you'll be on the road. Let me lay it out, and if you want to turn it down after I tell you about it, that's your decision. Okay? On Sunday night, you leave O'Hare International and fly to the Twin Cities. A day in St. Paul, and a day in Minneapolis. Tuesday night you fly to St. Louis, and spend the day there. Wednesday, you're in Iowa City, and maybe, every other week, you can make the hop to Butte on Wednesday instead of hitting Iowa City. Thursday you're in Indianapolis, Friday you're in Detroit, and by Friday night cocktail hour you're back in Chicago. If you want to, once in awhile, you can skip Detroit and spend the day checking out your detail men in Chicago. That'll give you a one-day breather once in awhile. The thing is, Hank, the midwest is our weakest district in sales. We've picked good young men with a lot of potential in those cities, but they aren't salesmen—not yet they aren't—but we're counting on you to move their asses, to make hotshots out of 'em."

"I just don't want to leave Miami, Tom. I think I'm doing a good job for the company here..."

"Good? You're doing a fantastic job down here! When was the last time Julie Westphal came down from Atlanta to critique your sales pitches?"

"I don't want to get Julie into trouble, Tom, but he hasn't been down here in more than two months."

Tom grinned. He sat on the desk, which made him still higher than me. Looking at the wall, he placed his left hand on my right shoulder.

"I know the score, Hank. And I've read Julie's reports. He doesn't come down here to check on you because I told him to leave you alone, and because, as he admitted, he was wasting his time checking on you. What can he tell you that you don't know already? We know how high the sales are down here, and if you weren't out there hustling they'd drop. Julie's a damned good man, but he's limited, too, and his position as Southeast district manager is his terminal job. That information's in confidence, of course."

"Of course."

"So instead of coming down here, Julie spends some extra time in Auburn and Birmingham where he can help two young salesmen who really need his help. But in your case, Hank, we've got some other plans. With quality production, our expansion is slow, but we *are* expanding. I told you on the phone that I hadn't slept for twenty-four hours, and now I'll tell you why. I spent that time with some lawyers in a hotel room in Boston, and we have just bought Franklin Toothbrushes. You've seen them in drugstores, and it was an additional line we needed. You'll have a sample case of toothbrushes within a week." He grinned, and when Tom grinned, his lips disappeared altogether and his mouth became a shallow U. "You'll never have to buy another toothbrush, Hank."

Tom took my glass, and fixed me another weak drink. I lit another cigarette from the butt I was smoking. I knew better than to chain-smoke, but the damned pressure was getting to me.

When he handed me my fresh drink, I rose, walked to the window, and pulled up the venetian blinds. There was no window; the raised blinds revealed a white concrete wall—how else could they soundproof a room with a plane passing overhead every thirty seconds? I dropped the blinds.

"I'm very flattered, Tom," I said. "But to leave Miami, to leave Florida..." I shook my head.

"Okay, Hank, I'll talk about money. Sit down on the bed. You'll be more comfortable there."

He sat on the desk again, and now, as I sat on the bed, the twelve feet of distance was back and he was still looking down on me from his desk seat vantage point. "As a single man, I know you have enough to live on, Hank, and you should be saving a few dollars. I did, when I was in the field, and we're pretty generous with our expense accounts. In some cases, too generous, but I won't go into that with you because you've never been an offender. But the midwest district means a five thousand dollar salary jump, and you'll be on the road five days a week. That means expense account money five days out of seven. Think about it. Don't say anything. Just think about it. Within five more years, and if you've done the job in the midwest we think you'll do, and we do, or we wouldn't have picked you for it, you'll be moving up. Lee Labs has some ambitious plans, and one of these days we're going to establish a Vice-President for Training. That's still a part of my load now, training, but with expansion, I'm going to have to let go of a few responsibilities. Not now, and not three years from now, but I'd say that within five years, or maybe four, that position will be an absolute necessity. I'm not promising it to you—I never promise a man shit. But I have a hunch that within five years—maybe four—you're going to *demand* it, and if we don't give you a vice-presidency or something comparable another company will. Yes, Hank, I'm afraid you're going to have us over the goddamned barrel."

"What happens to me if I decided to stay in Miami?"

"Speaking for the company, Hank, nothing could make me any happier! We won't be able to find a man half as good as you are to replace you, and as long as you're here this is one territory that Julie and I don't have to worry about. For the company, it would be a great thing. Fine. We could quit worrying about Miami—for about five years, anyway. But you're a person, Hank."

Tom jumped down, crossed to the bed, sat beside me, and put his right arm around my shoulders. He dropped his voice a full octave.

"Let me level with you, Hank. I like you, you horny fucking bastard! You know that, don't you?"

I nodded.

"You like me, too, don't you, Hank? Haven't we had a few good times together?"

"You know what I think of you, Tom."

"Right. So let me tell you a story. You've met Johnny Maldon, I know. He was at the last Atlanta meeting, and you've probably talked to him at other conventions, or seen him anyway. Has Julie ever talked to you about Johnny?"

"No," I lied. "Julie doesn't talk about his other salesmen, unless they've come up with a good idea."

"Good. Johnny hasn't come up with a good idea in ten years, but eighteen years ago he was a damned good man. He was never as good as you, but at least he got out and hustled. Awhile ago, when I told you that you were Lee's highest paid salesman, I didn't tell you all of it. How much did you make when you were first hired?"

"Nine thousand, and a car."

"That's what Johnny still makes now, Hank! Nine thousand a year and a car. He hasn't had a raise in seven years, and he'll never have another. But Johnny is really our highest paid salesman, Hank, because he's really making nine thousand dollars an *hour*—the *one* hour, if it's that much, he works for the company during an entire year."

Tom shook his head and signed.

"So let's say that you stay in Miami, Hank. For the next four or five years, fine. No problems. None for you, none for the company. But every year, inflation. If Johnny can't live on nine thousand a year in Alabama today, do you think you'll be able to survive in Miami on twenty-two thousand, five years from now? In Miami? You'll be bitter, and you'll be unhappy, and you won't blame yourself—no, you'll blame the company. And once you start blaming the company, you'll slack off. You'll work one day a week instead of three or four, and Miami sales will go down. Old Ned Lee won't be around in five years to save your ass, either. Next year, if he keeps his promise, Ned will give up the presidency and confine himself to handling the gavel at monthly board meetings as Chairman of the Board. You'll be thirty-seven years old, and you'll be out on the street, Hank. It's human nature. And even if you continue to do a good job, and I have a hunch that you won't let any bitterness influence your actual working habits, it won't help you. You aren't that kind of man, Hank. But all the same, the other company executives will wonder about you. And why? Because it's unAmerican to refuse a promotion, that's why. They'll think—right or wrong—that you haven't got any ambition. And if they think you haven't got any ambition, the next thing they'll think is that no matter how good your sales are in Miami—from Key West to Palm Beach—they should be even better, much better—no matter how hard you're actually working."

"Jesus, Tom," I said, "a lot of men keep one job for life..."

"Of course they do, Hank. But they aren't exactly ambitious men, are they?"

"But if they're happy men, what the hell?"

"Hank, if you're still only making twenty-two grand a year five years from now, I'll guarantee you that you'll be one unhappy sonofabitch in Miami. Believe me. How about one more drink, and then I've got to run you out of here. I've got to get a few hours sleep before my midnight plane."

"I'll pass on the drink, Tom."

"Okay. Don't make your decision now. Think about it—the decision's yours all the way, and I sure as hell don't want to influence you any. Either way you decide is fine with me. I may be your boss, but I'm a better friend than I am a boss, and I think you know that. So either way, I'll back you. Lee Labs is twice as big as it was ten years ago, but we still believe in the personal not the personnel approach to employee relationships. And if the company ever forgets that employees are *people*, I'm getting out myself and they can stick my seventy thousand dollars a year up their ass!"

He got to his feet, and so did I. I put the glass down on the desk.

"I'll be at the Coronado Beach in San Juan for the next week, or maybe ten days. Gonzales is the only Catholic in the company, and he wants to hire a black man for the Leeward islands. What do you think about that, Hank?"

"I didn't know that Gonzales was our only Catholic."

"Ned Lee hates Catholics. I thought you knew that. But we had to have a linguist in the Caribbean, and Gonzales speaks Spanish, French, and even Haitian patois. Besides, Gonzales is a native Puerto Rican with a B.S. from Tufts."

"I like Gonzales," I said, "I also think it's a good idea to hire a few black detail men—especially if you keep them in the Caribbean."

"I agree with you, Hank. In fact, if you take the midwest district, we're going to ask you to recruit a black detail man for Detroit. The guy we've got in Detroit now is afraid to drive a car into some of the sections in his territory."

I started for the door, and Tom grabbed my left elbow with a thumb and forefinger pincers grip.

"So you've got a week, Hank. Call me collect in Puerto Rico at the Coronado Beach when you've decided what you want to do."

"I can tell you right now, Tom..."

"I don't want to know now! I want you to think about it, and call me later."

"Right."

When I got downstairs I had a double-shot of brandy in the Dobbs House lounge, and then I left the terminal. Tom had manipulated me with a heavy hand. If he hadn't been so tired, and he had looked exhausted, he would have handled the matter much more subtly instead of beating me over the head. Nevertheless, almost half of everything he said was true. I would still get raises in Miami. If I didn't there were other pharmaceutical companies that would hire me at a much higher salary in another year or so. So if Lee didn't pay me what I was entitled to, I would get it elsewhere. But in seven or eight years—not five—I really would be frozen and unable to quit—like Johnny Maldon in Tuscaloosa. In ten years time, however, I hoped to own some rental property, maybe a small apartment house. All I had to do was save my money, but it is hard to save any money in Miami. I would have to work out a regular saving plan of some kind. And soon.

Thanks to Daylight Savings Time, the sun was still shining at eight p.m. I crossed the heavy traffic to the parking garage, and rode the elevator to the top floor. I unlocked my car, glanced at the back seat, and heard, before I accepted the physical evidence, the ticking of an alarm clock. There were four red-and-white wires wrapped around three sticks of dynamite, and these wires were attached to the alarm clock.

Without slamming the door, I turned and started running down the exit ramp, and I didn't stop running until I reached the ground floor.

19

On the ground floor, panting, I leaned with both hands against a concrete post and vomited a thin stream of sour bile. My stomach convulsed a few more times, but by breathing heavily through my mouth, I managed to regain control of my body and check my desire for further flight. My shirt was soaked through, and my seersucker suit jacket was damp beneath the arms. I removed my jacket, and wiped my streaming eyes and face with my shirt sleeve.

I had left my car key, on the ring with all of my other keys, in the car door. Cars raced noisily into the parking garage seeking, but not finding, a space on the first floor before they took the ramp on up to the second or the third or fourth. Because I could ride the elevator, I never wasted my time looking for a space on the bottom floor when I came to the airport. I drove to the top floor immediately, where there were almost always empty spaces. I tried to remember what the makes of the other cars up there were, but I couldn't. I also wondered if Mr. Wright was on the top floor, lurking madly about to exult over the explosion. I also wondered what the time was on the alarm clock attached to the dynamite in my back seat.

I looked at my watch. It was eight-twenty-two. If Wright had a sense of order, he would set the explosion for eight-thirty or nine p.m.—if he had a sense of order. A man crazy enough to put dynamite in another man's car was unlikely to have a sense of anything. My mind wasn't functioning too well either, or I wouldn't have taken a chance. But I took the chance, hoping, as I rode the elevator to the top floor that I would encounter Mr. Wright. If I did, I would disarm him, feed him his pistol, and then throw the sonofabitch over the rail from the fourth floor and watch him splatter when he hit the asphalt below.

I approached my car. The door was still hanging open. I retrieved my keys, glanced into the back seat, and noticed that the red paper on one of the sticks of dynamite was loose and flapping. I looked a little closer. The exposed end of the dynamite stick resembled a piece of sawed wood. I folded the driver's seat down over the wheel, and gingerly fingered the tissue paper, unfolding it back a little more. It was merely red tissue paper wrapped loosely around a short length of broomstick. So were the other two "sticks." The wires attached to the alarm clock didn't do anything either. There was no battery, and there were no dynamite caps in the three sticks of wood. The bomb was a fake. I threw the wrapped wooden sticks and the alarm clock on the concrete floor and got into the car.

I opened the glove compartment and discovered that my .38 pistol was missing.

There was no way, that I could figure, for Mr. Wright to know—in advance—that I was coming to the airport, unless, of course, he had a tap on my phone. But even so—and a tap was unlikely—he still couldn't know that I was going to park in this particular garage on the top floor. There are literally hundreds of places to park at the Miami airport, and the constant vehicle traffic is unbelievable. Somehow, though, Wright had followed me, watched me, and planted the fake explosive device after stealing my pistol. How, I wondered, did he happen to have a key that fitted my Galaxie? And why plant a phony bomb? Why not a real one?

The man was insane, that was all. He had to be. What he was doing, as nearly as I could determine logically, was playing around with, telling me, in one curious move after another, that he would kill me any time he wanted to, and there was nothing I could do to prevent it. The evil bastard was enjoying himself, and laughing at my antics.

Somehow, he was able to follow me about the city like a damned ghost, and he was able to get into my car every time I left it. He was probably close by now, watching me, even though I couldn't see him. I shivered. On the off chance (or on-chance) that he might have planted a real bomb under the hood this time instead of a Whiz-Bang, I checked under the hood, looked beneath the car, and rummaged around in the trunk. None of my samples was missing, nor had he ripped open any of the sealed cardboard boxes full of drugs in the trunk.

I sat in the front seat, closed the door, turned on the engine and air-conditioning and smoked a cigarette. I was bone-tired. With two bad scares that day, and what with the additional pressure from Tom Davies, my body was running out of adrenaline.

By the time I finished the cigarette, I had a plan. A stupid plan, maybe, but I was going to try it anyway. But first I had to eat something—the hell with my diet—I needed all the strength I could muster.

I pulled into the Pigskin Bar-B-Que on LeJeune, and ordered two pork barbecue sandwiches and a double chocolate milkshake. It was the first milkshake I had had in two years, and I had forgotten how good they were. I felt much better after eating, and although I wasn't too optimistic about succeeding with my hastily conceived plan, the fact that I was going to do something to counter Mr. Wright instead of just waiting to see what would happen next gave me a feeling of well-being.

Now, instead of worrying about his uncanny ability to track me through the crowded city, like some wily, city-wise Natty Bumppo, I began to worry about the possibility of losing him.

It was dark when I left the Drive-In. I took the Airport Expressway to Miami Beach, hugging the outside lane all the way without driving any faster than forty miles per hour. I didn't want to lose the bastard; I wanted to find him by making it as easy as I could for him to trail me.

In Miami Beach I cruised slowly down Arthur Godfrey Road, turned in to the side street behind the Double X Adult Theater and parked in the tiny parking lot. The old guy who gave me the parking stub asked me if I was going to the Double X Theater, and when I told him I was he reminded me to have the girl at the box office stamp and validate my stub before I came back for my car.

"Otherwise, buddy," he said grumpily, "it'll cost you a buck an hour to park here. This ain't no regular lot, you know, it's for movie patrons."

"I understand," I said. "I've been here before."

There were two films playing. I had seen both of them with Larry when they played at the Kendall mini-theater a few weeks back. The features were *A Hard Man's Good to Find* and *Coming Attractions*, and they were both one-hour length films. That gave me about two hours to see if my plan would work. I took the tire iron out of the trunk, and wrapped it in the oily pink towel I also kept in the trunk.

I gave the Cuban woman in the box office four dollars for admission. She looked sharply at the folded pink towel, and sniffed disdainfully, but that didn't bother me. She probably had a low opinion of all the patrons of the Double X anyway.

I found a seat, and watched a couple of naked blondes massage each other to rock music on the screen for about ten minutes, while I smoked a cigarette and got used to the darkness. There were about thirty people scattered about in the audience. Most of them were men, but there were two white-haired old ladies sitting together, and a couple of younger women—with their dates or husbands—who giggled a lot.

I left my seat and went to the lobby. I didn't see Wright in the audience, but I sensed, nevertheless, that he was somewhere about, or knew that I was in the theater. A man stood at the combination candy-and-porno glass counter. In addition to candy and popcorn, there was a wide selection of porno devices and still photos in the glass case. I waited until the man bought a box of popcorn, a Mounds bar, and a French tickler and went into the auditorium before I bought a package of gum from the girl behind the counter. I chewed two sticks in the empty lobby for a minute or so, and entered the men's room when I was sure that the counter girl was watching me.

The window in the crummy little toilet was about four feet

above the wash basin. It was three feet wide, triple-paned, and about eighteen inches high. I climbed up on the wash basin, unlatched the window and let it fall back inside against the wall. Then I unhooked the screen, and pushed it outside. The screen fell, clattering, onto the asphalt pavement of the parking lot. I could look out, but the old attendant was at the other end of the lot and he hadn't, apparently, heard the screen fall. The drop from the window to the ground outside was about ten feet, which was a safe enough fall if a man slid his body out belly down from the window, and then dropped with his fingers from the ledge.

I took a sheet of the brown blot-don't-rub paper from the container by the sink, and printed "OUT OF ORDER" on it with my ballpoint pen. I had to go over the block letters several times to make it readable on the brown paper. I stuck the improvised sign on the outside of the door to the toilet with chewing gum, and then locked myself inside the cubicle. There was at least a foot and a half of space below the closed door, and beneath the side panel separating the toilet from the urinal. I stood precariously on the seat and crouched down to hide my upper body. There was a tiny screw-hole in the metal side panel, and I could see through it with one eye. I could watch a man standing at the urinal, and I would also be able to get a quick glimpse of anyone who came in through the door.

It was hot in the john. The smelly latrine, unlike the rest of the smelly theater, was not airconditioned, and the slight exertion of climbing onto the wash basin and opening the window had opened my pores. Straight ahead, there was just enough space at the door hinge for me to see the mottled mirror above the wash basin, but not the basin itself. Crouching there, hot, uncomfortable, sweating, with my legs becoming increasingly cramped by the strained position I was in, I felt like a damned fool.

I clutched the wrapped tire iron in my right hand, and resigned myself to a long wait. I would wait out the full two hours, regardless of the discomfort. Sooner or later, Wright would discover that I was missing from the audience, and he would find out that I had come into the john. Perhaps he knew already. When he came in to check, and noticed that the window was open, I would jump him. Such was my simple plan, but the longer I crouched there the dumber it seemed to be.

A young Latin male of twenty or twenty-one came in, and combed his shaggy locks in the mirror. He ambled over to the urinal and unzipped his fly. He masturbated rapidly into the urinal as I watched him in about twenty seconds—zip, zip, zip. This was something I hadn't expected to witness, nor did I want to see it. My face flushed with embarrassment. I could feel the heat in my cheeks. He went back to the wash basin, combed his hair again and, without washing his hands, left the john.

I felt a fresh surge of anger toward Mr. Wright. Because of him I had become a voyeur. The fact that it was inadvertent didn't make me feel any better about the sordid spot that I was in. But what the hell did I expect? That's what most of the patrons came to the Double X Theater for and, in the next two hours, I would probably see another dozen men come in and jack off. This dismal prospect so unnerved me that I almost decided to give up my post and try something else, but then the door opened again.

The man who entered had a slight build, and long blond curly hair down to his shoulders. He wore rose-colored Bermuda shorts, tennis shoes with black support socks, and a heavy black denim CPO shirt with the long tails outside the shorts. His skinny white legs were hairless. He crossed quickly to the sink and climbed up on the wash basin. By raising my head slightly, I could see the back of his head above the door as he peered out the opened window. The long locks fluttered slightly as a gust of humid air came in through the window, and I suspected—and acted on it immediately—that this man might be, could be, Mr. Wright wearing a blond wig.

I flipped the door lock open and jumped down to the concrete floor simultaneously. My cramped legs tingled painfully as the circulation opened up in them again, but I ignored the pain. As I banged the door open, the man whipped about and jumped down from the sink. The long swing I had already started with the tire iron club caught him a glancing blow on his upper arm before his feet hit the floor. He slipped to his knees, grunted, grabbed his upper left arm with his right hand, and tried to scramble to his feet. My next downward blow, with plenty of leverage on it, caught him squarely between his neck and shoulder. His left arm went limp as it was momentarily paralyzed. He opened his mouth to scream, but I stopped him in time.

"One sound," I said, raising my pink club again, "and you'll be one dead sonofabitch!"

His mouth remained open, and as I looked back at him I could see the gold bridgework in his back teeth. He bubbled, but he didn't scream or holler. He whimpered involuntarily, but it was caused by the air being forced out of his throat. This was Mr. Wright, all right, with a blond wig. He would have been recognizable—even if he had shaved his black hairline moustache—if I had suspected a wig. But he had retained the moustache; and his wig, now that I knew that he was wearing a wig, made him look obscenely ridiculous. I didn't recall seeing him earlier. The chances are that I had seen him at the airport, or at the university, but hadn't given him a second glance. The disguise was perfect. Middle-aged men with long hair and Bermudas are commonplace, especially on Miami Beach, where this kind of outfit is almost a tourist uniform.

I waited a moment, letting him catch his breath, before I told him to stretch out prone on the floor with his arms in front of him. I lifted his wallet from his left hip pocket, and my .38 pistol from his right hip pocket. His heavy .357 Magnum was in a leather shoulder holster under his left armpit. The loose CPO shirt, with the tails outside the shorts, had concealed it well. When I felt the shouldered gun, I held the muzzle of the .38 at his head, and told him to roll over on his back. With my left hand I awkwardly unbuttoned the shirt, reached in and took the .357 out of the holster. I stuck the heavy weapon into my trousers, and buttoned my jacket in front with my left hand.

I had moved slowly and cautiously during the frisking and without taking my eyes off Wright's face. When a man is crazy, and I was convinced that Wright was crazy, the chance of some unpredictable move is great. Even with both pistols in my possession, and with Wright supine on the floor, with his blond curly wig getting damp from the pool of water and urine below the urinal, I was still afraid of him. Perhaps it was a good thing that I was afraid of him. He witnessed my fear, and he was probably equally fearful that I would do something crazy and unpredictable because I was frightened. But this was no Mexican stand-off. I had the .38 in my hand, and my hatred of this man was so intense I was anxious to squeeze the trigger.

My fury was controlled, however, and I surprised myself with my ability to talk calmly in a natural tone of voice.

"I don't want you to say a word, Mr. Wright. We're going somewhere where we can talk, but until we get there I don't want to hear a sound from you. D'you understand?"

He managed to nod.

"Good. If you had said 'Yes' instead of nodding you wouldn't have got the message. Now you can get up, and put both of your hands into your front pockets. Don't make any quick moves. I've practiced some dry shots with this thirty-eight, and it's got a very light trigger pull."

He got up slowly, and put his hands in his pockets.

"Okay," I said. "Now, when we leave the theater, I'm going to have the woman at the box office validate my parking ticket. So as soon as we leave the front door, you stand with your back to the ticket window and look out at the street. If you want to run, fine. I'll shoot you without thinking about it. But if you want to live, you'll just stand there, waiting until I prod you from behind. Then we're going to the parking lot around to the back, and you'll drive my Galaxie as I direct you. D'you understand?"

He bobbed his head, and the damp curls shook.

There was no problem. It was a dark night, and once we rounded the corner and left the streetlights on Arthur Godfrey Road, we left the pedestrians behind as well. I had the .38 in my right jacket pocket, and carried the towel-wrapped bludgeon in my left. Wright walked along slowly about three feet ahead of me. I gave the parking stub to the attendant, and when we got to the car I told Wright to use his key. He had a key all right, and he opened the door and got into the driver's seat. I slammed the door and walked around to the other side. He reached across and unlatched my door so I didn't have to use my key. This kind of cooperation, which was unexpected, only served to increase my wariness of the man.

He wasn't a good driver, but that was normal. He hadn't driven my car before, and he was listening to my directions at the same time, afraid to make a mistake.

I had remembered the Weinsteins, and their now empty Cresciente condominium apartment.

The Cresciente was on Belle Isle, the first island on the chain of filled islands that made up the Venetian Causeway. Like many of the expensive Miami Beach condos, there was a security man in uniform at the front entrance, and he checked on people who used the visitor's parking slots. The residents, or owners, however, were free to come down the access alley the back way and drive into their parking spaces beneath the building. Then, by taking the elevator from the parking basement, there was no way for the security man in front to check on their comings and goings. Like everything else in Miami Beach, security is merely another amenity that people pay for without really getting.

The access alley behind the row of apartment houses was barely wide enough for two cars, but there was enough space to park on a narrow back lawn before we got to the Cresciente, and I told Wright to pull onto it. After locking the car, I told Wright to walk ahead of me. We entered the parking garage from the alley, waited for the elevator and took it up to the twelfth floor.

21

There were four apartments on each floor of the Cresciente, so the Weinstein's had to be 12A, B , C, or D. I remembered that Larry had told me the Weinstein apartment was on the Bay side, which meant that it was either B or C. The name on the door to C, which I checked first was Ralston. I tugged on Wright's arm, and we went down to B. *I. Weinstein.*

"Open the door," I said.

"I don't have a key..."

"Open the door."

"What if I can't get it open?"

"Last time. Open the door!"

Wright took out his keys, and opened a slim silver knife attached to the ring (there were a dozen or more keys on the ring), and flicked out a shiny rod so thin it looked like a chromed piece of piano wire. He fiddled with the lock, poking around inside with the rod, and opened the door in about a minute and a half. I reached inside, turned on the light, and gestured for him to precede me. I closed the door, and put on the chain night latch. Then, turning on lamps as we went through the apartment, I pushed him ahead of me into the billiard or snooker room.

Some, but not all, of the furniture had been covered with sheets, mostly pastel colored sheets in pinks and blues. The snooker table was covered with a green, tight-fitting oilcloth cover. I told Wright to climb into one of the high rattan chairs against the wall. I went around to the other side of the table, flipped the switch on the long fluorescent table light above the table, and looked at Wright for a long moment, wondering where to begin.

Sitting there in his poorly fitting Bermudas, and wearing black support socks with his tennis shoes, he certainly didn't look dangerous. In fact, he had given me less trouble than I had expected. I felt much safer with the width of the snooker table between us. I knew what a poor shot I was, so I put the .357 Magnum down on the table within easy reach of my left hand. In case he jumped me and I had to start shooting, I figured that I would be able to get at least one of twelve rounds into him.

Behind me, the heavy, dark green velvet drapes were drawn. The room was so silent I could barely hear the hiss of the airconditioners. They were set high, about eighty, as is usual when you leave your apartment for an extended period of time. As soon as the temperature rose above eighty degrees, the thermostat would automatically kick in the condenser until it got back down to eighty. I would have reset it at seventy, but I didn't know where the thermostat was. I took off my jacket instead, and placed it on table.

"Now that I've got you here, Mr. Wright," I said, "I don't know exactly what I'm going to do with you, but first..."

"You're going to kill me," he said calmly.

"No," I said, "I'm not going to kill you, but I've got to do something or other, explain the facts to you, or something, to get you off my fucking back. First of all, I didn't screw Jannaire—your wife."

"I think you screwed her all right," he said, "but I don't care about that."

"If you don't care about that, why have you been trying to kill me?"

"I haven't been trying to kill you, Mr. Norton. I've been trying to scare you. If I'd wanted to kill you I could've hit you the first day I came to town, and taken the United Breakfast Flight back to Jacksonville. I knew it was a mistake, and I told Miss Jannaire so, but she wouldn't listen to me."

"Miss Jannaire?"

"That's right. I don't have to tell you nothing. I know you're going to shoot me anyway, but as long's I'm talking and you're listening I'm still sitting here. And sitting and talking is still living."

"Wait a minute. Why'd you call your wife, 'Miss Jannaire?'"

"She isn't my wife. She's my employer."

"Start from the beginning. I've been suspecting a set-up, but it looks worse than I thought."

"From the beginning?"

"From the beginning."

"Well, first I got this phone call from my contact here in Miami."

"Who was that?"

"I can't tell you that. It's unethical, but I can tell you the rest if you want."

"I want. Go ahead."

"Well, my contact said he had a contract for me down here, and he give me Miss Jannaire's phone number to call when I got down here, and my password."

"Password? How come?"

"That way, Miss Jannaire would know it was me, and not some guy trying to sell her dance lessons on the phone or something. So I called her from the airport. I had my bag and everything, and she told me to take a cab over to her apartment. She put me up in her guest room."

"When was this?"

"Two weeks ago. Almost. Twelve days, counting today."

"What took you so long to come after me?"

"We was dickering. I didn't like the set-up. Then my beeper set got messed up, and I had to drive up to Fort Lauderdale where there was a guy who could fix it. It's good when it works, but when it ain't working, it ain't worth a damn. I paid seven hundred and fifty bucks for it, and I thought at first I was gypped until I learned how to use it. My son and I practiced with it all over Jax, with him driving his car with a head start and me trying to find him until I finally got the hang of it."

"Wait a minute, Mr. Wright. What's the beeper got to do with Jannaire? You're getting off the track."

"Not with the beeper. You see, that's how I followed you. I planted the transmitter in your gas tank, and then with my sonic receiver I could sort of run you down. It takes a little time, and if you don't know how to work it, you might as well quit. But I know how to work it, thanks to my son having the patience to drive all over Jax for about six weeks with me chasing him. Of course, with Francis, it was sort of a game with him. But it was just hard, hot work for me. But I found out I wasn't gypped on the beeper set. I know how to use it now."

"Okay. That's interesting. You could trail me with a sonic beeper. That explains part of the mystery. How'd you get a duplicate key to my car?"

"From this same guy in Lauderdale. It cost me ten bucks. If I'd had more time, if Miss Jannaire had told me the make of your car and all before I come down, I could've sent away for one and got it for five bucks."

"Send away where?"

"Lots of places. They advertise keys in the car magazines. Don't you ever read the classifieds in the car magazines? You can get a key to any make car and year you want for five bucks. But this guy in Lauderdale, he charged me ten, and I give it to him because of the shortness of time."

"All right. Let's get back to Jannaire. She hired you, somehow, to kill me. Is that right?"

"No. That's what I thought it was when my contact down here called me. He told me he had this contract for me, and a contract means a hit, so that's what I thought. I think she had the same idea when she talked to my contact here, but she changed her mind later."

"Who was the contact?"

"I can't tell you that. It's unethical."

"Maybe it is, but I can't help wondering how she found out how to go about hiring a pro killer, that's all. She's a dress designer who dabbles some in real estate, isn't she?"

"I don't know. I don't care what people do for a living. I've got my living to make, and they got theirs. I offer a service, and if they can pay, they get it."

"How much do you get for killing a man?"

"Two thousand dollars. In advance. I've got more, but I won't work for no less. And I do it clean. I come in, I find the guy, and I hit him. Like that. Then I'm long gone back to Jax."

"Why'd she want you to kill me?"

"She didn't say, and I didn't ask. Besides, she didn't want me to kill you. She wanted me to run you out of town instead. That's what caused a lot more delay, you see. It's one thing to come into town, hit a man—nice and clean—and then get out. But to scare a man so bad he'll just pick up and leave, that's stupid. Maybe, in time, I could've scared you out. I just don't know about that now. But even if I did, you'd come back probably. And there was a lot of danger exposing myself to you that way, pretending to be her husband. That's why I couldn't say much to you in her apartment. Just the little we talked, you wondered why a woman like that would marry a man like me, didn't you?"

"Yes. I wondered about that. But I didn't think too much about it because I was surprised to find out that she had a husband in the first place."

"Well, I ain't him, Mr. Norton. She might have one someplace, but I ain't married to her. And I'm glad I'm not, neither. I'm a widower. There's just me and my son, Francis, and our little grocery store. And that's what I'd like to go on being; a widower. It was the money, Mr. Norton. I hope you know that I ain't got nothing personal against you. Tell you the truth, I felt sorry for you, all mixed up with that woman, a woman that don't shave under her arms or anything."

"It doesn't reassure me, Wright, to know that you didn't do all these things for personal reasons."

"I know. I just put that in. I know you're going to kill me, but it won't make it easy for you if you get to feeling sorry for me."

"I don't feel sorry for you, Wright. I've never met a professional killer, or a hit-man before, but I don't like you personally, Mr. Wright."

"I'm not a hit-man all the time, though. That's the problem. My son and me got us a small neighborhood grocery store, and the big chains've made it tough on us the last few years, what with cut rate prices and all. But the last year or so, what with rising costs, we been breaking even again. For the last year, and I could prove it to you if you want, there is hardly any difference in prices. With just me and Francis running the store, we don't have their big overhead, you see—not with inflation, so..."

"I don't care about your damned grocery store. I want to know why Jannaire hired you to kill me, and why she changed her mind, and why she wanted you to run me out of town."

"I don't know. I never hired out to no woman before, so it was different with her. Maybe she got chicken-hearted. Anyway, if I hadn't needed the money, I would've left as soon as she changed her mind. But we got to dickering, and I agreed to do it, with her giving me amateur advice ever step of the way. What I did, you see, was up the price to twenty-five hundred. If you kill a man, that's it. No danger. But fooling around this way, trying funny tricks and all, the man gets to know you, who you are, maybe, and then he comes after you instead of leaving town. Or, he leaves town, and then maybe he hires a man to hit you sometime. It's worth more, so I charged more. But she shaved me down to twenty-two hundred. I needed the money, and I would've gone back to my flat two thousand, but she ain't as good at dickering as she thinks she is."

"I never thought about it, Wright, but in a logical sense, the job was worth more than a flat two thousand. Because I did come after you, and I did get you."

"I told her that might happen. And now you're going to kill me."

"No," I said, "I'm not going to kill you."

But I was, and I had known all along that I was going to kill him, just as he had known all along that I was going to kill him. I certainly didn't intend to kill him at first, and I'm not sure when I passed the point when I knew I was going to kill him, that I was going to *have* to kill him, because I didn't allow myself to think about it. But everything he said was reinforcement. For some minutes now, I had merely been delaying the inevitable. I still needed more delay, and I still didn't want to think about it.

"How many men have you hit, Mr. Wright?" I said.

"Twenty-seven. But you're the first man I've ever tried to scare out of town."

"How many has your son killed?"

"None. He don't know nothing about what I do when I go out of town. He thinks I've got some investments that pay off just when we need the money for the store. The store's in his name, and he won't be coming after you, Mr. Norton, so you don't have to worry none about that."

"I was worrying about it, to tell you the truth."

"I know you were, but you don't have to worry none about Francis."

I took out a cigarette, and lit it awkwardly, without putting the pistol down. "Would you like a cigarette, Mr. Wright?"

"Are you going to shoot me now?"

"Of course not. I just asked if you wanted a cigarette."

"No, I don't smoke much. Sometimes a good cigar, but I don't care for cigarettes. I just thought..."

His voice was normal, resigned. He had had a pretty good run—twenty-seven murders, unless he was lying—and he had prepared himself for the same eventual ending. His quiet acceptance of the situation was unnerving, and I tried to close off my mind. I couldn't allow myself to think about it. Otherwise, I wouldn't be able to do it. Except for the patch of vitiligo on his forehead which had turned from pink to almost white, there was no evidence of fear in his face.

"Suppose, Mr. Wright, suppose, now, that I let you go? What would you do?"

"Well," he said, "I took the money from Miss Jannaire, and I mailed it to Francis, you see. He's probably paid a few bills with it, and all. But even if I still had it, I'd have to carry out the contract. That's the ethical thing to do. Once you take the contract, there can't be no mind-changing going on, because then word gets around. And if the word gets around that you welshed on one, they figure you lost your nerve, and they begin to wonder about the old contracts, you see. If you lost your nerve, you might be willing to talk about them."

"What 'they' is this? I don't believe that Wright is your real name, but I don't think you're any member of some crazy Cracker Mafia, either."

"I can't tell you about the 'they,' Mr. Norton. But I'm not Mafia, no, you're right there. I don't know if I'd do next what I'd planned to do next, but I'd still have to scare you into leaving Miami. That was the contract I took, you see."

"What nasty little trick were you planning next?"

"A beating. I was going to have you beaten. Not too bad, but enough to scare you. No broken bones, or not on the face, but a good beating with bike chains. I wasn't going to tell Miss Jannaire about the beating because I know more about these things than she does. And I think a good beating, with some bad bruises and all, would've scared you pretty bad."

"Yes, it would have. But if I let you go, you wouldn't leave Miami yourself and go back to Jacksonville?"

"It wouldn't do any good if I did. My contact here would get another man, and he'd have to make Miss Jannaire's money good. Even if I gave it back to him to give to someone else, it wouldn't help you any—or me neither."

"Suppose I gave you another fee—say three thousand—to hit Jannaire. Could you do that?"

"No. That wouldn't be ethical."

I put the cigarette out in one of the big sand-filled standing ashtrays.

Wright stiffened visibly, but that was the only movement he made. I shot him, and he tumbled forward out of the chair, curling his body slightly as he died silently on the white shag carpet.

The things I had to do took me much longer than they should have because I would pause all of a sudden, struck by the enormity of what I had done, and stand for long moments paralyzed in thought, or not thinking, in a state of dazed bewilderment.

Mr. Wright, a fatalist, accustomed to swift and sudden death, had died with dignity, as a right, as a rite long rehearsed in his mind. Or, to paraphrase the old cliche; "Dying well is the best revenge."

When my time came, as it must, there would be Wright's example to die up to, the measurement of a real man.

This murder of Wright, as necessary as it was, and I would always remind myself that it *was* necessary, and not a gratuitous act, had changed me forever. To kill a man, whether it is necessary or not, whether in anger or in cold blood, is the turning point in the life of the American male. It made me finally a member of the lousy, rotten club, a club I hadn't wanted to join, hadn't applied for, but had joined anyway, the way you accept an unsolicited credit card sent to you through the mail and place it in your wallet.

The report of the .38 had been loud, but here I wasn't concerned about whether the neighbors had heard the shot or not. In a $150,000 apartment, the walls are thick enough to deaden the sound of a .38.

The airconditioner condenser kicked in, and I felt a sudden whiff of cool air on my neck as I stood there, waiting, waiting to see whether Mr. Wright would move again. I couldn't see his upper body, but I could watch his white legs and the purplish snaky looking varicose veins climbing out of the tops of his black support socks.

I put the pistol down, staring at Wright's pale, almost feminine, legs, and willed them not to move. I had willed myself to shoot once because I had to, but I don't believe I could have shot him again, or put a round in the back of his head for a *coup de grace.* As I stood there, frozen, waiting, staring, I felt very close to Larry and Eddie. Larry had killed a thief, when he was still a cop, a legitimate shooting for which he was cleared. Eddie, as a fighter pilot, had killed a good many little brown men in Vietnam on strafing and bombing missions.

In every instance, the killing was justified, as I had so easily justified the killing of Mr. Wright. The thought bothered me, and it was difficult to brush aside. A killing can always be justified, or rationalized.

Perhaps I could have found an alternative, another option, but no other way out occurred to me. So I quit thinking about it. I also resolved not to think about it again, or at least to try not to think about it again.

The deed was done, and there would be no point to brood on the matter and come up with an alternative some five years from now, because I had had to do what I had done at the time.

I went through Mr. Wright's wallet. There was a Gulf credit card made out to L.C. Smith, a Florida driver's license, also in the name of L.C. Smith, and fifty-seven dollars in cash. There was no credit card for a rental car, so I assumed that he had driven his own car down to Miami from Jacksonville. If there is anything harder to do than rent a car without a credit card, I don't know what it is. But fifty-seven dollars was a very small sum of money.

I put the money into my wallet, and searched Wright's other pockets. I found a packet of Barclay's traveler's checks, all twenties, totaling $240.00. They were unsigned, neither on the tops nor the bottoms. I had no idea how a man could get traveler's checks from a bank without signing them first, unless they were stolen, and I didn't know what to do with them. But no one ever asks for I.D. when a traveler's check is cashed, and these unsigned checks could be used anywhere in the world. I decided to keep them. If I cashed them, one at a time, over a lengthy period, they would be impossible to trace to me.

I put Wright's key ring, with its peculiar collection of keys, in my pocket, too. One of those keys would fit Jannaire's duplex door, and I had a few things to talk about with that woman. There was a package of book matches from Wuv's, a folded length of copper wire, a theater ticket stub and a parking stub from the Double X Theater, and a plug of Brown Mule chewing tobacco with one small bite missing.

Other than that, Wright was clean. His other equipment, including the tools he had been using for his scary tricks, were probably locked in his car. His car was undoubtedly parked in the Double X Theater lot, but it could stay there. It would be just like him to booby-trap his own car.

I removed the green oilcloth cover from the snooker table, wrapped Mr. Wright's body in it, and carried him into the Weinstein's master bedroom. I placed the body on the bed, and turned on the bedside lamp. In another two months or within six weeks or less the Weinsteins would return. But within three or four days, even if I turned the airconditioning down to fifty degrees, the body would begin to stink. In fact, he smelled bad already. The heavy mattress would prevent the odor from seeping out through the bottom, but I need something more to put on top of his body. I went through the apartment and gathered up all of the sheets covering the furniture, and spread them, one at a time, over his body. There were blankets in the linen closet, and I spread these, one at a time, over his body until there were more than two dozen thicknesses, counting the sheets, over him. As well as I could, I tucked in the edges all around the bed.

By this time I was perspiring heavily, and I sat in the high pool chair to smoke a calming cigarette.

I then took my handkerchief and ran it over everything I had touched, or remembered touching, and turned the airconditioning-ing thermostat, which I found in the dining room, down to fifty degrees. I collected the two pistols, turned out the lights, and left the apartment. After wiping the outside doorknob, I took the stairway down to the tenth floor, and pushed the button for the elevator.

No one, luckily, was in the parking garage, and I walked up the alley to my Galaxie.

When I got to Coral Gables, and parked on Santana, two blocks away from Jannaire's duplex, it was ten minutes after one. I was tired and fuzzy-minded, and it took me a full minute to decide to leave the pistols locked in the glove compartment. Coral Gables, together with Hobe Sound and Palm Beach, is one of the best policed cities in Florida, and I didn't want to run the risk of being picked up with a concealed weapon on my person as I walked to Jannaire's house.

There was a light in the upstairs living room window, but that did not mean that she was still awake. It might have been a burglar light, but I had no intention of ringing her bell anyway. I found the correct key on Wright's keyring on the third try, let myself in, and climbed the stairs. No one was in the living room.

The door to the guest bedroom was slightly ajar. I flipped the switch. The bed was made, and there was a packed, but open, suitcase on the bed. Wright's suit jacket was draped over the back of a chair. The bed was made in a hasty, rumpled manner, and I assumed that Wright had made it, not Jannaire. I continued down the hall to Jannaire's bedroom. I flipped on the lights and she didn't waken. There was no overhead, or ceiling light, but both bedlamps came on, and so did a standing lamp, with a bamboo shade, beside a black leather lounge chair.

Jannaire, flat on her back, snored gently, almost daintily, but she slept hard. Her two brown fists, close to her head, were clenched tightly, and the muscles in her tanned forearms were tensed. She wore a pale blue nightgown, and was covered to her waist with a sheet and a bright blue blanket. The airconditioning in the apartment was about seventy, if not lower, and I was comfortable in my jacket.

I sat down in the leather chair, and lit a cigarette. The odor in the room was unpleasant, and I needed the smell of cigarette smoke. In addition to Jannaire's unique odor, the air was stale, and there was an overlay, hard to define separately, of baby powder, cold cream, wet leather, and the general odor of sleep itself. I had noticed this phenomenon before; a woman smells differently when she's asleep. The first time I had noticed this phenomenon I wondered if the subconscious overcomes the defenses of the sleeping body. Jannaire looked older in her sleep, too, and I wondered why I had ever thought that she was attractive. In her nightgown, with her apple-hard breasts partly uncovered, and all of her inky black underarm hair exposed, she was about as sexy as a squashed toad. Nor did I have to kiss her to determine how bad her breath undoubtedly was, either.

"Hey," I said lightly, from the chair, "wake up, Jannaire. There's a man in your bedroom."

"Wha'?" she said, stirring, but without opening her eyes.

"There's a man in your room, Jannaire, and he wants to talk to you."

She opened her eyes and blinked at me. She rubbed her bare arms with her hands, as she stared at me.

"Mr. Wright, your husband," I said, "sent me to pick up his suitcase. His son's sick, and he had to go home, so he asked me to mail him his suitcase, air freight. Incidentally, is Francis your son, or your husband's son by another marriage?"

"What?" She sat up in bed, and shook her head. "What do you want, Hank? I don't know what you're talking about. I took a sleeping pill, and it really knocked me out. What are you doing here?"

"It's foolish to take sleeping pills, especially at your age, Jannaire. They're a damned poor substitute for natural sleep, and eventually they ruin your health. A cup of warm cocoa..."

"I've gotta go pee. Put some coffee on, Hank. Until I'm awake I don't know what you're talking about." She got out of bed, walked primly—with her knees together—to the bathroom and closed the door.

In the kitchen I put on some water to boil for instant coffee, and discovered that I was ravenous. When Jannaire joined me in the kitchen a few minutes later, I had fixed two pieces of toast, and I was scrambling four eggs. She wore a quilted blue robe, and she had combed her hair and put on some pinkish-white lipstick. Her full lips were poked out surlily as she got down cups and mixed coffee and boiling water.

"D'you want some eggs? Toast?" I asked her.

"No. All I want is for you to get out of my house," she said. "If my husband happens to walk in..."

"Cut the bullshit, Jannaire. Apparently you weren't listening to me when I woke you up."

"How'd you get in?"

"I told you. I came for Mr. Wright's suitcase."

I showed her Wright's ring of keys. I took the scrambled eggs and the toast into the dining room, and she followed me with the two cups of coffee. I had to return to the kitchen to find a fork, and when I got back to the dining room she was sitting at the end of the long glass table, facing me, and staring with an expression that managed to convey fear, hatred, and loathing. I talked to her as I ate, and her expression didn't alter.

"Mr. Wright and I had a long talk, Jannaire, so you can forget about the marriage fabrication. He told me that you paid him to run me out of town. Fine, I am now on my way out, and I dropped by to tell you good-bye. Inasmuch as he asked me in such a nice way, I could hardly refuse, could I? But I want some answers from you before I go. First, you could have had me killed, but then you changed your mind. Why?"

She shrugged. "I didn't want your death on my conscience, although that didn't matter much to me at first. And then, after I got to know you, and realized how much Miami meant to you, it was a punishment of a sort—a banishment, and that seemed like a fair substitute. In the abstract, Hank, having you killed seemed like a good idea—and it still does—in the abstract. But when the time came, I had some second thoughts. The possibility that I might have become involved, in case Mr. Wright happened to be caught, occurred to me, and your death didn't seem worth going to prison for..."

"Okay. You chickened out. But why did you think about killing me, or having me killed, in the first place? I admit that I lusted after your smelly body, but that's no reason to kill a man!"

Jannaire got up, turned on the lamp in the living room beneath the black-and-white blow-up photo, and returned to her seat. She pointed to the picture.

"That's my sister."

"I know. You told me."

"But I didn't tell you her name. Her name is—was—Bernice Kaplan."

"So?"

"You don't even remember her name?"

"Should I? I don't remember any girl who looks remotely like that..."

"Bernice was twenty-two when she killed herself, and you're the reason she died."

"Bullshit. I don't know any Bernice Kaplan."

"She was a stewardess, and you knew her all right, you sonofabitch!"

"What was her uniform like?"

"Mustard yellow, with red piping. And she wore a little yellow derby with a red satin hatband."

"I remember her."

"I thought you would. Men usually remember the women they knock up. I know that Bernice had some emotional problems. Most girls do nowadays, and she didn't have to kill herself just because she was pregnant. If she had come to me, I could've paid for an abortion. For that matter, she had enough money to pay for one herself. But she wouldn't have killed herself if she hadn't got pregnant, and because you were the one who did it, you shouldn't be allowed to get off scot-free."

There was a great deal that I could say in self-defense, but I was unable to say anything. I was faced with a dilemma, a moral decision, and there was no way out of it—not a single way that I could prove my innocence.

I had met Bernice Kaplan at a party. She had been in uniform, and she had to leave early to catch her plane. When she started to call for a cab, I had offered to drive her to the airport. It was an excuse to leave a dull party, and I had been talking to Bernice and thought she was rather cute. In their uniforms, stewardesses always look ten times better than they do in their civilian clothes. It was a hilarious and exciting drive to the airport—a drive that was filled with suspense.

As soon as I got onto the Palmetto Expressway, she had taken off her derby, unzipped my fly, and started to go down on me. It was so unexpected I had laughed, of course, and then I began to wonder about the time. To get her to the airport on time I had to maintain a speed of at least fifty-five miles per hour, I estimated, but at that speed I was covering the distance so quickly I wasn't sure that I would be able to have an orgasm by the time we got to the terminal. The other traffic was distracting, too, and on the Palmetto you have to pay close attention to your driving. There are a lot of crazy people on the Palmetto, and that included, I decided, Bernice Kaplan and myself. As it worked out, however, my orgasm and arrival at the terminal coincided. I rezipped my fly in the yellow loading zone in front of Concourse Nine. Bernice had fewer than three minutes to make her flight, so all I could do was give her my card, with hasty note scrawled on it, and ask her to call me when she got back into town. She took the card and fled. But I never saw her again, and she never called me.

The point is, I couldn't have made her pregnant, but I couldn't tell Jannaire the truth about our brief encounter. To do so would be too cruel.

Besides, Jannaire wouldn't believe me anyway.

"Jannaire," I said. "I didn't impregnate your sister. I only met her once, and that was at a party with a dozen or more people around. I drove her to the airport and dropped her off at the terminal. There was just enough time to get her there, and we didn't stop on the way. That's the truth of it."

Jannaire jumped up, and started toward her purse on the couch. It was a leather pouch—a drawstring type bag—and huge. I left my seat hurriedly and managed to beat her to the purse. The thought hit me that there might be a pistol in the leather bag. I opened it, looked inside, and then handed it to her.

Her upper lip curled. "Did you think I had a gun in my bag?"

"Of course not. I was merely getting it for you, that's all."

She sat on the couch, rummaged around in the bag, and took out a wallet. She opened the wallet, removed a card, and handed it to me. It was my business card. On the back I had written: "You're the greatest!—Hank." I shrugged and returned the card to Jannaire.

"You admitted knowing Bernice, Hank," Jannaire said flatly, "and that isn't the kind of message a satyr like you would write to a young woman of twenty-two you only saw once, and on a short ride to the airport at that."

"It wasn't a short ride," I said defensively, "it was at least nine miles."

"I found this card in her purse when they sent me her effects from Atlanta. She didn't leave a suicide note, but she was four—or almost five—months pregnant. It had to be you, Hank. I wasn't sure until I met you and saw how you acted—like some sex-starved maniac—and then I knew damned well it was you. If there was any doubt before—which there wasn't—the fact that you've admitted that you knew Bernice cinches it once and for all."

"If you were interested in meeting me all along, why did you date my friend, Larry Dolman?"

"Your name was on his application as a reference. And you both had the same apartment house address. I thought, and I was right, that through meeting Larry I would meet you. And I wanted a natural meeting, to study you, before I made my move."

"All right, that worked. I was taken in. I certainly wouldn't suspect a woman who was dating through a dating service of being married."

"I'm not married."

"I know that, too. Mr. Wright told me. That also bothers me. I've been around the city a long time, but I sure as hell wouldn't know how to go about hiring a professional murderer. How did you go about it?"

Jannaire looked at me with surprise, arching her brows. "I asked my lawyer. How else?"

"And he told you? Just like that?"

"No. He said he would send me someone, and later on—about two weeks later—he sent me Mr. Wright. Why wouldn't he? I pay him a damned good retainer, and if he can't give me the services I need, I can always take my business to another lawyer. Do you know how many lawyers there are in Miami?"

I nodded. "Yes, strangely enough, I do. There are about twenty thousand lawyers in Dade County."

"There you are."

"There *we* are. I'm innocent, and yet, nothing I've said has made you change your mind about me—has it?"

"No. I know, we both know, that you're the indirect cause of my sister's suicide. And I think I'm letting you off lightly by banishing you from Miami instead of having you killed. Besides, it's better this way. If you didn't know why you were killed, it wouldn't have been enough punishment. This way, every time you think about Miami—wherever you are or happen to be—you'll be forced to think about that poor kid and what you did to her!"

Jannaire started to cry, and it made her angry because she cried in front of me. She tried to stop, but she couldn't, even though she kept throwing her head back and shaking it, and wiping the tears from her cheeks with the backs of her hands.

"I'll get Mr. Wright's suitcase and go," I said. "I promised to mail it to him."

I went into the guest bedroom, put the suit jacket into the suitcase, and then got Wright's toilet articles from the small guest bathroom. I packed these, and closed the suitcase.

In the living room, before reaching the door, I put the suitcase down and turned toward Jannaire. She had regained control of herself, and she held a crumpled Kleenex in her hand.

"Dark Passage," I said.

"What?"

"*Dark Passage*. That's the name of that Bogart film where he had the plastic surgery and turned out to be Bogart."

"No." She shook her head. "That wasn't the title."

"Maybe not. But in the movie, Bogey cleared himself, and didn't have to go back to prison."

"You aren't cleared. When are you leaving, Hank?"

"In about three, maybe four, days."

"I'll check, you know."

"Why don't you let your lawyer do it?"

"That's what I intend to do."

I left the apartment without saying good-bye.

I walked back to my car, and put the suitcase in the trunk. I would drop the suitcase into a Salvation Army collection box on the way home. Then, after I slept for about four hours, I would call Tom Davies in San Juan and tell him that I would accept the midwest district managership. He would be pleased. I would go to the New Jersey home offices for a one-week briefing—and then—Chicago, cold freezing, miserable Chicago.

I broke off with a short laugh that was a half-sob. But I didn't cry. Not yet. There would be plenty of time to cry during the long, cold, winter nights in Chicago.

Eddie Miller:

You can count on me, Don.

Don Luchessi:

You're ten years old, baby, and you're old enough to understand...

24

3624 1/4 Kelly Blvd. AA
Schiller Park, Ill.

Dear Eddie,

The reason you've only had a few postcards from me instead of a decent ltr is that I've been as busy as a cat covering shit on a marble floor. Also, I wanted to work out the report (inadequate as it is, I've enclosed it) on the contents of Gladys' handbag.

I've only got two of the three ltrs you said you wrote me, but I'm lucky to have that many. Notice my address above. First, there is the 3624 and *one-fourth*! There are four apts in each bldg, and if you leave off the 1/4th, the postman takes the ltr back to the PO or throws it in the dumpster or gives it to someone else. Nobody ever knows anybody else in these buildings, because the turnover is about every six weeks or so. After almost three months, I'm probably the oldest resident in these apts. Also, notice, after Kelly Blvd, the "AA." On the other side of Kelly, all the apts are listed with a single capital letter A. The same alphabetical double-talk goes for the other lines of quadriplexes on the streets beyond Kelly Blvd. What happened is that the first row on Kelly was called A through Z as they built them, and then when they build the second identical line-up adjoining across the street, they started with AA and went up through ZZ. The quadriplexes all look alike, the same shit-tone of dun, and they go on like that block after block through the alphabet. I would never ask anyone to meet me at my apt. To find me, you would have to be shown, as I was *shown* by the realtor. Anyway, I've put in for a PO box at the Schiller Park Branch PO, and I'm on the waiting list. Until I get the box, and the reason I have to wait is that everybody else who lives here also wants one, I can expect to miss about half of my mail unless it's addressed *exactly*, with the "1/4th" and the "AA" added after Kelly Blvd. (I even missed one of my paychecks and it was clearly marked because it was computer addressed from New Jersey. Somebody stole it probably and it will be cashed somewhere in Chicago.)

It's frustrating to know that you are usually in Chicago Tues and Wed nights before heading back to Miami, while I am out of town. When are you going to get your schedule changed so you can be here on a weekend and we can get together? I've got a duplicate apt. key made for you, and it's enclosed. So if you want to stay in my apt instead of the hotel during your layover go ahead (if you can find it). It's only a five-minute drive from my apt to O'Hare. In fact, every 30 seconds the windows shake as the jets take off. I moved in here because it's convenient to the airport, but that's the only advantage. Because I'm only here on Friday and Sat nights, I haven't done anything about getting a better pad. Besides, on wkends, I'm exhausted.

Outside it's colder than hell, as you know, with the damned black snow drifted up to about three feet along the sidewalks. And my car, which sits on the street (minus hubcaps, now) during the five days I'm out of town, has given me a lot of trouble. There are no garages within walking distance to park it in, and it seems stupid to have a car in a garage where you have to call a cab in order to get to it.

All in all, this is a miserable situation I'm in, and despite the money that keeps piling up in the bank, I'd rather be back in Miami at half the salary. But that goes w/out saying.

I did see Larry Dolman one Saturday night, two weeks ago, and we went out to have dinner and a few beers. He had—guess?—a club sandwich, and I had a steak, but he was so preoccupied about his new job that was all he could talk about. He is a Peter Principle textbook case, I think, at his terminal level of incompetency, but his superiors are crazy about him. Now that he's Director of Security Personnel for Cook County, one of the big jobs in the Nat. Sec. Pvt. Eye agency, anything he does in the way of recreation comes out of his sleep. He has to hire security guards for all of the building projects in Cook County, and when you can only pay a top of $2.20 an hour, you can imagine the kinds of men he's hiring!

Larry told me about one weirdo he hired. They issued the man a gun and a uniform, but before he reached the warehouse he was supposed to guard, he held up a man in the street (wearing his N.S. uniform, Larry said), and was arrested by the cops. But here's what's *funny*. Larry was worried, and thought he might get reprimanded for hiring the guy. They called him into the office after this incident, and all the top brass fell all over Larry to keep *him* from quitting! In other words, they thought Larry might get disgusted and quit because the hiring of people is so fucking hard. Larry has supervisors for his security guards, of course, but they're even harder to recruit, he said, or to keep once he hires them. If one of his men doesn't show up, you see, the supervisor has to take the shift until another guard is found, and sometimes a supervisor will be on duty 36 hours or so filling in for absentees. I suppose Larry has written to you about his new job, or will, eventually. If he hasn't yet, he is busy.

Except for two salesmen I've got—one in St. Louis and one in Detroit—who are really dogging it, the other men in the field seem to be okay. I'm going to fire the man in Detroit as soon as I can find a Negro with a B.A. degree to replace him with, but they are almost impossible to find. I've been running an ad in the *Tribune* for three weekends now, and haven't had a single response. But you can't blame them. A black man with a B.A. isn't anxious to move to Detroit, unless he's crazy—not when I can only offer him $10,000 to start (and a free car).

My love-life here for some reason has turned kind of nightmarish. You might find it hard to believe, but I haven't had a single piece of ass since I came to Chicago. It might be the cold, the wind, the atmosphere, the fact that I'm tired all the time, depressed—I don't know what. Anyway, about a month ago I went down to this bar about two miles away—The Shill—where a lot of stewardae hang out, picked up a neat Italian girl with short legs, brought her to my apt, and couldn't get it up. It never happened to me before. The girl took it pretty well, and said that because I hadn't screwed her at least she could take communion at Mass the next morning, so she didn't really mind, but it could've been a nasty scene. You know how some stewardae are when they get the upper hand. Since then I haven't bothered, and haven't thought too much about it, being so busy anyway. But I imagine the urge will come zooming back when Spring comes in and the snow leaves and I've got used to the grind of flying and going with so damned little sleep. It's hard to sleep in hotels on the road, and I usually just watch a lot of TV and drink a few scotch and waters in my room. My TV here in Schiller Park, thanks to the jets and O'Hare, has snow for 10 seconds out of every 30 seconds because of the vibrating antenna on the roof, and there doesn't seem to be any way it can be fixed.

You say that Don is pretty depressed. He has been, as you know, ever since *that* night, but at least you're there to keep an eye on him. He's really in an untenable situation with Clara, and perhaps if you could get him a sexy girl he could see a couple of times a week on the side, it might change his attitude. He can afford it, for Xst sake, and if he isn't getting it at home he should be getting it someplace. He told me once that he gets a rim job once in awhile from his secretary, Nita Peralta, but he only takes advantage of it when he's desperate. But he's worried that she'll tell the priest about it some time. They go to the same church, you know, and besides, Don should get more out of his life than a fat-assed broad like Nita. When we finally get together up here, you and I, we're going to have to work out some plan or other for Don to make him happier. He's a beautiful guy to be in such a terrible marital situation. Anyway, see him when you can, and call him once in awhile. I'll call him myself over the weekend if I can. The last time I called, Clara answered, and said he wasn't there, which was probably a lie. So if I can't get him at home, I'll call him at his office from St. Louis next week.

You didn't say much about your situation with Gladys, and I don't know if the short report I've enclosed will help you any, but don't forget that I'm your buddy, old buddy, and please call me or write soon. It's a lonely place up here, man.

Schiller Park sucks, Chicago sucks, Cook County sucks, and Illinois sucks.

—Yrs. HANK
Encls. The Bag Report
Apt Key - 3624 1/4, Kelly Blvd AA

GLADYS WILSON'S BAG

In this report I've disregarded some obvious things, Eddie, and I've drawn partially on my memory of Gladys, plus using some of the info you told me about her to reach my conclusions. So in some respects the report is not precisely objective. Because of Freud, Sullivan, Sykes, *Gestalt*, and some of the other holistic approaches to personality theories (including knotty old Laing, poor misguided soul) it's considered possible to construct a personality profile from objects; and Glady's profile, as drawn, is I aver, as valid as a horoscope, a phrenology chart, and every bit as meaningful as the cryptic message of a cock as decoded by a highly skilled alectromancer. But—combined with your personal knowledge of Gladys, you can extrapolate, man—*extrapolate*!

1. Tangee lipstick. God only knows where she found this, man. This orangey-pinky concoction was popular several years ago, advertised on full pages, etc., but it's fairly hard to find nowadays. It's dimestore lipstick for the very, very young; for adults it usually doesn't go with anything unless the woman has red hair, and a certain shade of red at that. Gladys has black hair, but because of the Tangee I maintain that it's dyed black hair, and she simply doesn't want to give up her favorite lipstick. From her use of Tangee I say that she was once a redhead, liked the color of Tangee, and did not switch lipsticks when she dyed her hair.

Unless she also dyes her pubic hair, it's a dark shade of orange, because pubic hair is usually one or two shades darker than the hair on your head. If her pubic hair is black, check the stubble under Gladys' arms, and you will find that it is red when it occasionally surfaces. In my opinion, Gladys will dye her pubic hair because redheads (at 47-50?) readily show gray, and it would defeat her efforts to look younger than her age to have red-*and*-gray pubic hair. Check underarm stubble for confirmation.

2. Driver's license. Technically, eyes are only blue, brown, or red (albinos). Gladys, on her license, you say, claims "hazel." Ah, she is a vain woman to claim hazel—but a confirming footnote to the possibility of red hair. Also, with hazel eyes, it's still possible to wear Tangee and get away with it—if the face is pale enough and unfreckled. And Gladys does have a pale complexion. To get off this minor point—a redhead averages 50,000 hairs on her head compared to an average of 100,000 for a blonde. So if Gladys has coarse hair, very coarse, and dyed black, the tines of her comb will be set well apart because she cannot use a fine-toothed comb. (To be positive on this point, you would have to count every hair on her head.)

3. Pills. Dexamyl (46), Elavil (120), and hormone pills. This is an incredibly small selection of drugs for a woman to carry in her purse—you don't even list aspirin. The chances are she has a lot more pills than this, but takes them at home on a regular basis. If she carries Dexamyl around, she probably pops more than one a day (I'd guess three). That's because the usual prescription for Elavil is 3 per day, which makes one sleepy, being an anti-depressant-tranquilizer of no uncertain strength. So the Dexamyl will clash and counteract with the Elavil, providing Gladys with mercurial turns of mood. Talky as all get-out and then a gloomy lapse into a deep brooding silence. She will also be a little jumpy. The sudden slamming of a door will make her jump, squeal, bite her nails, which will be followed by a smile, a shake of the head, and an apology for over-reacting.

She has a weight problem, and the dexamyl pills curb her appetite. The Elavil is to alleviate depression, and if she were not depressed, in fact, her doctor would not prescribe them—if she obtained them by prescription. So she has put herself in an ambiguous, ambivalent position. The Elavil will make her sleepy, and the Dexamyl will not let her sleep. She is weary, nagging, and happy by turns, and she will apologize following each time she scolds you about something. You also listed hormone pills which is inadequate evidence without the brand name, or generic make-up. I assume that they're female hormone pills, which means merely that she is going through the change of life. Once the change begins, hormone pills are needed to supplement what the body no longer provides in sufficient quantities to prevent backaches and osteoporosis. It isn't necessary to ask her if she is undergoing menopause. If she jumps up suddenly and turns the airconditioning down to sixty degrees, claiming that it isn't working properly, and then, if she just as suddenly turns it up to eighty again a few minutes later, she's had a hot flash. Your Gladys, Eddie, old buddy, will never see fifty again. You know how I feel about drugs, but if you don't get Gladys off this shit, she can have some severe physical reactions. (And find out what *else* she's on and let me know.)

4. Dental floss, Lifesavers, Binaca golden breath drops, chapstick, two No. 2 pencils with gnawed eraser ends, paper clip containing small amount of ear wax, Bub's red-hot bubble gum, 2 sticks of Juicy Fruit gum, 1 needle with beige thread, 3 Q-Tips, hair styling brush with ivory handle, aforementioned Tangee lipstick, nail file with ivory handle, gold ballpoint pen with engraved legend "I stole this pen from Gladys Wilson," set of car keys and house keys on chain with brass marijuana pipe attached, 2 Medico cigarette holders (1 blue, 1 green), ivory toothpick in leather case, and 1 rabbit foot.

Wow!

Before proceeding let me take time out to congratulate you on your list making ability, including the counting of the pills (above 3). As a pilot your life is devoted to checklists, pre-flight, in-flight, etc, but very few people wd notice or put down on paper "gnawed eraser ends," "small amount of ear wax" in the paperclip. You're a keen observer, but then you have Observer wings as well as pilot's wings. If you did not have a fulltime occupation as a co-pilot, I would have to put you down tentatively as an anal-retentive. But you escape or elude this impertinent classification the way medical students avoid being classified as psychopathic paranoids when they are given Rorschach tests. All they see is bones, blood, and organs—such is their preoccupation with such things—so it is as useless to give a medical student a Rorschach as it is to call you an anal-retentive. (Nevertheless, as an aside, Eddie, you'll feel a lot better about facing each day if you take a half-ounce of mineral oil before you retire each night.)

The oral orientation of 4, above, is staggering, indicating that this woman was arrested at the oral stage early on. If nothing else is handy, she sits or stands around with one finger in her mouth, and another in her ass. Her nails must be bitten down to the quick (ten times for ten fingers). Her interest in oral sex is keen to the point of being honed. Congratulations! It explains, in part, why you've lived with her for more than a year, and if you take offense at this surmise, it is time for you to reexamine some of the other facets of your relationship with Gladys for positive—if there are any—correlations. For example, do you talk to her or does she talk to you—and about what? The distinction is crucial because you might be drifting, man, drifting. And drifting, ancient pilot, with more than 3,000 hours in multi-engined flight, ain't soaring. It is one thing to have "I stole this *pencil* from Gladys Wilson" on a box of 50 Number 2 pencils (my sergeant did this once up in Pittsburgh), but when it is *engraved* on a solid gold *pen*, well, I'm sorry, man, her penial enviousness is majestically monumental. With Gladys, possession is ten/tenths of the law, and she will, if you allow her to do so, devour you completely. (I wish now, Eddie, I'd gone over this list with you the night you handed it to me in the White Shark parking lot.)

There was this black man with diarrhea who went to see a black doctor, recently graduated on the quota system. The doctor consulted his diagnosis book: "You got locked bowels," he told the patient. "But I got diarrhea, Doctor," the patient said. "That's because," the doctor said, "your bowels is locked *open*!"

In other words—and to make you smile, I hope—don't take my unlicensed diagnosis too seriously. The only textbook cases are in textbooks, and we were told in college to be leery of any so-called textbook case because it might be a shammer, don't you know. So disregard my advice (above) on the mineral oil, and take a tablespoonful of Metamusil in an 8-ounce glass of water before you go to bed instead.

5. Lumping the various plastic cards together, there is little significance in Gladys having courtesy check-cashing cards for Food Fair, Kwik-Chek, Publix, and fuel cards for Standard, Texaco, 66, Sinclair, and Soc Sec card, or checkbooks for three banks, plus one savings bankbook, nor even her Am Express, Diner's, bank I.D., and membership card for Fairchild Garden. Burdines, Sears and Jordan Marsh charge cards are merely handy, as is MasterCard. But it *is* peculiar that she only has two one-dollar bills in her wallet. You undoubtedly eat well, and I suppose that Gladys is a good cook, seeing that you get steak, mushroom gravy, and baked potatoes, even if she only eats four ounces of the meat and supplements it with a little cottage cheese, but if you wanted to borrow 2 or 3 hundred dollars from her you wd not be able to get it in cash. No cash will she provide for you (not that you need it), but her presents to you in the form of clothes, I'd say, are expensive, if you'll take them. But as I recall, you don't even own a suit or sports jacket. The only coat I've ever seen you wear is your uniform jacket. When we lived in Dade Towers, you slept in your underwear, but I have a hunch that you are now sleeping in silk pajamas, and you have an expensive dressing gown—a gown that you wear frequently because Gladys is frequently turning the airconditioning down to 60, or lower. If you want to make Gladys happy, let her buy you some tailor-made uniforms (you can always use them), but don't ask her for a twenty dollar bill if you're leaving the house by yourself (if you can still occasionally get away in the evenings by yourself). Also your old USAF leather flight jacket needs replacing: why not let Gladys order you a nice tailor-made leather jacket (about $350 or $400) from Spain? A new leather jacket will look good with your tie-dyed jeans, Ho-Ho T-Shirt, and flight boots, and you'll make the old lady very happy.

6. The photographs. Your descriptions read okay, but I

would still like to look at them myself before making a positive judgment. But, taken together, the four photos add up significantly. The wallet photo of the watercolor of Gladys by Augustus (Edwin) John—when she was 18—is more than just a conversation piece. Too bad he didn't date it (or if he did, you didn't put the date on the list). You told me about this photo before, and that her first husband kept the original painting. I'll tell you one thing, though, and I don't have to see the photo. She *never* looked that beautiful, man, not at 18, or any other age. And if you think this is a harsh and hasty critique, the next time you pass a library, enter at the risk of disillusionment, and compare A. John's watercolor of Dylan Thomas with a *photograph* of the poet. If you ask Gladys for an actual photo of herself at 18, she'll tell you—and I'll bet money on this—that she somehow lost all of her early photo albums. By now, though, I imagine that she actually believes she did look that good as a girl, and because she has still kept her lush, girlish figure, despite two children, why in hell shouldn't she?

Her son teaches Art History at San Francisco State, and her daughter is married to a *dentist* in Seattle. So why does she only have a photo of her son at age 14, and one of her daughter at age 12? Why not a few recent *adult* pictures? Because—I think—that's the last time she had complete control, or domination over them. Not only did they manage to get away, they got *far far* away. They have put a continent between them, they never visit Fla, and the last time she saw them both together was at their father's funeral. (Any woman who marries a man who spends his days with his fingers in somebody's mouth has got to be desperate to get away.) Her son—and this is a mean surmise—who became an Art History teacher instead of an artist, probably didn't get away *soon* enough.

The reason for this rude judgment is, of course, the 4th photo—the one she wangled from your mother in Ft. Lauderdale when you (stupidly, and I told you so at the time) took Gladys up to meet her. Why, for God's sake, would she want a photo of you in your Culver military academy uniform taken when you were only 12 years old? If she likes uniforms so much, why not a current photo of you in your airline uniform? Or in your USAF (Res.) uniform? There can only be one answer. Gladys sees in you the manly little boy she wanted her son to be, and if there isn't something incestual about her attachment (adherence is a better word), why does Gladys call your mother every week (when your mother doesn't call her first) to trade t.l.'s? If you don't want to think about such things, try, at least to extrapolate.

I've been thinking on and writing this report for about 4 hours, and I'll let the rest of the shit go. You can ask Gladys why she still carries a Wash. D.C. driving license that expired 15 years ago, and you might ask her why the business cards of her gynecologist, opthamologist, insurance man (Prudential), and lawyer all bear Anglo-Saxon names. Jesus, do you know how hard it is to find WASP gynecologists and lawyers in Miami?

But enough.

I reread the report, and I'm sorry about the negative tone of the over-all comments. Gladys is a beautiful and well-groomed woman, and it was quite evident from her possessive attitude toward you—on the night we went to Sloane's-for-Steak—that she is really crazy about you. Psychology works better with rats than it does with people, Eddie, and most of it is bullshit, but *propinquity* is valid. I have a lot of faith in propinquity, and it rarely fails: if you continue to live with Gladys she'll talk you into marrying her. In some respects, you and Gladys remind me of Wolfe's Monk Webber and Esther Jack in *You Can't Go Home Again*, except that Mrs. Jack was safely married, and Gladys is free...

"O lost, and by the wind-grieved, ghost, come back again."

Hank

Eddie Miller folded Hank's report on Glady's handbag and, without reading it, shoved it into the back pocket of his jeans. He had made his decision already, and to read the report now would be strictly academic. He would read it later on, when he had more time. He read Hank's letter three times. He read it hastily in the Miami Springs Post Office, where he kept a P.O. Box, and reread it twice more, taking his time, while he ate a breakfast of blueberry pancakes, sausage, and coffee at The Pancake House on Flagler Street.

Thinking about Hank's letter, Eddie came to the conclusion (if he read rightly between the lines) that the letter was somewhat in the nature of a cry for help. A man writing is not the same as a man speaking, but the tortured joviality, or tone of the letter, emphasized Hank's unhappiness, or disenchantment, with Chicago.

Eddie was familiar with Schiller Park, the suburban town within Chicago which was not unlike Miami Springs and Greater Miami. Miami Springs and Schiller Park, because of their proximity to International Airports—O'Hare and Miami—had restless transient populations, and a vast number of airline employees in temporary residence. Both towns had a substantial permanent population of steady citizens, as well, homeowners, who came into frictional conflict with the outgoing lifestyles of the transient residents. The homeowner residents of Miami Springs had not been overjoyed by the designation, "Miami Springs: Haven for Swingers," applied to the suburb by an enterprising *Herald* reporter who had dug the night life along the strip, and the singles-only apartment houses. In Schiller Park, the hard-drinking working men, who quaffed tankards of ale and dreamed of the day when Wallace would take up his residence in the White House, disapproved of young stewardesses with long-haired dates entering the dark, smelly, neighborhood taverns. There was no comparable high-life, or pick-up bars in Schiller Park as there were in Miami Springs, but there was no need for them: Chicago was a real city, not a group of sprawling suburbs like Miami.

Although Dade County boasted of an over-all population of more than a million, Miami itself only had a population of 350,000. The remaining residents were scattered over the county in twenty tight communities with their own shopping plazas, movies, and churches, all of them fighting the notion of becoming a single, unified city.

Miami Beach, a skinny sandy island, cut off from the mainland by Biscayne Bay, was, in Eddie Miller's opinion, merely Boyle Heights (in Los Angeles) without the hills. Eddie rarely went to Miami Beach. To see fifty guests sitting on a hotel veranda in metal chairs staring across Collins Avenue at another fifty guests sitting on a veranda of another hotel was too depressing. Old Americans used to go to Los Angeles to die before World War II. But the ancients now came to Miami Beach to die instead. Except, perhaps, for Brooklyn, Eddie had read somewhere, Miami Beach had more doctors and hospital beds per capita than any other American community of comparable population density, and Greater Los Angeles, with its polluted skies, had apparently lost the geriatric business to Miami Beach forever.

It was the clear bright skies and good flying weather of South Florida Eddie enjoyed. He did not love Miami the way Hank and Larry had, nor did he envy the dull, higher-styled suburban life, with country club-centered activities, that Don Luchessi and his family lived.

Ever since the swift and surprising departure of Hank,

followed by Larry, only three weeks later, the salty air of South Florida had lost its savor for Eddie Miller. Solitude and a few close friends were all Eddie needed when he wasn't flying, but he did not, and could not, have any solitude living with Gladys Wilson. And, as much as he liked Don—his remaining friend—it was increasingly harder for the two of them to get together. Eddie was free to go anywhere and do anything he liked—although Gladys usually went with him—but Don, to get away from the house at night, always had to make up some kind of lie to tell Clara. Don disliked Gladys as much as Gladys disliked Don, but Clara hated Gladys and Eddie equally. Eddie was indifferent to Clara, having dismissed her in his mind long ago as a typical American housewife, accepting Clara at her word when she had claimed that she was "a simple homemaker," so he neither liked nor disliked her. On the single occasion the four of them had gone out to dinner, however, the almost electrical enmity at the table, and the frequent manifestations of middle-class morality Clara had interjected into the dinner conversation had outraged Gladys, and finally, irritated Eddie.

As a practicing, professional Catholic mother, Clara had given an implicit impression that she would have to confess to her priest that she had eaten dinner with an unmarried couple who "were living in sin."

Before Clara consented to going out with them in the first place—not wanting to leave Marie, their nine-year-old daughter, alone—she had insisted that Don hire a registered nurse as a babysitter. During dinner, Clara had called the nurse three times, and Don had called her twice. Gladys, a past-president of W.A.S.P. (Widows as Single People), and quite active in women's liberation activities, found these calls amusing, at first; and then, turning serious, had lectured Don and Clara on the advisability of providing their daughter with Kung Fu lessons so the girl could become self-reliant. Gladys' rather generous offer to teach Marie a few basic lessons in Karate had been rejected with unnecessary force, if not rudeness, Eddie recalled.

When they got home to Miami Springs, Gladys said: "Never again, Baby!"

Eddie had grinned and nodded, visualizing a similar conversation taking place in Don's house in South Miami.

Eddie enjoyed his solitary breakfast. To prolong the pleasant feeling of being alone, he signaled the waitress to bring him another cup of coffee. He was going flying later this morning, and he decided to take old Don with him. He would feel Don out, and see how he was getting along. Perhaps he would have something to report to Hank when he saw him.

While he waited for fresh coffee, Eddie added the apartment key Hank had mailed to him to his key ring.

The window in Don's warehouse office was uncurtained, and in the mornings he opened the venetian blinds. He found it soothing to look through the slats at the traffic on the I-95 overpass. Almost a half-block away the noise of the traffic was a steady comforting murmur, and the sound only rose in volume when a heavy diesel semi rumbled south over the overpass in the near lane. Beneath the overpass, extending from the deeply shadowed bridge, were twenty colorful frame houses. The one-story houses, of two and four rooms, were about the last wooden houses remaining in Miami, but they were not destined to exist much longer. When Don had first moved into the warehouse office there had been seventy of these clapboard houses along Fair Alley, as it was called by the black residents (although there was no such street or alley listed on the city map), but fifty of them had been torn down, ten houses at a time, as new "Little HUD" housing had been constructed. The black residents had been "relocated," as the officials put it, in Liberty City, Brownsville, and Coconut Grove.

Sometimes, when he had nothing else to do, which was most of the time, Don stood by the window for hours, watching the remaining row of homes and the activity of the black inhabitants. The houses were painted in gay colors—bright mustards, carnation pinks, pastel blues. On the house closest to Don's window, a brown, misshapen, short-legged panther, with pink flowered decals pasted on the body, had been painted on the lemon wall. Don truly admired this lop-sided panther, and had considered the idea of buying the wall when the bulldozers came eventually to tear down the houses. He thought about framing the panther and part of the wall and putting the mural-sized picture on the patio wall by his pool. But he had merely considered the idea, knowing that he would miss the painting when the house was gone. He knew he wouldn't actually buy the brown panther and take it home. Clara would never stand still for it. Not in *her* house.

And it *was* truly her house now, in deed as well as in name, and so was the bank account and the bonds and jewelry in her private lock box at the Southwest Bank of South Miami, and the small waterfront lot on Marathon Key where he had hoped to build a weekend fishing cottage some day. The cottage was another plan that was out forever now that Clara had listed the lot and the price she wanted for it with a Miami realtor. The price was much too high at present, but eventually, as property values climbed inevitably, she would get it. She would get the money; not Don. He wished, somehow, that he had kept the Marathon lot a secret from her, but he had been unable to salvage anything when he went back to her. Nothing. Clara wasn't that bright, but Paul Vitale, her greasy lawyer brother, was a sharp, mean, vindictive sonofabitch. And Paul had drawn up all the papers to protect his "little sister."

An old black man, wearing a blue short-sleeved workshirt and a pair of pink-and-white striped bermudas, came out of the second yellow house. He sat on a bench beside the door, and opened a can of beer. He dropped the tab inside the can, took a long gulping pull, and leaned back against the wall, lifting his wrinkled, grayish black face to the hot morning sun. To the old man's left, along the wall of the house, there was a row of red and pink geraniums planted in five-gallon oil cans. Each can had been painted a different color—red, yellow, and blue—and the shadows of the geraniums against the yellow wall looked a little greenish to Don. That would make a hell of a nice oil painting, Don thought—the old black man, sitting there in the sunlight, with all that garish color in the background. Not a care in the world—except that he would be "relocated" in another month or so in some regulated concrete block-and-stucco housing development in Brownsville.

Don would miss the old man, the houses and brown panther, but if all went well, he, too, might be "relocated" by then. But how? How? And how could he take Marie with him? That was one thing he knew: he wouldn't leave Miami without Marie.

Don left the window, sighed, sat at his desk, moved the stack of yellow invoices to one side, and took out his ostrich leather wallet. He unzipped the "secret" compartment. Before removing the two bills, he glanced at the door to see if it was shut, and listened for a moment to Nita's hunt and peck typing in the outer office. He took out two crisp bills, and put them on the desk, placing the $1,000-bill above the $500-bill. He studied Stephen Grover Cleveland's face on the $1,000-bill, wondering again how this weak-chinned unmemorable man—at least Don couldn't remember anything about Cleveland—had been chosen for this honor. William McKinley was different. He, at least, had been assassinated, and it was decent of the U.S. Treasury officials, or Congress, or whoever it was that decided whose picture was engraved on money, to remember McKinley this way on the $500-bill. But why not McKinley, then, on the $1,000, and Cleveland on the $500? What in hell had Cleveland ever done to be honored more than McKinley? But maybe it worked the other way. Kennedy was assassinated, and his face ended up on fifty-cent pieces. The lower the denomination, perhaps, the higher the honor was supposed to be, like Lincoln's face on pennies.

But who remembered Leon Czolgosz, or if they did, how many people could spell his name? Don could, and he had won a few bucks in bars by betting he could spell it. How many people, in fact, remembered or knew that Czolgosz had assassinated McKinley? Or knew that McKinley, because he had been assassinated, now had his picture on the $500-bill? Don hadn't known about the faces on the $1,000 and $500 bills himself until he had changed smaller bills for them, and it had taken the bank three days to get the higher denominations for him when he requested them.

But it wasn't nearly enough money. He put the two bills away, zipped the compartment closed, and returned the wallet to his hip pocket. To accumulate this $1,500 had taken Don almost three months. To be able to leave Clara—and take Marie with him—Don had set an arbitrary sum of $10,000 as getaway bread. He would need at least that much. With $10,000, all in $1,000 and $500 bills, so his wallet wouldn't bulge in his pocket, he could go somewhere, anywhere he pleased, and set up housekeeping for himself and his daughter. He could change his name and have enough money left over to take care of the two of them while he established himself in business, or got a job of some kind, for a full year. Of, if he were frugal enough, the two of them could live for a year-and-a-half or even two, on $10,000. Surely, within a year-and-a-half he would be earning enough money again somewhere to support them in a half-way decent middle-class neighborhood.

With a pad and pencil, Don refigured his money and escape plans. By hoarding $500 a month—which was really rushing it—it would still be close to two years before he could make the break. But he couldn't hold out that long. In two more years, living in the same house with Clara, he would be as crazy as a shithouse rat...

There was a timid rap-rap on the door. Nita opened the door and entered. Her olive face had turned rosy, and she announced formally, "Mr. Miller to see you, sir."

Eddie Miller followed her in. The sound of his boots was masked by the clatter of Nita's wooden-soled wedgies on the linoleum floor. Winking at Don, Eddie stood a foot behind Nita. As she turned clumsily to leave, her breasts brushed his chest. Unsmiling now, his face solemn, but teasing the poor woman, Eddie side-stepped as Nita side-stepped, and they did a frantic skipping dance back and forth a few times before Eddie grinned and allowed her to escape. She closed the door behind her with a bang.

Nita would be upset all day about Eddie, Don thought.

Visitors rarely came to the warehouse office, and she would feel that the clumsy dance was all her fault—not realizing that Eddie was as agile and wiry as a mountain goat.

Don, blushing with genuine pleasure, got up and shook hands with Eddie. "Did you have any trouble finding the place?"

Eddie grinned and shook his head. "Not much. These warehouses down here all look alike, but once I spotted the brown tiger it was easy. I'm parked in a yellow loading zone, outside, though."

"That's okay," Don said. "I had it painted myself so I'd be sure to always have a parking place. You saw my Mark IV, didn't you?"

Eddie nodded, and looked incuriously around the office, shaking his head. "This is a crummy office, Don, for a man making your kind of dough."

There was a shrill whine and then a heavy thunking sound behind the plywood partition separating the office from the warehouse. Eddie raised his eyebrows.

"It's the printer," Don explained. "There was an extra storeroom in the warehouse I didn't use, so I rented it out to this guy. He prints bolita tickets, I think, and a few other interesting things. Fake I.D. cards, birth certificates, high school diplomas, and shit like that. But he's away a lot, so he doesn't bother me any—and I pick up an extra seventy-five bucks a month that way."

"Is that why you moved down here yourself, to save dough on office space?"

"No. It was too inconvenient being downtown. No place to park, and I always had to be coming here anyway for silver. All the flatware's in the safe here, you know, and I keep a black warehouseman. When I used to talk to him on the phone he got the orders wrong, so it was easier this way. Besides, no one ever comes to see me for orders. I go to them, so it was stupid to keep an expensive office on Biscayne Boulevard."

Eddie winked, and jerked his head toward the closed door. "If I'd known you had that around, I'd've been down before. How is she, Don?"

"Keep you voice down, man. I told Hank about Nita, and he told you, didn't he?" Don smiled sheepishly.

"Not the juicy details."

"It isn't that juicy, but Nita's been with me about five years now, and well, you know, I talked to her about some things. My problems, some, and about Clara. So—d'you remember when we got the vasectomies?"

"You're really something, Don," Eddie laughed. "That's an incident that would hardly slip a man's mind, for Christ's sake!"

"You remember *when*, I mean—it was when I was separated and living in the Towers with you guys. Well, Clara and I had always used the rhythm system, which is a bloody pain in the ass. You don't fuck when you want to, you have to wait until you *have* to, so to speak. I was living at the Towers when you and I and Hank talked about the vasectomy, so I never told Clara when I decided to get it done with you. Did Hank ever get his?"

"No. He chickened out finally. He read some study where about one guy out of every thousand or so has some side effects or something. He reads all those medical magazines, and he takes that shit seriously. You know how Hank is, Don."

"I got a postcard from Hank last week. From St. Paul."

"What did he say?"

"He said that when he got some time he'd write me a letter. Anyway, I think I knew at the time that I would eventually go back to Clara. Not consciously, you understand, but down there in my subconscious somewhere. And that was why—although I don't think I thought about it when we went to Dr. Silverstein—I got the damned operation. I must've thought, deep down inside someplace, that with a vasectomy, I wouldn't have to fuck around with the calendar and the rhythm system and all with Clara. So when we got back together, I told her about the vasectomy, and she got pissed, really pissed."

"Why?"

"We're Catholics, Eddie, as you know, but she's a woman Catholic, and they take all that shit seriously. Well, at first she wouldn't even believe me, so I told her to call the doctor. Dr. Silverstein—and you might want to remember this, Eddie—

wouldn't tell her shit over the phone. So the next day she went to see him. Meanwhile, you know, I was back home again, and still no ass, you see. She had to get this thing straightened out. So when she saw Silverstein, and proved who she was, he confirmed the operation—that I'd had it for more than six months, and we could screw our heads off if we wanted to."

"So everything was okay?"

"Hell, no! Then she had to see the fucking priest. He's a real prick, and he comes over to the house for dinner about twice a month. You ought to see the bastard drink my Chivas Regal—like wine, man. Here's the thing, Eddie. She would've done anything he told her to do, and he sure as hell didn't tell her not to screw anymore. I mean, he could've told her that, but he didn't. He merely let her figure it out for herself, which was worse. He told her that a woman could not deny her husband, which is right, but he also reminded her that the purpose of sex was procreation. This way, you see, she more or less had to make her own moral decision. And she decided, now that it was impossible for her to get pregnant, because I had the vasectomy, that there was no longer any purpose in having sex any more. She'd never cared much about it in the first place. I tried to reason with her—you know, what difference is there between the half-assed rhythm system, which is a way to avoid pregnancy, and a sure way—but she wouldn't accept the logic. She's too emotional."

"Well, Don. If you ever want a divorce, you've got grounds for one. No judge would ever go along with that crap."

"I'll never get a divorce, Eddie. If I did, I'd lose my daughter. The way things are now, I'm stuck, that's all. But I'm going to get out of it one of these days. Anyway, to get back to Nita Peralta. It took awhile, but she was so happy about Clara and me being reconciled it pissed me off. So I finally told Nita the truth about what was going on with my sex—or non-sex—life. She, too, you know, is a Catholic. And she's a virgin, too, believe it or not—"

"No!" Eddie laughed.

"No, she really is, Ed, and I feel kind of sorry for her. She's supporting her mother and her uncle, and about three teenaged kids—cousins or something. She's past thirty now, and she's still saving her box for a husband. But because she's taking care of all that family—her grandmother did live with her, but she died—Nita missed out on getting married. With Cuban girls, if they aren't married by the time they're nineteen or twenty, they can forget about it. Twenty-five is just about the outside limit, and then they have to settle for losers. The only chance for Nita to get married now, if she has any chance at all, is some old widower, unless she marries a white man—a Protestant. And she'd never do that."

"Hell, she's white, isn't she?"

"I guess so, but you know what I mean. All Cubans have got a touch or so of the old tarbrush. On an island like that, there is no way to avoid it. Even Castro is one-fourth nigger, you know.

"Anyway, Nita's still saving her box for someone. But not her ass. The way Catholic women work these things out in their minds is really something else, Eddie. But she began to brood about my lack of sex, and all, and she worked it out inside her head that it was okay for me to screw her in the ass, but I couldn't touch her anywhere else, you see. Not even a kiss—because a carnally-minded kiss, you see, would be a mortal sin. I wish to hell I'd had a tape recorder when she came to me with all this stuff. She had this real serious expression, and her big brown eyes were wide as she rattled through the whole explanation. It was hard for me to keep a straight face, but I did—somehow. A serious Cubano is weird enough, but a serious Cuban *female*—Jesus. She went on and on, and she kept throwing her arms and hands around as she got excited about it. But the upshot of the whole business was that I ended up by cornholing her over the desk here. I didn't mind. It was something to do, and at first I was slipping it to her every damned day. Then I got turned off somehow, and unless I'm desperate I just can't do it. Once a month, maybe—or five or six weeks go by, and then I call her in. She got worried when I slacked off, but I explained to her that it was like marriage. You do it a lot at first, and then only occasionally. I told her to talk to her girl friends about it—those who were married—and they'd tell her the same thing. So she did, and they did, and it worked out all right. What really turned me off, I think, was the fear that she'd tell the priest about it in confession. We go to the same church in the Grove, you see. I don't want that rummy bastard to get anything on me."

"Maybe she told him already, and he hasn't let on."

"No, not that bastard, Eddie. He drinks my Chivas like wine, man, and if he knew about Nita and me he'd be after a big donation."

"You don't believe in the church, do you, Don? How the hell can she possibly think that her ass is exempt from sin, if— " Eddie laughed, and then choked, shaking his head.

Don grinned. "There's nothing wrong with the church, Eddie, it's the people in it. People are always going to find a way to do what they want to do. Once Nita had worked this idea out in her squirrelly mind, she was set to carry through with it. She's loyal to me, she was worried about me, and she came up with a way to make me happy. In her heart, maybe, or deeply buried inside her mind, there's probably a doubt, but she's managed to suppress it. If she *didn't* have that doubt, she would've checked with the priest first, and asked *him* if it was okay. D'you see what I mean?"

"Sure, I see it. But I was asking about you, not Nita. What kind of Catholic does that make you, you bastard?"

Don shrugged. "I go to Mass on Sundays. I'm a pretty good Catholic. I believe in the church. I haven't been in a state of grace since I got the vasectomy. But I figure that sooner or later the church'll get around to authorizing vasectomies. And when they do I can go to confession, and get all this crap unloaded and off my mind."

"Suppose you die in the meantime, Don, and you aren't in a state of grace?"

"How'd you like some coffee, Ed?" Don crossed to the door and opened it. "We keep a pot— "

"Forget the coffee," Eddie said. "We'd better get along. I had three cups before I called you from the Pancake House."

"When will we be back?"

"In two, maybe three hours. We'll land in Ft. Myers, have lunch, and then fly straight back. But we'll have to take both cars.

I won't feel like driving back downtown from Opa-Locka, when it's closer for me to Miami Springs, so you'd better follow me out. I'm flying to Chicago tonight."

"Okay," Don said, nodding. "In that case I'll just call it a day."

Don told Nita Peralta that he would see her in the morning, and the two men drove to the Opa-Locka Airport.

27

Flying made Gladys sick. Eddie had seen to that.

To get away from Gladys once in awhile, to have a little time to himself, he told her that the airline had ordered all pilots to fly ten additional hours per month in light planes as "refresher" training. Gladys didn't know anything about airplanes or the airline, and she had accepted the story as the truth. It had made her angry, however, because it seemed unfair for the airline to give such an order and then make the pilots pay for their own rentals.

"If they're making you do it," Gladys said, "they should pay for the planes."

"They don't look at it that way," Eddie told her. "Besides, that's why they pay us so much money—so we'll have enough dough to pay for little extras like that. The way they look at it, they're doing us a favor. Most of us pilots like to fly light planes anyway, and by ordering us to do it, you see, we can take the expenses off our income taxes."

Gladys knew a lot about money, and she was mollified that Eddie could write off the plane rental fees.

Eddie didn't like to lie, and he had wondered, later on, why he really hadn't wanted to have Gladys along when he went flying, but flying seemed about the only area left to him where he could be completely alone. He didn't mind having Gladys around all the time. Most of the time, it was very pleasant. He liked to have her drive him to the Miami International Airport and pick him up when he came back from his regular flights. He avoided the parking hassle that way. He liked having her along when he went to a movie in the afternoon, or talking to her at dinner, or when they watched TV at night. But sometimes a man wanted to be by himself. Gladys often did things she didn't want to do, just to be with him. So Eddie had given up a few things he liked to do because he knew that she didn't really enjoy them. But she was with him all the time.

In the evening, around ten p.m., Eddie liked to stretch his legs. The four-block walk to the 7/Eleven store was just about right. He would walk down there, get a Coke and a bag of peanuts, browse among the magazines, and then buy the early edition of the next morning's *Miami Herald*. Gladys accompanied him on these walks, which meant that he had to wait for her while she put on fresh make-up and got dressed for the walk. When he wanted to take a little walk, that was what he wanted to do—then—not wait twenty minutes for Gladys to take off her old make-up and then put on all fresh make-up. But he went along with it, and waited, even though it made him impatient.

He still had the early morning jogging to himself, too. Gladys had bought a new sweat suit and red leather Keds with white racing stripes so she could jog with him in the morning, but she had only lasted for one morning and one block before she quit and walked home. Eddie had set a fast pace, and trying to keep up with him had made her breasts hurt. So all Eddie had left was the jogging and the flying. The rest of the time, during the three or four days a week he was in Miami, Gladys was with him. She was with him all the time, it seemed.

She had begged to go with him on the first Cessna flight, all excited about the idea, because she had never flown in a light plane before. This was about a month after he had moved into her house. As soon as he got some altitude he had sideslipped into a falling leaf, zigzagging sharply for a fairly swift drop of about 200 feet. Gladys had vomited all over her purple slacks and white sandals. He had flown back to the Opa-Locka airport only ten minutes after take-off.

"What caused that terrible drop?" she asked, as she scrambled out of the plane.

"Air pockets," Eddie lied. "They happen all the time, and I had to fight for control."

But even if she had given up flying with him, she usually drove him to the Opa-Locka airport and waited for him to come down. And this made Eddie a little irritated—knowing she was just sitting down there in the Twin Services rental waiting room, flipping through old *Aeronautical Journals*, bored out of her skull for two or three hours. The slight feeling of guilt he felt had diminished some of his pleasure in being alone up there.

If she hadn't been in Fort Lauderdale, she would have been with him today, not saying anything, but pouting jealously because he and Don were going to be alone for two or three hours without her. In some respects Gladys reminded Eddie of Schatzi, the German shepherd bitch he used to have as a boy. When he used to put his arm around his mother, or kissed her goodbye when he was leaving the house, Schatzi would bark and snarl. Until he broke her of the habit by beating her with a rolled newspaper, Schatzi would snap at his mother's legs.

But having Don with him in the plane was a lot different from having Gladys. Don probably had a hundred questions to ask, but Don could sense that Eddie didn't want to talk while he was flying. If Eddie had wanted to talk, why would he rent a plane for $55 an hour? So Don was quiet, and looked out the window. Gladys would have been asking "What's that?—and that?—and that?" Of course, just to have Don or anyone else along was distracting, in a sense, because if Don hadn't been with him Eddie wouldn't have been thinking about him. But then, Eddie didn't mind thinking about Don, because if he thought about Don he wouldn't have to think about Gladys. And thinking about Gladys, now that he had made his decision, was painful. He wanted to wait until he had some more distance, until he was in Chicago, maybe. Then he would think about Gladys.

Don, Eddie thought, was like a chameleon—a social chameleon—because he could adapt himself to almost any group or social situation—blend right in and be accepted, even though he never said much of anything. Basically, though, Don was a sad guy, a sufferer. Although he didn't show his pain or complain about anything much unless he was fairly close to a man, as he was with Eddie and Hank, and Larry, sometimes. But even then Don had to be coaxed a little to get him to talk about his problems.

That story about Nita and the rim-job was probably true. Otherwise, Don wouldn't have told it on himself. Eddie would never have told a story like that to anyone if it had happened to him. And yet, in a curious way, he had admired Don's courage, or humility, in being able to tell him about it. Don could talk about it, Eddie supposed, because he was a Catholic. Catholics were used to making confessions, or conditioned, as children, to talking about intimate matters to nuns and priests, and so it probably didn't bother them any. Also, Don being an Italian and all—that probably had something to do with his crying when he got drunk. Italians were very emotional. Eddie hadn't cried since he was twelve years old, and that was when Schatzi was run over. She was a good old dog, Schatzi. Eddie had refused his mother's offer of a new puppy. He hadn't wanted another dog. Another dog wouldn't be old Schatzi. Some things were just too damned intimate to discuss.

Eddie certainly couldn't talk about his sex life with Gladys to anyone, although Hank had asked him questions about it several times. Every time, Eddie had merely grinned and shrugged. He had driven old Hank right up the wall. But what he and Gladys did together would never be told to anyone. He didn't even like to think about it. Jesus. He had had his share of ass in his time, but he had never done *that* with anyone before! Eddie wasn't a prude. He didn't mind talking about sex, in general, like admitting you balled some chick three times in one night, or something like that, but going into the intimate details was just too gauche.

Anyway, Hank, in his letter, had been right about Don. Don was really depressed. He was way down there. But Hank's suggestion about getting Don a girl to shack up with on the side wasn't the answer. Besides, Don had never had any trouble getting laid. Women liked Don. He was good looking, in a dark way. A lot of women had told Don he looked like John Derek—in that movie where John Derek had been in a wheelchair. No one could ever recall the title of that movie, but Eddie remembered two or three times when women had brought up Don's resemblance to John Derek, and none of them could ever recall the name of the movie, either. But each time, they added "in that film where John Derek was in the wheelchair." That was when the four of them used to hang around the Turf and Surf in Hialeah, before the new manager took out the pool table. Eddie and Hank would meet there for lunch, and then play pool all afternoon. Don would arrive by two-thirty or three, and Larry by five-thirty. Sometimes, drinking beer and playing pool, they would close up the place at midnight. Those were the really good days, when Don was still living in the building. But after the new owner had taken out the pool table, they had started to hang around the White Shark instead.

Eddie still didn't know what to do about Don, though, and now it was a little too late to do much of anything. He should have gotten around to Don before now, instead of spending all that time with Gladys. Well, when they got to Ft. Myers he would tell Don about his promotion to captain. He could do that much. It always made Don happy when something nice happened to one of his friends.

The plane was approaching the huge abandoned concrete slab in the Everglades that was supposed to have been a new jetport for Miami before the environmentalists had forced the state to stop work on it. The plans had been made and more than three million dollars expended on the jetport before "ecology" had become a fad. But the landing field was still there, a vast, flat-out wasted expenditure of taxpayers' money. It was used occasionally by private planes and even for training purposes by some of the airlines, but that limited use would be curtailed soon—as soon as there was a bad accident on the uncontrolled field. Eddie liked to shoot a few landings in the Cessna when he came near the field, especially when the weather was nice, as it was today. But as he looked down he could see thirty or forty parked cars and a crowd of people at the southern end of the slab. Drag racers. He would skip the touch-and-goers today. Drag racers were crazy, and some of their home-made vehicles, with parachutes for brakes, zipped down the middle of the slab at 250 miles per hour.

Eddie made a slow banking circle to give Don a closer look at the crowd and the cars, and then flew straight across the 'Glades to Naples. From Naples, he followed the shoreline up to Bonita Beach, turned inland, and put the Cessna down at Page Field in Ft. Myers.

Instead of taking a cab into Edison Mall, they ate lunch, at Eddie's suggestion, in the small cafe in Hangar Three. Eddie ordered the special—meat loaf, blackeyed peas, corn bread and string beans—but Don, who said he wasn't very hungry, asked for a hamburger and a chocolate milk shake. While they sat in the booth, waiting for their food, Don polished his purple sunglasses with a paper napkin.

"While we were flying over, Ed, I had an idea," Don said. "I don't know if it would work or not, but if it did, it would be a way out for me."

"A way out for what?"

"You know. The situation I'm in. I don't work very hard, as you know. In a way, I hardly work at all. I just take orders from the stock I have in the warehouse. I haven't had to get out and hustle any sterling for about three years. Most of the time, as it is, it takes about two months to fill a big order. A replacement order—like a new forty-five dollar spoon to replace one some housewife's thrown away in the garbage—takes from three to six months.

"So I'm not overworked. In fact, Nita handles most of the Dade County orders. My main job is keeping my boss in Gunnersbury, England, happy, and checking on my salesmen in Tampa and Jax. Considering the bread I make, I sometimes feel guilty about how little I do."

Eddie grinned. "I feel the same way sometimes. In fact, I just got a raise, Don—and my promotion to captain."

"You did? Congratulations!"

"Thanks. I've been putting off the promotion for some time, Don. I could've had my fourth stripe two years ago, but I waited until I could get my own Seven-twenty-seven. If I'd taken it two years ago, I'd've been hauling cargo and taking most of the lousy runs. Moving from co-pilot to pilot only means another twenty-five hundred a year to me right now, but a lot more eventually. The point is, I'd probably fly for nothing—or for just enough to live on, if that was the only way I could get to fly. But other pilots in the Association, fortunately, don't feel that way, so now I'll be drawing down twenty-eight, five a year."

"You sure as hell deserve it, Eddie. As the captain, you'll be the man, now, and if anything goes wrong it'll be your ass."

"I know. That's what they really pay us for—the responsibility, not for flying the plane. If they only paid us—say—six or seven thousand a year, the passengers would lose confidence in flying, I think. It's like psychoanalysts. They charge fifty bucks an hour so you'll trust them."

"I never thought of that, but you're probably right. Let me ask you a couple of questions, Eddie, before I test my idea on you. Okay?"

"Anything, man."

"The Cessna. Could it haul you and me and about twelve hundred additional pounds?"

"No. Not this one. The ten-passenger job could, though—the Cessna Four-oh-two. If it didn't have the ten passengers along, I mean."

"Could you check one out—a Four-oh-two?"

"Sure. I've got more than thirty-five hundred hours in multi-engined planes, for Christ's sake."

"I know that. But are they available for rental, these ten-passenger jobs?"

"If you've got the hundred bucks an hour. The rate is, or used to be, about sixty-five cents a nautical mile. They might've gone up some on rentals, though, just like everything else."

"How long would it take you to fly to Tampa and back from Opa-Locka?"

"I'd have to check the maps first for an exact schedule, but I can give you a rough idea. It's about one hundred and twenty-five miles to Tampa from Miami—nautical miles—and the Four-oh-two can fly at about one hundred and eighty knots. So roughly, give or take a few minutes, it would take about an hour each way. At Tampa, however, you can't always land when you want to. Sometimes they make small planes wait—both to land and to take-off. They've got priorities, you see."

"D'you need a flight plan?"

The waitress brought their food. As she put down the plates, she stared at Don and smiled. "You've got beautiful hair," she said.

"Thanks," Don said, nodding pleasantly, "I just had it styled yesterday. Twelve bucks a crack."

"In Fort Myers?"

"No—in Miami. I go about twice a month."

"I didn't think it was in Fort Myers. I didn't mean to be rude. But my husband's got long hair like yours, and his looks like a rat's nest."

"That's okay. It's always nice to get a little feedback. So maybe the guy's worth twelve bucks." He grinned at Eddie, "Where do you get your hair styled, Eddie?"

"Miami Barber College. It's a buck-fifty for white sidewalls."

"I'd rather see my husband with short hair like yours," the woman said to Eddie, "instead of having it look like a rat's nest."

"That's a nice diplomatic comment," Eddie said.

The waitress left, and Don nodded solemnly. "D'you see how it is, Ed? If you'd let your hair grow, they'd be all over you."

Eddie grinned. "I can't stand it down over my ears that way, but I've been wearing it a little longer since I've been living with Gladys. Lately, though, I've been thinking about going back to the flat-top. That was the best hair style men ever had, and George Peppard's gone back to it. I saw his picture in the paper the other day."

"Where was I? Before my fan came over?"

"On the flight plan. The answer is no. It isn't necessary to file a flight plan, not on a rental plane. If you were going outside the continental limits—like to Nassau or somewhere—you'd need one. But that's because you'd have to have a Customs agent check your plane when you got back. What is it, exactly, you've got in mind?"

"Well, what I need, you see, is some money. Twenty-four complete sets of flatware, about fifty pounds each in its neat little case, are worth about twenty thousand. My plan or idea was to steal twenty-four sets from my own warehouse, have you fly me and my daughter and the silverware over to Tampa. You could fly back alone, you see, and I could rent a car over there, and take off. We could settle somewhere, in New Orleans, or Dallas, and I could change my name. Then, once we got settled, I could find another job and start a new life."

Eddie shook his head. "Don, Don, Don—you really haven't thought this thing out, have you?"

"Not the details, no, but in general, I have—as we flew over."

"How would you get the silverware and your daughter to Opa-Locka?"

"I could rent a panel truck, I suppose."

"And leave it at the airport?"

"Sure. You could turn it in for me when you got back from Tampa."

"Here's a better way. You visit your salesman in Tampa once a month, right?"

"I'm supposed to, but usually it's about every other month. It's easier to phone him, and Henry's a pretty good man. I do go to Jax once a month though. I take the breakfast flight up, and the dinner flight back. And I never tell the bastard when I'm coming, either."

"Okay. How about this idea. You drive over to Tampa, and you establish that you're in Tampa—an alibi—because you're checking on Henry. Then that night I pick you up in Tampa, and fly you back to Miami. You have a stolen car staked out at the Opa-Locka airport. You take the stolen car, drive downtown to your warehouse, pick up the silverware and drive back to Opa-

Locka. I fly you and the silverware back to Tampa. All in all, you'll only be away from Tampa about three hours."

"But what about Marie? I'm not leaving without my daughter."

"Wait'll I finish. You stay in Tampa all night, and then you drive back to Miami the next day. Then you discover the missing silverware and call the police. You're clear. You couldn't possibly have taken it because you were in Tampa, and Henry Messinger'll prove it. Meanwhile, the silverware is all hid out over there somewhere. When things blow over, in another two or three months, let's say, you can quit your job, pick up Marie, and go to Tampa. *Then* you can get the silverware and take off for New Orleans, or wherever."

"That plan sounds better than mine."

"It's a plan, at any rate. You didn't have a plan. You just had an idea. A bad idea."

"Would you do this for me, Eddie?"

"Sure. Why not? If that's what you want to do. But I'll tell you one thing, you'll have one hellova time finding another thirty-thousand-dollar-a-year job like the one you've got now."

"Hell," Don said, "I don't expect to. But the way Clara's got me boxed in now, I can't keep any money anyway. My paychecks and commission checks go directly into her account, and then she gives me a weekly allowance. It's an adequate allowance, but that isn't the same. The house, and even the Mark IV, is in her name. Marie and I, we won't need a lot—but I'll need at least ten thousand to start over, and twenty would be even better. D'you see what I mean, Eddie?"

"Yes. But if you try to start over as a fugitive—you and a little girl trying to begin again somewhere with new names—you'll get caught, or you'll worry about getting caught all the time."

"No, Ed, I won't get caught. I'm going to work on this plan, get it all together, and with your help, pull it off."

"You can count on me, Don."

Eddie was genuinely happy to see Don's face so animated, with his dark eyes shining and wearing the superior elevated smile of the blind. It had been a long time since he had seen such an exultant look on Don's face. Of course, he had no intention of helping Don rob his own company, but it didn't hurt to let Don think that he would. Look how happy it made Don now. The present is all a man has anyway, and Eddie had managed to make Don feel good three times today already. First, by taking him out of his dreary office for a flight to Fort Myers; second, by telling Don about his promotion; and third, by giving Don the impression that he would help him in his foolish plan to steal $20,000 worth of silverware from his company.

They ordered desserts and coffee. Eddie got the apple pie, and Don asked for strawberry jello. Unable to eat the tough crust, Eddie merely ate the apple-and-cornstarch filling as he watched Don put away all of the rubbery jello. It was the worst lunch Eddie had had in months.

On the flight back to Opa-Locka, Eddie skimmed along at 200 feet in an effort to make the trip more exciting for Don. But Don was no longer interested in looking out the window. Smiling, he spent most of the flight in jotting notes and writing down figures in his black leather notebook with a silver ballpoint.

After promising each other that they would get together very soon, they parted at the Opa-Locka airport at two p.m.

When Eddie left the Opa-Locka airport, after settling his bill for the rental of the plane, he drove directly to Mel's Foreign Car Exchange on West Flagler, and sold his M.G. to Mel for the prearranged price. The sum wasn't as much as he could have gotten for the car on a trade-in, but it was above the book price and more than he had expected to get. The forty thousand miles on the M.G. were very hard miles, but Mel didn't know that.

"Look, Mel," Eddie said, after he signed the papers and got his check. "If I'd taken the radio out before I brought in the M.G., would you have knocked anything off the purchase?"

"Of course not. But what good is a car radio without a car?"

"It's worth thirty or forty bucks, isn't it?"

"If you could find someone to buy it, I suppose. But a car is expected to have a radio in it."

Eddie grinned. "I'm trying to make a point. If the radio's worth thirty bucks, let's say, and I gave it to you free, absolutely free, you ought to have one of your salesman give me a free ride home. A cab from here to Miami Springs'll run five or six bucks."

"Sure," Mel laughed, "you cheap bastard. I'll run you home myself. You've been a good customer, Eddie. I'll even let you take the radio."

"I don't want the fucking radio," Eddie said, grinning, "I just want a ride home."

Gladys Wilson's house, set on a jungly one-acre lot,

prompted Mel to whistle when he turned into the semi-circular pebbled driveway and stopped in front of the copper-screened porch.

"You airline drivers live pretty high," Mel said.

"It's only got three bedrooms," Eddie shrugged. "It just looks big because of the screened pool and the way the garden sections are separated."

"Right," Mel grinned. "One full acre of deception."

The two men shook hands and Eddie thanked Mel for the ride.

Eddie still had plenty of time, and he took it in packing. If possible, he wanted to get everything into his old U.S.A.F. val-pack, and that took careful planning and arrangement. The two new, unworn tailormade suits presented him with a dilemma. Gladys, on several occasions, had wanted to take him to a tailor for some suits and jackets, but he had always refused. She had then, without his knowledge, taken his oldest uniform, his favorite, to a tailor, and had the two suits—a blue gabardine, and a dark gray whipcord—made from the uniform measurements. It had taken three weeks. Every time Eddie had wanted to wear the uniform she had told him it was at the cleaners and that she had forgotten to pick it up. The tailor had taken the uniform apart to make his measurements, but when he sewed it back together again the worn material had ripped under the arms. The uniform had only been good for another month or so of wearing anyway, but Eddie had raised hell with Gladys. He was irritated by the gift of the suits, not by the destruction of the old uniform (he had three other uniforms), and he hadn't even tried on the new suits. He decided now to take them. After all, they were tailored for him, he would need some suits in Chicago, and if he didn't take them, what would Gladys do with them?

There wasn't too much to pack after he got his uniforms and the two suits arranged in the val-pack. His shirts, his jeans, and extra black silk socks went into the outside pockets with a little squeezing. He had his dark blue melton-cloth bathrobe and two pairs of black flight boots left over, however, and he had to put these into a brown paper grocery bag. His other personal possessions, what little he had, including his banjo and his Vietnam souvenirs, were still stored at his mother's house in Lauderdale. He could send for that stuff later, after he was settled.

Finished, he mixed a light scotch and water, with one ice cube, and took the drink into the living room. There was a color photo of Gladys in a silver frame on the Yamaha grand piano, and he deliberated, as he sipped his drink, whether to take it, too. The photo was his, Gladys had given it to him, and he had bought the expensive frame himself. It was an arty photo, self-consciously posed. Gladys, with her coal black hair tossed back, and smiling with her teeth exposed, reminded Eddie of a Gypsy. It's the looped gold earrings, he thought. But no one, he concluded, could tell from the photograph that her lower front teeth, the entire row, was a removable plate.

Eddie knew, from experience, if he didn't see Gladys for a couple of years, in person, her face would gradually fade from his memory. He would always remember what she looked like, of course, but not exactly, and perhaps that was the better way. The photo was several years old already, and she didn't look that fresh even now, so there was really no point in taking the photo with him. Gladys wouldn't live alone for long, and she could give the photo, with the expensive silver frame, to her next lover. If she could find him, she could find someone else.

Eddie had removed his leather jacket while he packed, but now he found himself shivering. He checked the thermostat. Sixty-five degrees. Jesus. He moved the needle up to 75 degrees, and slipped his jacket on again. He unpinned his inside pocket, and took out his savings and loan company passbook. $73,583.14. He had gone down the day before to draw out the money and to get a cashier's check, but the teller reminded him that there was another dividend due in ten days, and he would lose the interest if he took the money out before that date. So Eddie had decided not to withdraw his savings. But he would have to eventually, after he found a better way to invest the money. He should be getting better than five and three-quarter percent interest on that much money, but he had been too lazy, or too cautious, in looking around for a better investment. But he still didn't need any money at the moment. There were still two paychecks in Chicago that he hadn't picked up and cashed. Perhaps it would be best just to leave the $73,000 in Miami until the sum built up to $100,000 or so, and start over with a savings account in Schiller Park. His savings would build up—eventually—in a few years, and he wouldn't have to worry about checking on investments. He returned the passbook to his inside pocket, and refastened the safety pin.

Eddie looked forward to seeing Hank again. Old Hank would certainly be surprised to see him in his apartment when he got home to Schiller Park, but Eddie felt bad about leaving Don all alone in Miami.

He took Don's business card out of his wallet, and telephoned Don's office.

"Miss Peralta," he said, when the secretary answered the phone, "this is Captain Eddie Miller—from this morning, remember? I've got a message for Mr. Luchessi. Have you got a pencil? Good. Tell him that I've been transferred unexpectedly to Chicago. Yes. Chicago. That's right. I'm going to be flying from Chicago to Seattle now, and the airline wants me to make Chicago my home base. That's right. Anyway, I'll be staying with Mr. Norton in Schiller Park. Mr. Luchessi has his address and phone number. I'm sure he has it, so there's no use in me giving it to you again. I'll write or call him from there about the business deal we discussed today. Okay? You're a good girl, Miss Peralta, and you take good care of your boss, d'you hear? Thank you. And good luck to you."

He racked the phone. That was that. If Don called him in Chicago, and really bugged him about the stupid plan to rob his company and use the plane and so on, he would offer to lend Don $10,000—at eight percent interest. Don would be good for it, in time, and eight percent interest would be a lot better than the five and three-quarters he was getting from the savings and loan company. Even if Don only paid him back at the rate of $108.00 a month, he would get the $10,000 back eventually, and anyone, nowadays, could scape up $108 a month. He had a hunch, however, that Don would stay put right where he was—in his dead-end $30,000-a year job, In the long run, even living with Clara, Don would be better off. Besides, some people are born, or programmed, to be unhappy. Like Don. Like Gladys Wilson. Like his widowed mother.

Eddie took out the report on Gladys Wilson's handbag that Hank had sent to him, mixed another scotch and water, and then put the lp soundtrack album of *2001: A Space Odyssey* on the hi-fi record player before settling down to read.

He read the report twice, chuckling at the same place both times. Hank, when he wanted to, could be funnier than hell. But Hank's report had saved him from a painful task. Eddie hated to write letters, and he had been putting off writing a letter to Gladys telling her that he was leaving and wouldn't be seeing her again. There was no good way to write such a letter anyway, but now, all he had to do was to leave Hank's report on the coffee table, and Gladys could read that instead of a farewell letter from him.

Pleased with this tidy solution, Eddie called a cab and took his val-pack and bulging paper sack out to the front porch. He re-entered the house, took the house keys and the extra keys to Gladys' Cadillac off his ring, and put them on top of the report. When Gladys read the report, she would probably have a hot flash, Eddie thought. He thoughtfully re-set the thermostat to fifty degrees, and went outside to sit in the afternoon sun and wait for the cab that would take him to the Miami International Airport.

30

In 1967, puzzled by the static state of their sales in the United States in a time of burgeoning prosperity, the board of directors, of Gunnersbury Silversmiths, Ltd., engaged the Reinsberg Research Institute, in Baltimore, Maryland, to make a national survey. In addition to fifteen pounds of unwieldy computer printout sheets filled with binary statistics, the board received a report of twenty-four single-spaced typed pages outlining a few valid and several specious suggestions based upon the statistics.

A conservative firm, but a practical one, the board acted somewhat reluctantly on some of the suggestions with, of course, its own modifications. As a consequence, Gunnersbury Silversmiths' silver flatware sales, by the end of 1969, rose almost twenty percent in the United States.

Young American couples did not, the Reinsberg researchers reported, entertain more than two other couples at dinner, except on very rare occasions; therefore, the complete silver service for twelve, which was quite expensive for newlyweds, was hard to sell because at least half of it was rarely, if ever, on the table.

New and much more attractive leather silverware boxes were then designed, and the sets of twelve were divided and reduced to two smaller boxes of six service sets. Sales zoomed. Four sets were not quite enough, and eight sets were still too many, but six sets were just about right for young and newly affluent middle-class American brides.

During its 127 years in business, enterprising and artistic silversmiths had designed and developed sixty-eight different flatware patterns. Some of these patterns, heavy and grotesquely Baroque, were seldom purchased by the young, and, when grandparents bought them for their granddaughters, the young brides, more often than not, returned them to the jewelers and exchanged them for lighter, simpler, and more "modern" patterns. The vote was five to four, with the twenty-four-year-old family descendant chairman of the board casting the deciding vote, but fifty-seven patterns were discontinued abruptly and the extant sets retired to the vaults. The retired sets were then cannibalized for replacements, as replacements were ordered, and each implement of each retired pattern was doubled in price.

A new patternless plain pattern was developed, at the suggestion of the chairman of the board, with just enough room on each "streamlined" handle for a single, narrow intaglioed initial letter; and this beautiful and purely functional pattern was named, at the insistence of the young chairman of the board, "English Danish." In spite of the ambiguity, or perhaps because of it, the "English Danish" pattern, within two years, became the most popular flatware pattern in the history of Gunnersbury Silversmiths, Ltd.

Other minor changes were adopted, as suggested by the Reinsberg Report, but they were not as radical as the discontinuance of the fifty-seven patterns. A few implements, for example, were eliminated from the complete sets. Americans were trained, when they received any table manners at all, to place their knife, when it was not in use, on the edge of their plates. The intricate and difficult to manufacture cut glass-and-silver kniferests were not used by American housewives because these puzzled young women did not know their purpose, and were either too intimidated or too embarrassed to ask their jewelers. It was easier, and cheaper, to eliminate items such as kniferests and gherkin prongs from each set than it was to prepare an accompanying booklet—as the Reinsberg Report suggested—explaining their function. If someone demanded kniferests, however, they could be ordered separately—and dearly.

The tax-deductible Reinsberg Report was worth every cent the United Kingdom and the United States did not receive in taxes in 1967, and a good deal more to Gunnersbury Silversmiths, Ltd.

Don Luchessi, as he disengaged the burglar alarm, prior to opening the walk-in safe in his rented warehouse, was thinking about the Reinsberg Report. As a consequence, he selected eight boxed sets of "English Danish," two sets of "Wheat," and two sets of "Victoria" to load into the trunk of his Mark IV Continental, which he had backed into the warehouse alongside the safe. The wholesale value of the twelve sets was approximately $10,550 (the value of a "Victorian" set was at least a third more than that of the cheaper "English Danish" set), but Don expected to get, when he sold these sets, one at a time, and as he needed to sell them, a good deal more than the wholesale price recommended by Gunnersbury Silversmiths in England.

Don locked the trunk, drove his car outside and parked in the yellow zone in front of the outside office door. He opened the glove compartment, removed the .45 caliber U.S. Army semiautomatic pistol, checked the magazine, pulled back the slide, and released it to let a round enter the chamber. Without pushing up the safety, he placed the pistol, butt first, back into the glove compartment and closed the little door without locking it. Don had carried a pistol in his glove compartment ever since *that* night, but he only kept it loaded and ready to fire when he was carrying silver in his car.

It was seven-thirty a.m. when he closed and locked the warehouse door, and opened the front door to his offices. George, Don's black warehouseman and general handy man, who had his own key to the warehouse double door, would show up at—or about—eight-thirty. Nita Peralta would appear promptly at eight-forty-five. Ordinarily, when Don arrived at nine-fifteen, the coffee would be ready, and Nita would serve him his coffee, already creamed and sugared, together with a small plate of *sobre mesas* in his private office.

But today was the day, and so far, everything was on schedule and according to his plan. He reread the three-by-five card, as he sat at his desk, and checked off 1 and 2. Number 3 was to fire Robert C. Matlock, his salesman in Jacksonville, a man he had never liked, but had hired because he was a conscientious salesman. He wrote out the letter for his secretary to type and then added a note to Nita, telling her to predate the letter by two days, to sign his name, and to send a carbon copy of the letter to Gunnersbury Silversmiths, Ltd., in England. With a little luck, Don thought hopefully, the embittered Matlock, fired without cause or reason, would steal some of the flatware he had on hand in Jacksonville, and disappear with it. Perhaps and probably not, but Don had never liked Matlock, and as long as he was absconding, it wouldn't hurt anything to throw some suspicion on Matlock while he was at it.

He crossed out No. 4 on his card, and then unlocked the file cabinet in Nita's office. He removed the inventory folder, ripped it into four sections, and placed the quartered sheets of graph paper into a brown paper sack he had brought to the office for that purpose.

Don sat at Nita's desk and wrote her another short note telling her that he would be in Tampa for the next three days with Henry Messinger—checking out his sales talks. As an afterthought, he told Nita to have George sweep the warehouse and to give the handy man two days off and a salary advance of ten dollars for doing such a good job. If she needed to contact him, which he doubted, she could call him after eight p.m. at the Ramada Inn in Tampa.

Don picked up the paper sack containing the trashed inventory file, locked the office, and left the warehouse area. He ate the breakfast special at the Biscayne Boulevard Hojo's, drove to the back parking lot of Jordan Marsh and parked his Mark IV. He locked his car, dumped the paper sack into a trash can beside the back entrance, and entered the door just as the floorwalker opened it from inside with his key.

In the children's department he purchased three pairs of blue denim bell jeans, size ten, a red wool topcoat, size ten, three long-sleeved cotton T-shirts (one with "Marlins" printed on the front, and two with "Dolphins" printed on the back), size ten, and two pairs of cowboy boots, one black and one white, size six-D.

Downstairs in the luggage department on the first floor Don bought a red leatherette suitcase with white leatherette straps and packed his clothing purchases into it. In the cosmetics department, still on the ground floor, and near the back exit doors, he bought a clothes brush, a hair brush, a tortoise comb, and a toothbrush. He added these items to the red leatherette suitcase. He paid for all of his purchases with a Jordan Marsh credit card that belonged to his wife, a card he had removed from her purse the night before while she was busy in the kitchen cooking his dinner.

Don crossed off 5, 6, and 7 on his three-by-five card, left Jordan Marsh, and ripped the credit card into two halves as he reached the trash can. He dropped the two halves into the can. He unlocked his Mark IV, placed the red suitcase on the back seat beside his own, and drove south on the Dixie Highway, turning left on Twenty-seventh Avenue to the Lilliput School in Gables-by-the-Sea.

Ms. Dubina, the headmistress of Lilliput School, didn't like it. She didn't like it at all. "I've told parents, Mr. Luchessi, and I've told them again and again, orally and in writing. We don't like to have children taken out of school for doctor or dental appointments during school hours. There's plenty of time after school for such appointments. Marie's only been at school two hours, and what little she's learned this morning will be knocked out of her head completely by the excitement of going to the orthodontist."

"I'm sorry," Don lied, "but the orthodontist said that it was at least a two-hour wiring job, and we didn't tell Marie about it. She's afraid of dentists, you see—"

"That's perfectly normal," Ms. Dubina said. "So am I—"

"At any rate," Don said, "her mouth'll be pretty sore when he's finished, so I won't bring her back this afternoon."

"Very well. But next time, I want at least three days notice in advance, whether you tell your daughter about it or not. You have your problems with Marie, and I have mine. Your daughter, Mr. Luchessi, is not a tractable child."

"I know. My wife spoils her, I think."

"Somebody has." Ms. Dubina nodded grimly. "Wait here. I'll get her..."

Marie was so excited about getting out of school to go with her Daddy to Disney World that she almost wet her pants. Three blocks away from the Lilliput School Don had to stop at Lum's to let Marie go to the bathroom. When she came out of the restroom, he bought her a Lumburger and a stein of root beer, and then they were on their way again, driving north on I-95.

Now that he was actually on the road to somewhere with his daughter by his side and with the ten thousand dollars worth of silver safely stowed in the trunk, Don allowed warm waves of elation to wash over him. His skin tingled, and his face was hot with pleasure. He had done it by himself, without any help from Eddie, or Hank, or anyone else. The black depression that had clutched him every morning for the past two weeks, after he had learned of Eddie's transfer to Chicago, was completely gone. Until he had made his decision and his new plans, Don had been popping Librium capsules like peanuts.

Marie, sitting quietly beside him in her school uniform (white scalloped blouse, pink pinafore, and white patent leather shoes), looked solemnly out the window at the flat green countryside.

That had been his only mistake, Don thought, telling Marie he was taking her to Disney World. Of course, Disney World was nowhere near Tampa, where they would be looking for him, if they looked, and he could be damned certain that Clara would demand a search, but all the same, there would be at least a one-day delay if he took Marie on an all-day visit to Disney World. Was there any way out of it? He guessed not. He didn't want the girl to suspect anything, so he would stay overnight near Orlando—but not in Orlando—and take her on the damned tour tomorrow. Marie's excitement had died down, the doubled excitement of missing almost a full day of school today and another day tomorrow, with the Disney World trip thrown in as well, and for at least five minutes she hadn't said a word and she hadn't squirmed.

"Daddy?"

"Hmm?"

"How come Mommy isn't going with us?"

Don cleared his throat. It was time to tell Marie the truth. If not now, when? So why not now, and get it over with?

"Your mommy isn't coming because you and I, after we see Disney World tomorrow, are leaving her for good. From now on, it will just be you and me, sweetheart, and we'll never see your mommy again."

"We'll never see Mommy again?" Marie's voice broke.

"No. Never."

Marie began to cry.

Shit, Don thought, maybe I should've waited until tomorrow to tell her—while she was having fun, like watching an exciting puppet show or shaking hands with Mickey Mouse, or something like that, so she wouldn't have time to think about her mother. All the same, he was a little surprised by her tears. If Marie had told him once she had told him a thousand times that she had wanted to be with him all the time. And now that she had her wish, here she was, crying like a damned baby.

31

At ten minutes after midnight Don was awakened by three imperative raps on the door. He was groggy because he had only been asleep for about an hour and a half, but the desk lamp was still on, thanks to Marie's inability to sleep without a night light, so Don was not disoriented. He knew, from the moment he was awakened, that he was in an Orla Vista motel room, that it was late at night, and that there was no excuse, or valid reason, for anyone to pound on his door, unless, perhaps, it was some drunk who had mistaken Don's room for his own.

Still in his underwear, with his eyes half-closed, and shivering slightly in the chilled airconditioned room, Don hoped that the rapping hadn't awakened Marie. He had had a difficult time getting Marie to go to bed. She had cried for almost an hour after they checked into the room—although her appetite at dinner had not been noticeably affected by grief—and then she had sulked for the rest of the evening, refusing to talk to him. Shaking his head to clear it as he crossed, barefooted, toward the door, Don glanced at Marie's bed and noticed that she was not in it. His relief was immediate. It was now evident that Marie had gone outside for some reason or other and had locked herself out.

But such was not the case.

The man in uniform who stood on the narrow concrete porch beneath the overhead porchlight was a full head taller than Don, and he was pointing the barrel of a .38 police special at

Don's midriff. The officer smiled shyly, exposing brutal, metal-studded upper front teeth, reholstered his pistol, and said apologetically, "Excuse me, Mr. Luchessi, but if you'll ask me in I'd like to talk to you for a few minutes."

Nodding, Don backed away as the big man in khaki chinos, with a round eight pointed badge pinned above his left shirt pocket, entered the room. Before closing the door he said something Don didn't quite catch to another man in uniform who was still outside, and then he edged warily into the room between Don and Don's opened suitcase on the baggage rack. Don was trying not to panic, although he was almost certain now that something terrible had happened to Marie, or else this sheriff, or deputy sheriff, would not be in his room, and Marie would be. Don sat on the edge of his bed, staring at Marie's rumpled bedclothes and, to have something to do, began to put on his socks and shoes. The sheriff nodded approvingly as Don started to dress, and pawed idly through Don's suitcase with his large left hand.

"That's good, Mr. Luchessi," he said. "I was going to suggest that you get dressed."

"What's going down?" Don said thickly.

"A few questions—that's all." The sheriff removed the contents from Don's pockets before handing the trousers to Don. He took Don's key-case to the door, opened it, and handed the case to the man outside. "Here, Red," he said, "take a look through his car."

"There's valuable property in my car," Don said.

"Sure. But it won't hurt any to look at it, will it?"

Don stood up, zipped his fly closed, and crossed to his suitcase. He slipped a clean white knitted shirt over his head, and then lit a cigarette, taking it from the pack on the bedside table. He switched on the bedside lamp and sat on the edge of his bed. His legs were trembling.

"Listen," Don said, "if something's happened to my daughter, you'd better tell me about it." His tongue was thick and his throat was tight.

The sheriff sat at the desk facing Don. He removed his

broad-brimmed hat and placed it on the other side of the desk lamp. The shadowed brim had made it difficult for him to read the cards in Don's wallet.

"You daughter's okay, Mr. Luchessi," he said. "That's your real name, isn't it? Luchessi?"

"Yes, sir. Where is she?"

"She's all right. Mr. Rouse, the motel manager, brought her over to my house, and my wife made her some hot chocolate. She's probably having some oatmeal cookies with it. I just want to ask you a few questions is all."

"About what?"

The big man chuckled. "For one thing, about these two big bills. Are they real?"

"Yes, they're real. But what happened to Marie?"

"She said her name was Marie Luchessi, so you must be her father. Is that right?"

"Of course I'm her father. Is she hurt or anything?"

"No, no, she's fine. Why're you carrying around a thousand-dollar-bill and a five-hundred dollar bill?"

"If I carried fifteen hundred dollars in one-dollar bills I couldn't fold my wallet," Don said.

"That's right, that's right," the big man chuckled, exposing his metal-studded teeth, "I guess you couldn't at that." He counted Don's traveler's checks. "Four hundred and twenty bucks in traveler's checks, too. Right?"

"I think so, yes," Don said.

"Where're you heading, Mr. Luchessi? A little vacation? New York, maybe?"

"No. I'm the state representative for Gunnersbury Silversmiths. You can see my business cards there. I'm visiting my salesman in Tampa, a regular field trip. Our main office is in Miami, and I make a trip to Tampa and another to Jacksonville about once a month, sometimes every other month."

"You're the boss, then, right?"

"That's the way it worked out. I've been with Gunnersbury for almost ten years now. I was the Miami salesman at first, and then when the English representative retired, they gave me his job, too. So I'm both: the Florida district manager, and the Miami sales representative. Two hats. But what—?"

"This is a lot of money. How long were you planning to stay in Tampa?"

"Look. Tomorrow I'm taking my daughter to Disney World. We'll go on to Tampa for one or two days, and then we drive back to Miami."

"In the middle of the week? What about school? Doesn't Marie go to school?"

"It won't hurt to miss a couple of days. She's very smart, and I've been promising to take her to Disney World for a long time."

There was a knock on the door. The sheriff was on his feet and had the door opened before Don could stand. Don sat again as the deputy entered. He was a short man with curly red hair, and his expression, as he looked at Don, was a curious mixture of anger and loathing. He carried Don's .45 semiautomatic pistol loosely in a red bandana handkerchief.

"Look what I found in the glove compartment, Ed," the redhead deputy said. "Not only is it loaded, he doesn't even have the safety on."

"Where does your little girl ride in the car, Mr. Luchessi?" the sheriff said, no longer smiling.

"She rides in the front seat, but she's been told not to touch my pistol. After all, I've got some ten thousand dollars worth of silverware to protect, and it isn't against the law to carry a gun in your car for protection."

"What about the silverware?" The sheriff turned to the deputy.

"The trunk's loaded with it," the redhaired deputy said. "What about the pistol?"

"Put the safety on, and stick it back in the glove compartment. Then lock the car and wait outside for a few minutes."

The deputy left, carrying the pistol, pausing at the threshold to glower for a long moment at Don before he closed the door.

The sheriff chuckled. "Red's got four kids, you see, and he won't even take his pistol home with him. Keeps it locked up at the substation when he's off-duty. But he's right, you know. It isn't a good idea to keep a loaded pistol where kids can get it. They're curious, you see, and—but that's your business. If I were carrying valuable silverware in my car, I'd want a pistol for protection myself."

"I'd like to know what's going on, Sheriff," Don said.

"Well, Mr. Luchessi, we have a small problem here. I think we can work it out all right, but here it is. About an hour ago your daughter woke up the manager, John Rouse, and told him that she was being kidnapped—"

"That's ridiculous! I'm her father!"

"Yes, I know. She even looks like you. Anyway, John drove her over to my house and brought her in. He could've taken her to the substation, but he knew I was home and they'd've called me anyway, so he figured that was the easiest way. As he said, he brought her over without waking you up because he didn't want to take any chances, you see. I talked to your daughter, and she told me you were her father all right, but when she told me you had a gun I didn't take any chances myself. I asked her where you were supposed to be taking her, and when she said that you were going to Disney World tomorrow, I didn't take much stock in her story. She would be the first little girl to ever complain about being kidnapped to Disney World!" He chuckled. "Anyway, Mr. Luchessi, I checked the thing out before I drove over here, and sure enough, it was on the wire tonight that you kidnapped your daughter, or that you're suspected of kidnapping her. What do you have to say about that?"

Don shook his head. "I don't understand. I left a note for my wife," Don lied, "telling her that I was taking Marie with me. The only thing I can think of is that Clara didn't find the note. Why would I kidnap my own child, for Christ's sake?"

"I don't know, Mr. Luchessi, but your wife might think, that is, if she didn't find the note, that you were running out on her or something. So that's the position we're in right now. You and your daughter have been reported missing, and you are alleged to have her—well, illegally, I suppose. Anyway, that's what we're faced with, and although it isn't a big problem it is a problem, and we'd better work something out."

"I could call my wife," Don said, "but if she didn't find the note she's probably hysterical by now, and it wouldn't do much good to have her tell you to forget the whole business, and withdraw the allegation. I have a hunch she'd be sore, and she'd want Marie back in Miami immediately."

"Yes, I think you're right. She wants her back, all right."

"Meanwhile, I've got to go to Tampa on business, and I don't feel like driving back to Miami and then up again to Tampa tomorrow. So I'll tell you what, Sheriff. I'll let you call the Miami police, or the sheriff, whoever put out the missing report, and then I'll give you the money for expenses and transportation. You can send someone down to Miami with Marie, and I'll go ahead over to Tampa and complete my business. By the time I get home again, two or three days from now, my wife will be cooled off some and I can talk to her and straighten everything out. What do you say to that?"

"It's an intelligent way to solve your problem." The sheriff looked at the ceiling for a moment, and then put on his hat. "In fact, I might take the trip down to Miami myself. I'll bet it's been six—no, closer to eight—months since I've been down to Sin City."

The sheriff got to his feet and stretched, and Don joined him at the desk. Don picked up his silver ballpoint pen and signed seven twenty-dollar traveler's checks. He handed the filled-in checks to the lawman.

"Will one-forty be enough? I know it is if you drive down, but if you take a bus—"

"I'll drive my own car down, Mr. Luchessi. Now, I suspect you'll want to talk to your daughter, won't you?"

"For a minute. I'm wide awake now, so I'll just go ahead and check out and drive to Tampa afterwards. Let's get Marie's clothes in the bag."

Don checked out of the motel, and followed the sheriff's car with its flashing blue light to the lawman's house. He waited at the curb while the sheriff went inside to get Marie. She came out shyly and reluctantly, wearing her new jeans and one of her Dolphin T-shirts. The sheriff and his wife remained on the front porch, and the red-haired deputy sat in the front seat of the police car. The blue light on top of the sheriff's vehicle was on and whirling, and Marie's pale face looked a ghostly blue to Don as she came down the walk. Don dropped down on one knee and opened his arms. Marie started to cry and then ran into his arms. He enveloped her, hugging her tight, and kissed her wet cheek.

"You're ten years old, baby," he whispered, "and you're old enough to understand. And if you can understand, you'll be able to remember this night. Do you understand, Marie?"

"What, Daddy? Understand what?" Marie wiped her streaming face with the backs of her hands.

"It was *your* choice, not mine. I'm leaving now, and you'll never see your daddy again."

Don rose. Marie clung to his legs, crying, "No, Daddy, no!"

Don disengaged her arms gently and got into his Mark IV. He waved to the sheriff and his wife on the porch, backed up a few feet to clear the sheriff's car, and then drove away. For two blocks, before Don turned right to get to the Interstate, the blue light continued to flash in his rearview mirror.

Every time, Don thought, every time Marie sees a blue light flashing, every time for the rest of her life, every time she will remember me.

Part 4

Larry "Fuzz-O" Dolman

Any man who is willing to accept responsibility is always loaded down with more and more of it, because there aren't that many men around who will accept responsibility.

It was a stormy March night, but Hank and I, after talking about it on the telephone that afternoon, decided to go ahead with Don's birthday party. Besides, it was more than just a birthday party for Don; it was a celebration for me, as well. Don, after sitting around in Eddie's apartment for a month doing nothing, except for watching TV all day and drinking Pagan Pink Ripple wine, had finally snapped out of his lethargic depression and had gone out and found a job selling Encyclopedias Americana. And I, because of Merita, had taken possession of the apartment above Hank, the one Don was supposed to get, and all of my furniture had been shipped up to me from Miami.

I liked the apartment, and so did Merita. Eddie, who enjoyed having Don live with him, or said he didn't mind at any rate, had told us—Hank and I—that Don wasn't ready to live alone yet, so I had taken the vacant apartment two weeks before Don's new birthday. My furniture was installed, with everything the way I wanted it, so the party was a combination housewarming and birthday celebration.

I was above Hank, and Eddie and Don were across the hall from me. There was an inside stairwell, and Hank's apartment was directly below mine. There were a fireman and his wife living across from Hank, in 3624 1/2, a middle-aged Polack who was planning to buy a house with a yard in a few months. When the fireman moved out, we had already made arrangements with the real estate agent for Don to get his apartment, and the four of us would then have the quadriplex to ourselves.

Meanwhile, everything was working out well. The fireman, Mr. Sinkiewicz, was on duty at the fire station for one full twenty-four hour day out of every three, and on the two days he had off he worked at a Philips 66 gas station. His wife, Anna, cleaned Hank's and Eddie's apartment one day a week, and I had Merita to keep mine spotless. Merita had polished my harpsichord, and it was more beautiful now than I had remembered it. She had used a full can of New Gloss wax on the harpsichord.

When Don had arrived in Schiller Park, Eddie and Hank had been concerned all out of proportion to the problem he presented. Without consulting me they had talked to Don at length, trying to persuade him to go back to Miami. Their arguments were rational enough, based, as they were, on practicality, but they either did not understand or take into account Don's emotional commitment. They worried about all of that silverware Don had appropriated, and they were also afraid that Clara would report the Mark IV Continental as stolen. She had the legal title, not Don, and they were afraid that Don would go to jail, both for stealing the silverware and for stealing his own car. This was a possibility, of course, but there were ways to get around it. If Don went back to Miami, time was also on his side, because Don's bosses were far away in England, and it was possible for Don to absent himself from Miami for two, three, or even five weeks without his company even finding out that he still wasn't in his office. He mailed them two reports a month as a general rule, but even if they didn't get a report for a few weeks, he could always say that he had mailed it and that it was lost by the Post Office. So Don could go back to Clara easily enough, and keep his well-paying job without his company knowing that he had spent a fortnight's vacation in Chicago.

Don listened to them patiently, but he told them that he was not going back, ever. They heard him, but the tone of his voice was so despairing they didn't believe him. He had left Clara once before and had gone back to her, so they felt that a precedent had been set.

When Don had failed consistently to respond to "reason," they asked me to talk to him. Eddie and Hank had listened to themselves, but I listened to Don. Don was not going back, ever, and he meant exactly what he said. What they took for despair in his statement, "I'm not going back to Clara, ever," was resignation—not despair.

"Okay, Don," I said, "if you aren't going back, what do you want to do?"

"I don't know yet, Fuzz-O, but I'll have some dough after I sell the silverware, and I can decide later. Right now, I don't want to think about it, and I don't even feel like going out to hustle the silverware."

"What about child support? If you send Clara money, you'll be traced, you know."

"I'm not sending Clara shit."

"Then you'll have to change your name and disappear. Either that, or we can ship the silverware back to Miami, which'll clear you of that charge, and you can mail in a letter of resignation to your company."

"I can't do that, Larry, I'll need the money."

"All right, then," I told him, "I'll take care of it for you—the whole business, and you can start all over again here in Chicago with a new name."

"You can fix all this for me?"

"Sure. Pick a name, and I'll get it for you."

"I don't care about the name," he said. "A kid can't pick his name when he's born, so if you're going to handle the whole business for me, I don't give a shit about the name either."

I used the resources of National Security to get Don a new identity—"Donald Lane." If he didn't get into any major troubles with the law, the new identity would hold up for all ordinary and practical purposes. I got him a Social Security card with a new number, a driver's license, a birth certificate, and a transcript from the University of Chicago in the name of Donald Lane with forty-eight college credits. In time, I told him, if he joined a few clubs and had some calling cards printed, no one would ever question his identity unless he got into trouble. Insofar as a work record was concerned, he would have to come up with a list of previous employments on his own, jobs that couldn't be checked out very well—like farm laborer, counterman, and so on.

"That will more or less disqualify me for any decent position," he said.

"Not exactly. That's the new dropout lifestyle these days, and if you want to—you've got forty-eight credits already—you can always go back to the University of Chicago and work on your degree."

"Is this a genuine transcript?"

"Of course."

"What happened to the real Donald Lane?"

"He dropped out of college five years ago. I don't know what happened to him. You'll also notice that the Don Lane on the birth certificate is two years younger than the Don Lane on the transcript, but you'll have to work out these discrepancies and make up your own phony biography and memorize it. I can't do everything for you."

"I know that, Larry. I didn't think you could do this much."

I didn't do very well on the car and the silverware, but I didn't want Don to go around the city trying to sell the sets one at a time and risk getting caught with hot silverware. So I checked our N.S. files again, and sold the Mark IV and the silverware to a fence in Peoria, Illinois, for a total of $7,400. If Don was disappointed in the sum, he didn't say so. He took the cash and opened an account in the name of Don Lane at the Schiller Park Bank and Trust Company, and he established credit at the Sunset Drugstore and Karl's Liquor Store in the shopping plaza four blocks away from our quadriplex.

Hank Norton, of course, as was to be expected, had two long distance calls, one from Nita Peralta, and one from Clara Luchessi. Both of these women were charged emotionally on the wire, Hank told us, but Hank was able to convince them that he had neither seen nor heard from Don in several weeks. He also promised to telephone them immediately if he did get a letter or call from Don.

There were no more calls from Miami.

In summary, all of this sounds simple enough, but it wasn't. Getting a new identity for Don was complicated and time-consuming, and during this period I had a few problems of my own. I had two chipped knuckles on my left hand, and my hand and part of my wrist was still in a cast. These knuckles hurt constantly. The company doctor told me that they might hurt ("give me some discomfort") for a year or more, and that they would easily break again if I banged my fist into anything hard. To minimize the pain, I carried my left wrist in a black silk sling, and I tried, without much success, not to move my fingers. Every time I moved my fingers, the grating pain in the knuckles grew sharper. But at least I was alive.

Frank Devlin, one of the security guard supervisors, had called me at the Stevens Hotel and told me that one of his watchmen was drunk and waving his pistol around. The watchman was stationed at an all-night park-and-lock on the North Side. There had been a good many car break-ins in the huge parking lot, and the male cashier in the one-man lighted box by the exit had been held up twice in one week before the stingy owner had called N.S. and hired a night watchman.

Our security watchmen wear powder-blue uniforms with black Sam Browne belts and .25 caliber pistols. Usually it is safeguard enough just to have one of these uniformed men walking around to discourage car prowlers and stick-up men.

They are all lousy shots, with only four days of security training before they are sent out on jobs like this one. In 1973 we decided to arm them with .25 caliber pistols, instead of .38s they used to carry, so they wouldn't be so likely to kill someone. I would have preferred to arm them with .22s myself, but a warning shot with a .22 sounds like a pop gun, so we settled on the .25 caliber pistol as an uneasy compromise. At least half of the men I employ for these uniformed security jobs are hired against my better judgment, but I'm like the Dutch kid plugging the dike with ten fingers instead of one, and I have to hire the kind of men I can get. And the kind of men you can get for $2.20 an hour to work twelve-hour shifts—in many cases, but not all, thank God—are often the kind who could and do make more money panhandling, stealing milk bottles, or bagging groceries than they get from National Security. I screen out the worst ones, but to fill the thinning ranks every week I have to take on a good many borderlines. Luckily, I lose the worst of the borderlines during the four days of training.

Every Monday morning we start a new four-day course. The recruits get lessons in courtesy, some basic city and county law, do's and don'ts, and weapons training. We show them how to use a riot gun, although they don't get to fire one. But we do give them dry and wet run firing with the .25 caliber pistols in the basement range of the N.S. Building. On the fifth morning, Friday, they are issued uniforms and pistols. Tom Brady, the Chicago Director of N.S., gives them a pep talk.

We start every Monday with from 25 to 30 new men, and by Friday, when we issue the uniforms, we are fortunate if we have 15 of them left. During the week, they melt away. N.S. has learned to save money by issuing the uniforms on the fifth day instead of on the first, as the agency did formerly. (The men who didn't show up again took their uniforms with them, of course.) Also, on Thursday night, the new men are given their pay for the first four days—even though their work was merely training, and easy training at that—but that first small paycheck means that at least four or five of them will not show up the next morning for graduation.

At any rate, the survivors, now in uniform, come back to me, and I send them out on jobs. Two months later, after being out on all-weather jobs, there are only one or two men left who started out originally with a group of 25 in a four-day training session. It's a headache to me, trying to recruit and keep manpower, but I can't blame these men for quitting. For good men, intelligent men, the work is too boring after a week or so, and it is cold out there in the open spaces and lonely in the warehouses. But the work they do is light enough. Visibility is the main idea, and the biggest problem they have is in staying awake and walking around. But if, on the job at night, a man gets too bored, or too cold, he simply walks away and goes home. When this happens, the man's supervisor has to find out that the man has gone before the company who hired us does, and replace the watchman with another man or take the position himself until the end of the shift.

Good supervisors are the key to running a smooth operation, and the supervisors I hire are never borderline cases. I check these supervisors out closely, and fortunately there are still a lot of American males who will work for less money if they are given a uniform to wear and the rank of "Lieutenant." If many of my supervisors are ex-servicemen who would have had a hard time making sergeant in the Army, I still have a lot of retired NCOs with a good retirement pay already who are willing to work as supervisors because they can wear a powder blue uniform with red stripes on the legs and gold lieutenant's bars on the shoulders.

Frank Devlin was a good man, an ex-first sergeant of Infantry, so when he called I told him, "You don't need me, Frank. Fire the sonofabitch, and replace him."

"Not in this guy's case," Frank said. "I'm in uniform, and I've chewed him out twice this week already. He's drunk, and he's got a loaded pistol. If he spots me in my uniform, he is liable to start shooting."

"Okay," I said, "I'll come down. Where're you calling from?"

Frank had phoned from an all night café two blocks from the parking lot. I put on my full-length leather coat, rode the elevator down, and took a cab. When I reached the café I went inside and Frank and I discussed strategy.

"I caught him drinking the other night," Frank said, shrugging, "and I should've fired him then. But it was cold, and he only had a half-pint on him, so I let it go."

"Did you take the half-pint away from him?"

"Yeah. I did that. And I got word today that he was bitching about it to the other men. Personally, Mr. Dolman, I don't think either one of us should take a chance. We should get a couple of cops to pick him up."

"If we did, we'd both be on the mat with Tom Brady in the morning. Every time one of our uniformed men is picked up by the fuzz, it's another black mark against the agency. Don't forget that our N.S. watchmen have eaten up a hellova lot of security jobs that off-duty policemen used to get. We can handle it. You can take off your uniform hat and wear my leather coat. Then he won't know it's you in uniform. I'll go into the lot straight on, and you circle around behind. While I wander around, pretending to look for my car, you come up behind him. I'll grab him from the front, and you can sap him behind the ear. Have you got your sap?"

Frank nodded.

"Okay. Where's the cashier?"

Frank grinned. "He was here, in the café—he called me from here. But after I talked to him, and told him I'd call you, he went home."

"That's good. Let's go."

The plan was simple, and it should have worked out all right, but the watchman, instead of having his pistol in his holster, had it concealed in his right hand. His arm was hanging down and I didn't notice it. When I jumped for him, he stepped back clumsily and raised his arm with the pistol. In mid-jump, I swung my left hand and arm in a backhand. My knuckles hit the pistol hard, cracking, knocking it out of his hand. I heard it skittering across the wet asphalt of the lot but I didn't see it because everything went red, then blue, and then black in flat wavering sheets of color like a Mark Rothko painting. I must have passed out, or fainted, momentarily, but only for a second or a fraction of a second, because when I opened my eyes again I was on my knees. The drunk watchman was out cold, sapped from behind by Frank Devlin. Because of my injured hand I wasn't much help to Frank, but we got the watchman into Frank's car and drove down to the N.S. Building. I told Frank to get the man out of his uniform—he had awakened by then, and was sobering up as well—into his civilian clothes, and to dump him over on State Street some place. Still hugging my smashed hand, I went back to my room at the Stevens, which was only a block's walk from the N.S. Building.

I soaked my hand in hot water, ate a couple of aspirins, and drank four ounces of whiskey. It didn't do any good. The swelling was getting worse, and so was the pain. At two a.m. I called the hotel doctor. He taped my hand, and gave me a shot. I took a few more slugs of bourbon, and fell asleep at four a.m.

The next day, after x-rays, which showed the chipped bones on the first two knuckles, and following the cast-setting, Dr. Haas, our agency doctor, asked me how many hours a day I worked.

"Twelve, fourteen, why?"

Dr. Haas pointed to the cast. "This," he said, "shouldn't have happened. As Director of Personnel, you've got a responsible job. Going out with Lieutenant Devlin last night was like a colonel playing P.F.C. By playing games, and taking on everything, you're doing yourself and National Security a disservice. It isn't your place to— "

"Look, Dr. Haas, don't tell me how to do my job. Somebody had to help Devlin, and he had to call me because there was no one else to call."

"In that case— " Dr. Haas grinned "—appoint Frank Devlin as the night supervisor, and then your other security supervisors can call *him* when they get into similar jams, and he'll have to handle it. You can stay in bed at night, and get your sleep for the next day's work. No man can work for twelve and fourteen hours a day without making mistakes through being overtired. And last night, you made one hellova mistake. You could've been shot and killed. And Devlin, if you *had* been shot, would have, in all probability, beaten that drunken watchman to death with his sap. And *that*, Mr. Dolman, would've resulted in much worse publicity for the agency than calling a couple of cops in a patrol car to pick up the watchman."

Dr. Haas was right. He ordered me to take two days off before going back to the office, and I lay on my bed at the Stevens thinking about my life, the job, and the way things were going.

A man who is willing to accept responsibility is always loaded down with more and more of it, because there aren't that many men around who will accept responsibility.

The agency kept two hotel rooms at the Stevens at all times. These rooms were reserved for visitors, directors from the field who were visiting Chicago headquarters for a few days, and for clandestine meetings with clients who, for one reason or another, did not want to come to the N.S. Building for conferences. There were more of the latter than one would suppose—husbands or wives who wanted spouse surveillance, for example; and also, we could meet privately with our ops who were engaged in industrial espionage and discuss their reports in these rooms.

When I came to Chicago, Tom Brady gave me the use of one of the hotel rooms "until I got settled." The room was convenient, only a block from our building, and with the hotel desk acting as a message center and answering service, I was in touch with the office all of the time. The room was bug-free, swept regularly; and it was always spotlessly clean when I returned to it, with fresh sheets; and my laundry was picked up and returned on the same day. As a consequence, I spent additional hours at the office because I had very few personal matters to take care of, and those few I did have to worry about were taken care of by my secretary. And so, because I was there, in the office, I was doing a great many things myself, making a good many decisions, and taking on too many additional responsibilities that could have and should have been delegated. My full-time presence at the agency made Tom Brady's job easier, so he never reminded me that I was living in a rent-free hotel room because it was to his advantage that I live at the Stevens and be on tap all of the time.

I decided to pull back and establish some kind of normal life.

Merita Orfutt, I also concluded, would be part of my new resolve to live more normally, and she would be helpful to have around during the transitional stage. Merita Orfutt was a seventeen-year-old black girl from Dothan, Alabama. She had been picked up for shoplifting, and had been given probation. She had been living with a female cousin who had also moved to Chicago from Dothan, and her cousin was on welfare. The cousin had two illegitimate children already, and was pregnant with a third.

The probation officer started screwing Merita, and moved her into a housekeeping room, which he paid for, on Cermak Street. It was a mixed block, and he could come and go without too much curiosity from the people in the neighborhood, but he got scared—or so he said. He was afraid that his wife might find out about Merita, and besides, he really didn't make enough money as a probation officer to support the girl, even minimally. And Merita was unable to find enough work to support herself. She found some occasional day-work but she didn't earn enough to live on.

So I took Merita over, the payments of the room on Cermak, and gave the girl an allowance of thirty dollars a week. Merita was a very black black girl, the color other blacks call a "blue." She was sexually inexperienced and a very poor lay. But she was quiet and amenable, only spoke when she was spoken to, and she ironed beautifully.

Actually, Merita and I had so little in common that there wasn't much of anything to talk about. She truly ironed beautifully, and liked taking care of the apartment. She was awkwardly efficient, and funny to watch at the same time. If I gave her two things to do at once, like ironing a fresh white shirt and taking the garbage downstairs, she jumped around for a few moments like a woman suddenly tossed a couple of bouncing tennis balls. For a slim girl, Merita had fairly large breasts, and the typical high rounded ass of a black girl, but she didn't really turn me on sexually—or at least, not very often. If she had, I would have taken the time to teach her a few things, but I never bothered, and only took her into my bed once or twice a week. When I had kept her in the room on Cermak Street I visited her about twice a week, and thought, at the time, that the reason I didn't see her more often was because I was too busy. But after I had her living with me in the apartment, where she was available every night, I still only tapped her once or twice a week because that was enough.

She didn't sleep in my bed, of course. She slept on the Castro convertible in the living room. When she woke me in the morning, bringing me a cup of coffee and telling me that my breakfast was "on the fire," her bed was already made up in the living room and the white leather cushions were back on the couch.

At any rate, our arrangement, if anything, was temporary. Knowing that the end was vaguely inevitable, I took her into downtown Schiller Park and signed her up at the Schiller Park Beauty College. In six months, or nine, or however long it took her to master the hairy lessons they taught her there, she would become a beauty operator. When she got her diploma, I planned to put her on a Trailways bus back to Dothan, Alabama. With a trade, I figured, she would be able to earn a decent living down there. Our arrangement, in my opinion, was fair enough, and if Merita had any objections she never voiced them. She only spent three hours a day at the beauty college, with a twenty-minute bus ride each way, so she still had plenty of time to do the shopping, keep the apartment spotless, watch dayside television, and play the One and Only B.B. King on the stereo.

Except for weekend-stands, I had never lived with a woman before, and it wasn't nearly as depressing as I had thought it would be. But now, looking back, I think that it was a mistake not to indoctrinate Merita with some advanced sex education.

One afternoon, about a week before the party, and after I had provided Don with the documents for his new identification, I called Hank and told him to get Eddie and to meet me at The Shill at six-thirty p.m.—without Don. I wanted to show Eddie and Hank the letter I had written to Clara Luchessi.

Hank was only visiting his salesmen in the field every other week now instead of once a week, and faking his reports during the week he stayed at home. It consumed a lot of desk time for him to make up his phony reports, but now that he had his men in the field straightened out he could slack off without any decrease in sales, and he was tired of living in hotel rooms four days a week, every single week. Eddie was home three days a week one week, and four days the next, and during his layovers in Seattle he was staying at a waterfront hotel and trying to learn as much as he could about salmon fishing. When the summer fishing season came around, the four of us had made some tentative plans to spend a week together fishing for salmon on the Columbia, and camping out. The way my hand was hurting all the time, I didn't think it would ever stop so I could enjoy a camping-fishing trip, but I kept my reservations to myself.

When we met that evening in The Shill and ordered drafts,

I brought out the letter on N.S. stationery I had written to Clara Luchessi. I also had a Xeroxed copy of the letter to send to Nita Peralta.

"The reason I wrote this letter—a report really—" I told Eddie and Hank "—is to forestall Clara's hiring an investigator to come up here and look for Don. The only lead she has to Don is through Hank and us, so by sending her this official report, telling her that I had the airport, bus, and train terminals covered and that I was continuing to have an operator checking on the hotels, she'll think we're all as concerned with Don's disappearance as she is. So I can continue to send her, from time to time, some additional faked negative progress reports. The cover I got for Don is primarily for his psychological benefit. It wouldn't hold up for ten minutes if a plainclothes investigator started looking for him, but it'll give Don the kind of security he'll need to pull himself together. Don, as you guys know, is square as hell and very straight. This runaway business is out of keeping with his way of looking at the world, and it's much better for us to keep him here with us, instead of having him all alone and disturbed mentally down in Miami."

Hank read the letter, grinned approvingly, and passed it to Eddie. "What makes you think Clara'll believe a negative report like this? As far as she knows, you're as much Don's friend as I am."

"The language for one thing," I said. "It's in officialese. *Couched* in officialese. And for another, if she tries to hire an investigative agency to look for Don, and finds out that it'll cost her from one-fifty to two hundred bucks a day, she'll settle for my free report."

"I like it, Fuzz-O," Eddie said. "But what about Don's company? They're going to be out a few thousand bucks, so—"

"I called Nita Peralta on the phone the other day, and I've got a Xerox copy of the letter to Clara to send her." I showed them the copy.

"I didn't know you knew Nita Peralta," Eddie said.

"I know her pretty well," I said. "In fact, I took her out a couple of times in Miami and banged her, so I know her damned well."

"I thought she was a virgin." Eddie gave me a puzzled look.

"Not when I took her out, she wasn't. I never said anything about it because she didn't want Don to know. She has a crush on him, you know—one of those things—so she was awfully afraid Don would find out about us. So after a couple of dates, we just dropped the whole business. Anyway, because I never said anything about it to Don, she trusts me. So when I called her, I told her I'd send her a copy of the report I was sending to Clara, and if the company ever looked for Don in the Chicago area they should have the investigators contact me first. Because, as I told her, we're all as concerned about Don's whereabouts as she is. I think that'll do it all right, and we can keep Don with us in the quardriplex as long as he wants to stay there. This is all pretty devious shit, but I can take care of the paper chase without any trouble as long as an investigator comes to see me down at N.S. first."

"Send the letters," Hank said. "You're brilliant, Larry."

"I intend to," I said, "but I wanted you guys to know what I was doing. We all agreed never to mention *that* night, but I want you to know that I feel a lot better about having Don up here with us instead of having him running around loose in Miami."

"Don would never say anything about that night," Eddie said.

"Not unless he were subjected to pressure, he wouldn't," I said. "But he was under a lot of pressure with Clara, and if a man's under too much pressure the top of his head can blow off."

"He's not under any pressure with us," Hank said.

"That's right," Eddie said. "This afternoon he was talking about looking for a job."

We had a few more beers, and then we went out to a steakhouse for dinner. We switched to martinis, then to scotch, and when we got in a fairly jovial mood, someone—I think it was Eddie—brought up the idea for a First Birthday party for Don, and we made the plans.

33

Don Lane, his ordinarily olive face a dusky rose, was smiling as he speared an onion in his Gibson with his right forefingernail. Today, March 15, he was one day old. This was the first day of the rest of his life, and "officially" he was only twenty-six years of age.

To top it off, he had sold three encyclopedias in less than an hour: one to Mr. Sinkiewicz, one to Hank, and one to me. I had gone for the whole package, the encyclopedia, the two-volume dictionary, and the maple bookcase to hold the set. By my taking the entire package, Don was able to throw in a free 24-volume set of *The Book of Knowledge,* reduced to twelve double-volumes. When the crates of books arrived, I planned to give *The Book of Knowledge* to Merita.

We were in Hank's apartment, all of us dressed and having preprandial Gibsons before going out on the city. Reservations had been made, and after we had done everything we planned to do, we were going to come back to the quadriplex, and my apartment, for birthday cake and for the opening of Don's presents.

I had given Merita her instructions. She was baking an apple snack cake and making trays of canapes up in my apartment. She had plenty to do to keep her occupied until we returned.

"Shall I make another batch?" Hank said.

Hank had gained twenty pounds since he left Miami. His round red face was puffy, and I knew he had been drinking all afternoon. He knew his capacity, however, and he spaced his drinks. The torrid Tanqueray Gibsons were just beginning to hit him, and he had loosened the knot, as big as a boxing glove, of his white silk tie, and unfastened the top button of his yellow Viyella shirt. He wore a new brown tweed suit, rough and twiggy in texture, which added another ten pounds to his bulky appearance.

"I don't think there's time," I said. "We've got reservations. But why not fix us one more apiece to drink in the car?"

"Not for me," Eddie said. "If we're going to have another at dinner, and then wine—I'd rather wait." In his new gray suit, Eddie had never looked any sharper. He wore a blue-and-gray striped U.S.A.F. tie with his blue uniform shirt. His black flight boots were, as usual, highly polished. Eddie was usually a beer man, with an infinite capacity for tall drafts, but he was celebrating tonight, and he didn't have to fly again for three days. When he was flying on the next day, Eddie wouldn't even drink a draft beer. Wanting to last out the evening, Eddie was drinking his lethal Gibson in a tall six-ounce glass full of shaved ice.

"I think I'll wait, too," Don said. He got up and struggled into his new pile-lined trenchcoat. It was a complicated coat, with a dozen suede straps and waist belt, and shiny in various places with useless brass buckles and D-rings.

Hank and I carried fresh Gibsons in plastic glasses when we left. We sat in the back of Hank's new Galaxie. Eddie drove, with Don up front beside him.

In traffic, and there is always traffic, it usually takes me about forty-five minutes to drive to the Loop on the Kennedy Expressway, but Eddie, whipping expertly in and out of the stream, made it in thirty-five minutes to the Congress exit. We didn't say much in the car because we were listening to Hank's tape of The Allman's, "Brothers and Sisters." With the music blasting out of four speakers, it was too difficult to talk anyway. After turning North on Michigan, Eddie drove into the parking garage behind the John Hancock Building and found a slot on the twelfth floor. We rode the elevator down and, because there was still plenty of time and Don hadn't been in there before, we went into the Playboy Towers—not the club, although we all had our cards from the Miami Playboy Club—and had a drink at the bar. This bar and lounge is as big as three gymnasiums, and a good pick-up place. But it was crowded, noisier than hell, and distorted band music filtered in from the other rooms.

We left and walked the one block south on North Michigan to the Hancock Building, entered via the subground floor, and took the nonstop, twenty-nine second ride on the express elevator to The Ninety-Fifth Floor Restaurant. I told the *maitre'd* who I was, and he took us to our table immediately. We got the table I had requested, but the night was too stormy for the usually impressive view of the Loop I had wanted Eddie and Don to see. The pitchy blackness of Lake Michigan was somewhere to our left, but we could at least see the lights of the First National Bank Building.

The service impressed Don and Eddie, who hadn't eaten there before. Hank and I enjoyed watching the Korean waiter work. He had a half-dozen assistants, and while we drank champagne cocktails, he prepared most of the food at the table, snapping his fingers, and the steaming plates appeared like magic. We had a smooth vichyssoise, lobster Newburg, Brussel sprouts, baked potatoes, and a great salad, plus two bottles of champagne. By the time we finished the French pastries, and lit the cigars I had brought along, we had eaten ourselves almost sober.

Hank ordered B&Bs and coffee all-around. I unfastened my belt two notches, and looked out the thermal window at the starred lights and swirling fog. Eddie and Hank had partially glazed eyes from eating too much, but Don, who had hardly touched his food, looked almost pensive.

"Two or three years back," I said, "some woman threw herself out of the window on the ninety-second floor, and bounced all the way down."

"There's a technical term for that," Hank said. "Auto-defenestration."

"What's it mean?" Eddie said.

"Throwing yourself out the window." Hank laughed.

Don got up, walked two paces to the window, and tapped the thermal glass. He sat down again, shaking his head. "No way—that glass is doubled and almost an inch thick. It would be impossible to throw yourself through the window."

"Not if you had some help," I said. "Besides, Don, this is Chicago, and the police said it was suicide so that's what it was."

"I'm miserable," Eddie said. "I ate too damned much. Let's get the hell out."

I paid the $156 tab with my credit card, plus writing in a 25% tip for the Korean waiter, who was well worth it, and we left the Ninety-Fifth Floor.

The icy air and the brisk walk revived us a little, and the drive back on the Kennedy Expressway to the River Road exit and the Regency Hyatt House sobered me completely. This hotel is in Rosemont, Illinois, but the corner of the building is only ten feet away from Schiller Park. In the Blue Max, we had two double-scotches apiece, in an effort to get the glow back, before the floor show began.

The M.C., finally, introduced a "Famous Star of Radio, Stage, Screen and Television." Hank had seen him on the old Ed Sullivan show, but I had never heard of him before. He was just another fat, dead-pan comic to me. He had a screen and a slide projector on the stage with him. The house lights dimmed.

"I just got back from my vacation in the Florida Everglades," he said sadly. "I had a good time."

Click!

There was a color picture of a wide-mouthed alligator on the screen.

"That's an alligator," the comic said.

Click!

A black-faced Seminole Indian in a colorful striped jacket appeared on the screen, staring.

"That was our guide," the comic said, "a Seminole Indian."

Click!

The expressionless Indian appeared again; this time he was up to his waist in sand.

"There's our guide in quicksand," the comic said.

Click!

"There's his hair—"

"Let's get the hell out of here," Hank said. Everybody in the lounge was laughing except us, but then, what the hell did they know about Florida? Florida was Paradise, for Christ's sake.

When we got back into the car, Don started to cry. "I miss it, I miss it!" he said. "I can't help it." He dug his pudgy fists into his eyes.

"Cut it out, Don," Hank said. "This is your birthday, man, and you've got presents to open later."

"And some other surprises," I added.

"I'm sorry," Don said. "I'm having a good time, I really am, and I'm okay now."

"You know what's the matter with you, Don?" Eddie said. "You used to be an Aries, and you just aren't used to being a Pisces yet, that's all."

"Jesus," Don said, "am I a Pisces now?"

"Your new birthday's the fifteenth of March, and Pisces runs from the nineteenth of February to March twentieth," Eddie said.

"I never even thought about that," Don said. "It'll give me a brand new way of looking at the world."

"Just be grateful you aren't a Capricorn, like Larry and me," Hank said. "To us the world looks like shit. Right, Larry?"

"Not tonight," I said. "I'm having a good time."

"What are you, Eddie?" Don said.

"Scorpio. November fourteenth. But I don't believe in that crap."

"I—I don't either," Don said quickly. "But it's interesting to think about it."

Eddie half-turned to look at me. "Do you need to stop for anything, Fuzz-O? Liquor? Ice?"

"Nothing," I said. "It's all there."

Eddie and Don got out of the car first when we parked on Kelly, in front of the quadriplex. Eddie handed Hank the car keys, and then Eddie and Don took the walkway to the front door. Hank grabbed the sleeve of my leather overcoat as I got out of the car. "It isn't too late, Larry," Hank said. "Let's go get Don a girl."

I grinned. "I'm giving him Merita for tonight," I said. "That's my birthday present to Don."

"So *that's* why you didn't want me to get him a girl before!" Hank laughed. "How does Merita feel about it?"

I shrugged. "It's all set up, man. I gave her instructions before we left."

The difference between my apartment and Hank's was apparent the moment you stepped inside my door. Hank had had all of his odd-sized mismatched furniture shipped up from Florida, and he hadn't added anything new to it. Mrs. Sinkiewicz cleaned his bedroom and half of his living room, but the other half of his living room was still stacked with unpacked cardboard boxes. His sailfish, with just the sword sticking out, was still wrapped up in a foam-rubber blanket. Hank's apartment was depressing, but mine was light and cheerful. The way my white leather furniture was placed, my living room looked almost twice as large as Hank's. Eddie, of course, had rented his apartment furnished, and he didn't give a damn whether he furnished it with new stuff or not. But there were twin beds in Eddie's bedroom, which was at least convenient, with Don living with him. My apartment was the logical place to have the party, and I had insisted on it.

Merita looked so damned good, when we came into my apartment that even I was astonished. I had never seen her short natural hair in anything but braided corn-rows, which made her look almost bald, or close to it; but she surprised us—me most of all—with a giant Afro wig when she opened the door. It was a huge wig, and I supposed she had bought it at the Beauty College—or borrowed it for the night—and it had changed her entire appearance. The long kinky hair stood out for a full foot all of the way around her head, and she looked as feminine as a mother cat. She wore a white satin pants suit, with lace at the cuffs and collar, and the same matching lace bordered the bottom of her bell trousers. She was nervous, of course, and her long fingers fluttered, but everything in the apartment was perfect. She had fixed the buffet on the white parson's table just outside the kitchen door. The liquor glasses, ice bucket and mixes were neatly arranged on the coffee table, we could all fix fresh drinks from a seated position without getting up.

Merita took our outer coats into the bedroom to hang them up. Hank looked at all of the finger food displayed on the buffet, grinned and shook his head. "You really overdid it, Fuzz-O. It's beautiful, but who can eat anything else after that dinner we had?"

"You'll probably be hungry later. Fix your own drinks," I announced. I crossed to the stereo to take off the James Brown, which I replaced with my favorite Van Morrison album—"Hard Nose the Highway."

Eddie and Hank mixed themselves Chivas and sodas. Don stared glumly at the table, twisting each bottle one quarter turn. "I don't see any wine," he said.

"Hank and I have been meaning to talk to you about that, Don," I said. "You've got to get off that Ripple kick. I've got plenty of champagne in the fridge for you—or for anybody else who wants it, but you'd probably be better off drinking Chivas."

"I just don't like the taste of scotch, is all," Don said.

"I'll get the champagne."

Hank laughed. "It was pretty funny, though. I didn't think Korean's were capable of showing any emotion on their faces until Don asked that guy for a glass of Pagan Pink Ripple."

"I just said that to be funny," Don said, flushing slightly.

Eddie laughed. "It was funny all right, but I thought that Korean waiter was going to piss his pants."

I brought in the champagne and four glasses. I handed the bottle to Don to open, and lined up the glasses on the coffee table. "Let's all have one glassful for a birthday toast to Don before we start drinking seriously," I said.

"I'll drink to that," Hank said solemnly, and he drank half of his Chivas and soda.

Merita was standing over by the buffet. Don poured the

champagne, and then he said, looking at me, "Where's Merita's glass?"

"I'll get another one," I said, snapping my fingers. As I went into the kitchen, I told Merita to sit down on the couch directly behind Don's chair.

After Don handed the filled glasses around, Eddie said, "I want to be the first to wish Don a happy first birthday, but if anybody here wants to sing the happy birthday song, he's going to beat the shit out of me first!"

"And me," Hank said.

"Happy birthday, baby," I said to Don. We all drained our glasses, and Don blinked his eyes.

"Thanks," Don said, bobbing his head, as he poured another glass of wine, "this is a great party. It really is, and I appreciate it."

I winked at Merita, and jerked my head. She put down her glass, which she had only sipped, and went into the kitchen. A moment later she brought in the apple snack cake. There was a single lighted candle in the middle. The cake sagged slightly at one end, but she had done a smooth, even job with the white icing, and it looked nice. Merita carried the cake over carefully, and held it low for Don to blow out the candle. We all applauded, and Merita took the cake over to the buffet.

I fixed a Chivas and soda for myself, checked to see that everyone else was all right, and then went to the bathroom, gesturing for Merita to follow me. I took the wrapped presents—Eddie and Hank's presents to Don—out of the closet, where we had hidden them earlier, and placed them on my bed.

"Do you remember what I told you do?" I said to Merita.

She bobbed her head vigorously, and her long hair trembled as though wind blew through it.

"Okay. Then *smile*, and keep smiling. I don't want you to act as if you're doing Don a favor, for Christ's sake."

I picked up a package, handed the other one to Merita, and she followed me out. Back in the living room, we put the packages on the table in front of Don. He was well-pleased with his presents. Hank had given him a beautiful all-leather traveling liquor case, with silver-plated bar accessories and two four-ounce silver drinking cups inside. Eddie had given him a Mark Cross pigskin briefcase. Don had always like leather, and we knew that he would like these gifts whether he ever used them or not. He was so pleased he kept saying "Wow!" and "Thanks!"

I gathered the paper wrappings, and folded them into small squares. Hank winked at me. Eddie, who wasn't in on the surprise, merely mixed himself a fresh drink without giving any outward indication that there was no present from me for Don to open.

I put the folded paper under my chair, freshened my drink, and said: "Oh, yes, I almost forgot, Don, I've got a present for you myself."

Don looked at me. Merita sat quickly on Don's lap, dangling her long legs over the arm of his chair, put her arms around his neck, and kissed him on the neck. Her wild Afro hid his entire face from us.

Hank and I laughed, and Eddie grinned.

Don struggled slightly, and Merita sat up, still on his lap, smiling.

"I'm overwhelmed," Don said, laughing a little. "But you're kidding, of course?"

Merita got up, walked to the front door, swaying her high round ass, turned, and took off her white jacket, slowly unbuttoning it from the top as she smiled at Don. Her long-nippled conical breasts, defying gravity, pointed upwards. She held her jacket in her right hand, and put her left hand on the doorknob.

"No joke, Don," I said seriously. "She's yours, man—but just for the night. Happy birthday, from me to you."

"You aren't just kidding, then?" Don said.

"He isn't kidding, for Christ's sake," Hank said. "Go ahead."

Don got up, grinning sheepishly. "In that case, if you'll excuse me for a few minutes, I'll be back after awhile. Don't take off anything else," he said to Merita, "I like to unwrap my own presents."

"I'll get you a fresh bottle of champagne," I said. When I returned from the kitchen with an unopened bottle, Don had two wine glasses in his right hand, and was handing his apartment key to Merita with his left. I gave Don the bottle, and they left, without closing my door, to cross the hallway to Eddie's apartment.

I closed the door, and took off my arm sling and suit coat. Hank removed his bulky tweed jacket and gave it to me, but Eddie shook his head. I draped the two jackets over the back of Don's vacated chair. Then I slipped my arm sling on again.

"How come," Eddie said, "you guys didn't let me in on the surprise?"

"I didn't intend to let Hank in on it," I said, "but when you and Don walked ahead, when we got back, Hank was all set to return to the Playboy Towers or somewhere to pick up a girl for Don—so I had to tell him."

"That's right, Eddie," Hank said. "Don was getting depressed again, I thought, so I figured that a woman might cheer him up. But it's better this way."

"Well, it sure as hell surprised me," Eddie said. "I wouldn't mind some of that myself, if my luck ever needs changing. Try and remember *my* birthday, Larry—November fourteenth!"

I laughed. "By November, Merita'll probably be back in Dothan, Alabama, where she belongs. This is just a one-shot deal. You and Hank can get your own poontang."

"What I wish," Hank said, "what I wish, is that I had a Polaroid color shot of Don's face when she sat on his lap. That's what I wish."

"I've got a Polaroid," I said, "but I never thought of it. We could've taken some shots of all of us when Don was opening his presents. On the other hand, the fewer the pictures of Don around the better, especially of Don since he came to Chicago. In fact, I was thinking this afternoon, one of us should be with Don all of the time, until he's really straightened out."

"I like Don," Eddie said, "but having him around all the time with me isn't the best solution. But now that he's got a job, and will be out there making money again, he'll be all right. He's really excited, I think, about selling encyclopedias. He told me yesterday that the only thing he didn't like about it was that you had to sell to families who could least afford them."

"That's nothing to worry about," Hank said. "Nowadays no one can hardly afford anything—except for guys like us, who aren't mired down with wives and children."

I heard the shot—the sound of the .45—and I was on my feet, taking my left hand out of the sling, before Eddie said, "Was that a shot?"

"Yeah," I said, "and it came from your apartment. Give me your keys, Eddie." I had inadvertently clutched my fingers into fists the instant the shot was fired, and my hand, which hadn't hurt all evening, was tingling with pain.

Eddie got up, took his keys out of his pocket, and said: "Let's all go over together."

"No," I said. "You and Hank wait here. I'll just check and come right back."

I crossed the hallway, opened the door, and went inside. There was a light on the floor in the bedroom. I entered the bedroom. The lamp, which had been on the bedside table between the two beds, had been knocked over, but the light was still burning. Merita, who had been sitting naked on Eddie's bed, stood up as I entered. Her eyes bulged whitely in her black face. Don, except for his heavy blue-and-yellow Argyle socks, was naked on his own bed. The drawer of the bedside table was open, and the pistol was on the floor by the lamp. I picked up the lamp, put it back on the table, and looked at Don. The bullet had entered his head from his chin, shattering it, and had ploughed upward through the back of the roof of his mouth. The pillow and the padded yellow headboard were a messy mixture of blood, scattered brains, and hair. I closed his staring eyes with the thumb and forefinger of my right hand.

"What happened, baby?" I said.

Merita started to cry, but I told her sharply to stop, and she managed to quit in a moment or so. I got her pants suit from the closet, where she had hung it up neatly, and told her to get dressed. She put on her pants and jacket, but her fingers were shaking so much she couldn't button the front. I did it for her, and led her into the living room, closing the door to the bedroom. I turned on lights, and told her to sit down. She shook her head.

"He was trying to hurt me," she sid. She patted her high round ass, unable to say it. "Back here. I—I wouldn't let him do it, and he got the gun and said he'd make me. I thought maybe he was funnen me, but he was mad, really mad. So when he kept on, I tried to get the gun and it went off. It was so quick, so quick, quick— "

"Who pulled the trigger? You or Don?"

"I don't know, but not me. I didn't do nothin'. I just tried to get the gun and it went off."

"That's all right," I said. "Let's go back to my apartment."

I locked the door, and we went back to my apartment. I didn't worry about the Sinkiewicze's hearing the shot. They went to bed at ten-thirty when he wasn't at the fire station, and nothing would wake them after midnight. They had lived in Chicago for forty some odd years; all their lives.

"Don's dead," I told Eddie and Hank. "He shot himself. It wasn't Merita's fault."

"Jesus!" Eddie said. "Are you sure he's dead?"

I touched my chin with my thumb. "It went in here, and came out back here." I patted the back of my head.

Hank reached for the scotch bottle. "You never know, do you? He seemed so damned happy when he left," Hank said.

"Pour a double for Merita, Hank," I said. He did, and I handed the glass to her. She shook her head.

"Drink it, girl," I said. She held the glass with both hands and drank it down, shuddering.

"What do we do now, Fuzz?" Eddie said.

"Let me think a minute." Cradling my left hand, I walked back and forth across the room a couple of times, thinking. Then I snapped the fingers of my right hand. "Okay!" I said. "Here's the first thing we've got to do—!"

"Oh, shit!" Hank laughed. "Here we go again!" He kept on laughing, and Eddie joined him. I caught a glimpse of Merita's startled face. Her mouth was a large round carmine O, and her humid eyes bulged from her head as she looked at Eddie, then at Don, and then at me. She performed her awkward, shuffling dance from one foot to the other, back and forth, and a big wet stain appeared on her white satin trousers as she wet them. I had to laugh myself. All three of us were laughing, and we couldn't stop.

Poor Merita.

She probably thought we were crazy.

ALSO BY CHARLES WILLEFORD

WILD WIVES

Forthcoming from Vintage Crime/Black Lizard . . .

Amoral, sexy, and brutal, Charles Willeford's *Wild Wives* is a classic hard-boiled tale of an insane woman, her jealous husband, and the man who gets caught between them. Jake Blake is a private detective short on cash when he meets a rich and beautiful young woman looking to escape her father's smothering influence. Unfortunately for Jake, the smothering influence includes two thugs hired to protect her—and the woman is in fact not the daughter of the man she wants to escape, but his wife. Now Jake has two angry thugs and one jealous husband on his case. And as Jake becomes more deeply involved with this glamorous and possibly crazy woman, he becomes entangled in a web of deceit, intrigue, and multiple murders. Brilliant, sardonic, and full or surprises, *Wild Wives* is one wild ride.

Crime Fiction/1-4000-3247-4

ALSO BY CHARLES WILLEFORD

MIAMI BLUES

After a brutal day investigating a quadruple homicide, Detective Hoke Moseley settles into his room at the El Dorado Hotel and nurses a glass of brandy. With his guard down, he doesn't think twice when he hears a knock on the door. The next day, he finds himself in the hospital, badly bruised and with his jaw wired shut. He thinks back over ten years of cases, wondering who would want to beat him into unconsciousness, steal his gun and badge, and most important, make off with his prized dentures.

Crime Fiction/1-4000-3246-6

NEW HOPE FOR THE DEAD

Hoke Moseley is called to a posh neighborhood to investigate a lethal overdose. There he meets the alluring stepmother of the decedent, and begins to wonder about dating a witness. Meanwhile, he has been threatened with suspension unless he leaves his beloved, if squalid, suite at the El Dorado Hotel and moves downtown. His difficulties are amplified by an assignment to reopen fifty unsolved murders, the unexpected arrival of his daughters, and a partner with an unwanted pregnancy.

Crime Fiction/1-4000-3249-0

SIDESWIPE

Hoke has had enough. Tired of struggling against alimony payments, two teenage daughters, a very pregnant, very single partner, and his low-paying job, Hoke moves to Singer Island. Meanwhile, career criminal Troy Louden is hatching plans of his own with a gang including a disfigured hooker, a talentless artist, and a clueless retiree. But when a simple robbery results in indiscriminate bloodshed, Hoke hurls himself back into the world he meant to leave behind forever.

Crime Fiction/1-4000-3248-2

THE WAY WE DIE NOW

When Miami homicide detective Hoke Moseley receives an unexplained order to let his beard grow, he doesn't think much about it. He has too much going on at home, especially with a man he helped convict ten years before moving in across the street. Considering Hoke has his former partner, who happens to be nursing a newborn, and his two teenage daughters living with him, he doesn't like the situation one bit. It doesn't help matters when he is suddenly assigned to work undercover outside of his jurisdiction. Impersonating a drifter, he tries to infiltrate a farm operation suspected of murdering migrant workers. But when he gets there for the job interview, the last thing he is offered is work.

Crime Fiction/1-4000-3250-4